When I
Snap My Fingers
You Will
Remember
Everything

When I Snap My Fingers You Will Remember Everything

Stories

J. Morris

No Record Press
2016

NO RECORD PRESS
www.norecordpress.com

Morris, J.
When I Snap My Fingers You Will Remember Everything
J. Morris.

Publisher's notes:
This is entirely a work of fiction.
The stories in this collection were first published elsewhere:
"Sid Badloss Sings…" *Missouri Review*
"When I Snap My Fingers…" *Green Hills Literary Lantern*
"A Childhood" *Green Hills Literary Lantern*
"Screamer" *High Plains Literary Review*
"Would I Lie to You?" *American Literary Review*
"Me and Martin and Our Wives" *Other Voices*
"Set List" *Potomac Review*
"A Dream That Paul is Dead" *New Delta Review*
"The Twenty-First Rule" *Five Points*
"Twenty Visions of Poor Alice Rosenbaum" *Western Humanities Review*
"Roaches Crawled Across My Chicken" *RE:AL*
"A Finger in the Pocket" *The Styles*
"The Liontamer" *Antietam Review*

ISBN: 978-0-9835860-9-8

Cover design by Katie Fisher

Printed in the United States of America.

to Katie

THIS SIDE

THE OTHER SIDE

THIS SIDE

Sid Badloss Sings "The Malignant Wandering Spirit of Darkness"

Here is Sylvia, in the audience again. She's hunkered down on the rec-center Astroturf, surrounded by kids, but none of them are hers.

I play my guitar and sing "The Squeak Squeak Song." *Squeak up!* goes the refrain, *Squeak now or forever hold your peace!* Cute. All the kids get the idea and start squeaking. I stop the song and vamp while I teach them how to do an excellent squeak. The moms, and the two or three dads, check all this out with nervous smiles (and eyes foreseeing future squeaks at the kitchen table, at lights-out time, in church pews and Burger Kings and cross-country car trips along about Nebraska) while their heirs and progeny squeak hysterically, and properly, on the downbeat. It's a trick of the trade: nothing a kid likes more than making a totally obnoxious noise that has been solicited by a strange singing adult with a beard and an O's cap turned the wrong way around.

Sylvia sits amid the squeakers and aims her smile at me. When the gig is over the moms bring their children to meet me, if they care to. Most of them do. My ex–committed relationship used to say that the secret of my success with kids is: I treat 'em like everybody else. Talk funny to 'em, ignore 'em if I feel like it, ask 'em stuff they can't answer. This could be so; they definitely dig me. One of these days I will get around to having some myself.

Several moms have brought my CD for me to autograph. *Sid Wicker Sings "Great Green Gobs of Greasy Grimy Gopher Guts" and Other Childhood Favorites.* Actually, my version of "Great Green Gobs" isn't the childhood favorite one. Mine is G-rated, so as not to offend. Colby Dunn, my agent, insists that my public is pre-K through 4th, and he's supposed to know. Though lately we've had a disagreement or two about that.

There on the edge of the crowd, her permablonde hair shining in a bar of October afternoon sun coming down through the skylight, is of course Sylvia. Smiling and clutching another manila envelope.

"Here you go," I say to a mildly hysterical girl child, handing her back the CD. She pounds on my flank and says, "Did you sign it? With my name?"

I tell her, "I signed it with *my* name, to *you*, Ms. Carolyn French."

"Carolyn French," she agrees doubtfully, her face flushed. She jogs from foot to foot.

"Come on, sweetie," the mom says. "We have to go pee-pee."

Carolyn French slugs me again, on the same rib. "More

music," she suggests. "Sing more about the worms crawl in, the worms crawl out."

The mom tells me she sure does remember that one from when she was a girl. "I don't know how you sit up there and sing those silly songs. But they just love you, for a fact!"

I tell Carolyn, "Don't let those worms crawl into your spinach tonight, baby." Then smile at the mom and say, "Thank you so much for coming by, ma'am."

They go away. Now the Frenches will be hearing about worms at dinner. That's entertainment.

Slowly the moms and dads and kids disperse. "Come on down, Sylvia. Your turn," I mutter, putting my Martin back in its case as I smile and wave to the last of the little ones. Now she's approaching closer.

"I can't wait to see you on YouTube," says the last mom. (Closer still: Sylvia, incoming.)

"Dollar-Brite's all-new We're Kidding! channel, starting in November, also streaming, and don't forget to shop at Dollar-Brite," I tell her. I'm about to become a local media celebrity. Thank you, Colby; thank you, Dollar-Brite, my dear sponsor. No doubt Sylvia will have some observations to share with me about celebrityhood.

Just ignore her. I pick up the guitar-and-case and move my boots across the Astroturf, heading for the double doors. Every time, *every time*, I fancy myself rude enough to ignore Sylvia. Why don't I know better by now?

"Hello, Sid," she says. That sweet, square, determined voice.

My boots slow down, I slump my shoulders, look

longingly at the bright afternoon, and then set the guitar on the Astroturf. I turn to Sylvia Goodwin. "We've got to stop meeting like this," I say.

"I realize you're ignoring me, Sid." Her tone is tolerant.

"Trying," I say.

"I know it is," says Sylvia, not punning. "I realize it's difficult for you to believe that the love I feel for you is the same relentless love Jesus feels. But you just haven't met Him yet."

"Sylvia, I don't think, that time in Wheaton, for instance, that Jesus would have—"

I've martyred her. Her pretty baby-blues blink, she juts her chin at me to show that she deserves this scourging and will suffer it bravely. "That was a long time ago, Sid," she says.

"Yeah. Seven whole months."

She shakes her head. "I was weak. And anyway you made it clear you were in a 'committed relationship.'" The quote marks come through; in Sylvia's book—you know, *the* Book—I was just wallowing around in sin, committed to nothing but fornication. "I realize" (big word with old Sylvia: it means *I understand but don't approve*) "that you disbelieve in a love that can transform itself from carnal to holy."

"Whatcha got there for me, Sylvia?" I say, pointing to the manila envelope.

Sylvia looks at it, turns it around in her hands as if to make sure it's the right one. "I want you to take this and read it, Sid. These are my thoughts concerning the YouTube show you're going to do. I realize you've chosen not to respond to my letters, but I'm asking you to please read it. Will you do that for me?"

"Yep," I say, and reach for the envelope, but Sylvia hangs on to it. "I also realize," she says, "that you wouldn't want to get together and talk about it, but if by any chance that's incorrect"—she shrugs—"if you have a little time perhaps to enjoy a cup of coffee?"

"No can do."

Sylvia nods and says, "Please take this, then," and I'm handed her epistle. She shakes a teasing finger at me, looks healthy and winsome and girded with all manner of weapons of the spirit. "You're my prayer project, Sid. Jesus and I, we've got you in our gaze. When you do meet Him, you're going to realize He's known all about you for a long time."

"Yeah, well, I'm familiar with *his* rep, too," I say. "We'll have a lot to talk about."

"I don't mind if you joke," says Sylvia, minding.

I say to Sylvia, "Thank you for this envelope. I'll see you around, I'm sure."

"God bless you."

"Dig it."

I wave at Sylvia from the rec-center doors, waving with the manila envelope, my other hand holding the guitar-and-case and my shoulder pushing open the doors to freedom.

"Sylvia *Goodwin*," I say that night to Colby Dunn at Barnaby's. I drink from a beer bottle. "Is that an unfair name, or what?"

Colby nods, looking around for the waitress.

"Good, win," I say. "Maybe I'll change my name to Sid Badloss."

"That's pretty powerful," Colby agrees. "Wear a black hat, never smile on stage, sing about runaway women. Rack up DWIs and stuff."

"But the kids wouldn't go for it, now would they, Colby."

"Oh no, that appeals to a different public."

"Speaking of which—"

"Is that one ours?"

I look where he's pointing. "No, ours was older."

"Her name was Constanza," Colby remarks.

"Is that right." I have forgotten to smoke any cigarettes. This only happens to me when I feel down about myself and more or less welcome a jones. I have to smoke constantly when I'm not in front of my public, so as to put enough nicotine in my bloodstream to last me through the times when I *am* in front of my public. Remembering, I take out a Marlboro, fire it up, and blow smoke at Colby. "Have you listened to the mp3 I sent you? Called 'Excellent New Direction for Sid'?"

"Sure have." Colby nods with vigor and turns completely around in his chair, so I'm staring at his bald head as he scans the restaurant for Constanza.

"And?"

He turns back. "I want a couple fellows down in Nashville to hear it."

"You want a second opinion."

"Exactly."

"You didn't like it."

"Hell, Sidney, it's all right." Colby looks down at his empty beer. "Powerful," he says.

"'Convenience Store of the Heart'? The first song? That happens to be a hit," I tell him. "That has Country Top 20 written all over it."

"There's Constanza!" he says happily, and flags her down. We order beers. Constanza reminds me I can't smoke in here, and I pop my ciggy into an empty beer bottle.

"But of course it's not 'The Squeak Squeak Song,'" I say.

"Well, exactly."

"You don't believe I can write songs for grown-up people."

"I'd like to get a second opinion. I don't want you making any sperm-of-the-moment decisions." He giggles at himself.

"Colby," I say sternly, "now is the time to do a break-out. *Super Seance*"—this is the name of the spooky-themed show on the We're Kidding! channel that will feature me—"will put my name before a wider public. I believe those were your words."

"A wider public of *children*."

"And their moms. Now is the time. I am, we agree, a country music artist first and foremost. This is major exposure, Colby. Seven guaranteed minutes for every half hour of new programming on the show. As my agent, I'm expecting you to have vision."

Colby allots himself a major exposure to his bottle, puts it down, and says, "I got vision. *Super Seance* is gonna earn you beaucoup bucks, especially if it goes viral, is that what they call it?, and all this streaming shit I don't really understand yet. And speaking of that, I'd like to describe the efforts I'm making to—"

I make a gesture for Colby to shut up, which he recognizes from long association with my moods. As the artist half of this relationship, I'm entitled to have a mood or two. I slide down in my chair until I can feel my tailbone hurting. "According to Sylvia Goodwin's latest communiqué, *Super Seance* is going to earn me a one-way ticket straight to the Devil."

"Yeah, well, fuck her, okay?" Colby responds briskly. "Don't read that stuff she gives you. Have her arrested."

"Spiritual warfare," I mutter. The manila envelope sits in front of me, getting wet from the condensation off my many beer-bottles. I'd intended to toss it but Sylvia had block-printed on it: SID I MUST ALSO WRITE ABOUT THIS TO YOUR YOUTUBE SHOW. "The *hell* you must," I'd said out loud in the car, and read its contents at the table—a three-bottle project —waiting for Colby to show. Now I tell him, "That's what we're engaged in here, Colby my man: spiritual warfare. Did you 'realize' that?"

Sid you must realize that the use for so-called "amusement" of New Age occult practices (ie. seances crystal balls channeling guided imagery et.al.) is only opening the door to Satans power. And she teaches school.

"It's unrequited love," says Colby. "She still thinks she's

gonna sink the old hooks into you."

"You and your public school strategy."

Colby looks offended, and rightfully so. It's true he got me the gig that took me into Sylvia Goodwin's first-grade classroom, running some kind of "elements of music" educational scam, but I have only myself to blame for the rest. Though she did take the lead, that much is also true. After admiring my performance, she asked me if I wanted to perhaps enjoy a cup of coffee sometime soon, discuss music and kids. I believe she also mentioned Christian values but it got no particular big play. I said sure, thinking, Hey, recommendations, contacts. And Sue and I were at that point just about finished, so I wasn't totally averse to some pleasure with the business. We had the coffee, and she was glowing like neon, and saying not much about Jesus but quite a bit about me, and when I hugged her goodbye, here came a soul-kiss. I disengaged myself and spoke up and mentioned my committed relationship but it's possible I did not sound stalwart. And Sylvia played it like a pro. She made sure there was more to talk about, music-wise and ideas-about-Sid-and-kids-in-schools, etc. So it seemed natural enough to invite her to come to one of my weekend rec-center gigs. This one was out in Olney, and it snowed that morning, and just about no one showed up except me and Sylvia. I sang for the ones who did make it, and then Sylvia and I repaired for another enjoyable cup of coffee, this time at her place. Of course I knew what was in the air. What can I say? She was easy to look at and I'd been out of circulation for two years, and feeling it. I told myself

I wouldn't make any first moves—kind of clearing my conscience in advance. This time, all snug at her place, she rapped me with Jesus pretty hard. And then jumped me on the couch, saying What a team we'd make for Him, Sid! Better than a cold shower: I told her no, not likely, I wasn't ready to be for him (not that I was against him either, just uncommitted), and as for teaming up, there was still the matter of the relationship I *was* committed to. She got small and red-faced and said, You're right, you're right, Sid, forgive me, I was weak. And I left into the snow, figuring adios for good. Except she showed up at a gig in Wheaton the very next weekend, as if nothing had happened, followed me out to my car, handed me the first of her famous epistles, and said, Please take this and read it, Sid. This is goodbye. Okay, goodbye, I said. Goodbye, she said again, staring at me, and then she grabbed me and doled out another major sultry kiss. I hadn't been too keen on seeing her just show up like that, and had decided anyway that her rap was a touch demented, so when she kissed me for the third time I got as stern with her as I probably ought to have been from the beginning. Forget it, Sylvia, I said. I am committed.

End of personal contact—but the letters marched on, and on.

These are little children we're talking about Sid. They are as empty vessels that are filled either with the love of our redeemer Jesus Christ or the malignant wandering spirits of Darkness.

"Malignant wandering spirit of Darkness," I say.

"She sure is," says Colby.

"Sid Badloss Sings 'The Malignant Wandering Spirit of—'"

"Hey, did you write down October thirty-first? The Dollar-Brite opening?"

I tell him I haven't forgotten about October thirty-first. The *Super Seance* contract calls for Sid Wicker's presence at Dollar-Brite grand openings, "to perform no fewer than five (5) songs to be featured on the All-New Dollar-Brite We're Kidding! Channel program entitled *Super Seance* (hereafter 'The Program'), and to greet, mingle, converse, sign autographs free of surcharge, and in all other reasonable ways assist the aforesaid grand openings (hereafter, singly and severally, 'Grand Openings') and promote positive viewer expectations in re The Program," and similar mumbo jumbo.

I say to Colby, "I expect to hear the second opinion as soon as you do. I have a great deal of faith in that demo." Colby nods, and looks sad because he knows I'm about to tell him, again, how sick I am of the gopher-guts circuit. But tonight I just don't have it in me to argue.

I tell him to pay the check, I've got to be getting home, it's been a long day.

To be perfectly honest, kids make me tired.

"Who is Sylvia Goodwin?"

We're at Ace Video doing a run-through of my first *Seance* spot. The woman who wants to know is Ronda Loewenfels, the producer. She's hoarse and no-nonsense—I dig her as the mother I wish I had—and we share smokes out in the courtyard while the techies do their endless light-readings and sound-samples and all.

"She really did write to you," I say.

"Yes," says Ronda.

"So isn't it clear what she is?"

"Certainly." Ronda thumb-flicks the ash from her cigarette onto the courtyard floor. "We get cranks all the time. I'm a tad concerned, however, about two things. Three things." Ronda gives me a digit for each: "One, she's got a church. Two, she's a public schoolteacher. Those are the most important points of concern."

"I should think so."

"But, plus, three: she says you're about to undergo a conversion to the Lord, and that when you do, you're going to denounce *Super Seance* and, ah, all its works, was I believe the way she put it."

"Goddamn it," I say.

"Is that any way for a Christian to talk?"

"Hey, Ronda, look at me." I put a hand on each of her shoulders and stare into her eyes. "Am I a man about to enter the Middle Ages?"

"Well, Sid, that depends on what you consider middle-aged. You're what, thirty-eight, thirty-nine—"

"Thirty-six. Very comical. The *Dark* Ages. Demons, spooks, all that crap."

"No," says Ronda carefully, "you don't appear to be such a man."

Sylvia Goodwin, I tell her, is a loony-tune who believes in things that haven't existed since the Salem witch trials. An alternate world of evil critters hovering around us like bad weather, like mini-helicopters, trying to land inside our brains and drive out all hope of Jesus. I explain how one of these predators got inside Sylvia's brain seven months ago—"a lust demon, Sid"—and made her kiss me with full-tongue penetration on three separate occasions. "Of course," I say to Ronda, "she only started calling it a lust demon after I told her forget it. So that's the whole picture. She's a woman scorned, is all."

Ronda pats my arm. "Okay, Sid, I believe you. No conversion for you. Do you happen to know if she really has a church and is really a public schoolteacher?"

"I'm afraid so."

"I'll see-see you on the letter we send her."

"I'd appreciate that."

"It will be a very conciliatory letter."

"Fine."

"We're Kidding! is open to a diversity of opinion, and enjoys hearing from its viewers."

"I hear that."

"Any chance you could talk her around to laying off us?"

"I very much doubt it."

"Would you be willing to try? I'd really hate," says Ronda, still being careful, "to see your debut spoiled by an organized protest from the Christian Right."

"Ooooooh."

"Yes. Dollar-Brite in general, of course, feels the same way. All the more so because this organized protest will commence, according to Ms. Goodwin, at the Dollar-Brite grand opening."

"I'll try, Ronda. I absolutely will."

A techie with headphones comes calling for us. I walk back into the studio to greet my innocent little public. (We've imported some for the video.) I'm nearly through the doors before I realize I've still got a Marlboro fired up in my hand. I ditch it just in time.

Two nights later, here is Sylvia, in Wheaton again, my hometown. It's one of the few D.C. suburbs with some character left. The shopping mall dominates, naturally, but there are still a few non-chain stores outside the mall's drawbridge, and beat-up neighborhood bars, and an Army surplus joint that doesn't sell designer warfare garb, and an outstanding used CD and record store. None of the upscale Washingtonians are quite sure what to do with Wheaton, so we're managing to get along okay without 'em.

I've asked Sylvia to dine with me at Crouching Panda. She eats a piece of orange beef and looks at me a little breathlessly. Maybe the MSG is getting to her.

"So about your letter," I say, sipping beer. "Your letters. I want you to know, first, that I respect your position. As I believe Ms. Loewenfels does."

"Thank you, Sid. I've never doubted that."

"All right. Now I would like you to respect *my* position. This," I point out with my fork, "is America. We are into life, liberty, and the pursuit of happiness. Everybody gets to follow their own star. You with me?"

"Of course, Sid. You don't have to talk to me like I'm—"

"Yeah, I know, you're a teacher, you *teach* this stuff. Bear with me." Sylvia locks her eyes on mine, using chopsticks to take a grain or two of rice into her mouth at intervals and chewing softly as I explain to her that here is a classic example of American principles: everyone has rights, we value diversity, no one will force any empty vessels to watch *Super Seance*, ultimately it's a family-values issue, parental prerogatives, refusing to permit censorship, et cetera. "Which is your *thing*, I believe, Sylvia: family values, mom and dad making their own decisions. Et cetera," I conclude.

Sylvia smiles. "Sid," she says, "I have such respect for your position, and the way you articulate it."

I thank her and swallow beer, thirsty from my oration.

"You are a talented and articulate man, and these are the very qualities which drew me to you from the start, and also, not that you want to hear this but it does bear repeating, also the very qualities which will make you such a blessed soldier in the army of the Lord."

"Aw, shucks," I say, in the spirit of parley.

"I mean it. And so good with children." She gives me one of those cute finger-shakes, holding a chopstick. "Why you're not a father I'll never know. Have you and your"— Sylvia pauses scrupulously—"your fiancée set a date yet?"

She wasn't a fiancée, and anyway she's history, I explain.

"Oh." Sylvia goes inward for a second or two. Uh huh, I think: should have lied. "Well. However." She sits upright and puts her utensils down, along with her smile. She begins to speak. She speaks for fifteen minutes. After the first thirty seconds it's clear my civics lesson was a waste of time. I stop listening and start glaring. Eventually, Sylvia says, "So in the last analysis, Sid, as I've tried to make clear, this is a matter of conscience which Christians are pledged to carry into the public weal."

"I believe you used that very phrase in your recent letter. Letters," I say. My beer mug is empty and my appetite is gone. Why, every time, do I imagine there is some way to affect Sylvia Goodwin for the better? Reason will never do it; how could it?; if she was a fan of reason she wouldn't be torpedoing my career in the first place, because reasonable people do not fear that I will unleash creepy spiritual entities into the public goddamn weal.

"Sylvia, I'm appealing to you on personal grounds." I take her hand. I feel the fingers start to jerk away, but then she lets me hold on. "Let's cut to the chase: you have the power to mess me up in a fairly major way here. Not that I believe the We're Kidding! people will change their minds about the show just because of your churchladies, but the effect will be to tar me with a brush, you understand? My public? Or rather their parents? They see headlines on Facebook, they read a word here and there—DEMONS, SATAN, OCCULT, CHILDREN, SID WICKER—they make assumptions without troubling themselves to understand the fucking issues."

"Sid, really." The fingers jerk again.

"I'm sorry. I'm a little upset. What I'm saying is, you can hurt me, Sylvia Goodwin. And I'm appealing to you, in memory of certain shared moments which I won't go into, to just let me alone here. I mean, would Jesus really want you to hurt me?"

"Oh, Sid." Her hand grips mine, her lips part. "Jesus knows this is for your own good. You're worried about your career but Jesus is worried about your soul. You're building your house on sand. And it will fall, it *has* to fall. With a mighty crash. Before you can open your heart to Him. That's your destiny, Sid."

When I told Ronda Loewenfels it was hopeless, I meant it. But I'm still angry enough, now that I've been proved right, to want to kick Sylvia Goodwin's ass all the way up to Destination Heaven and back. Keeping hold of her hand, giving the palm a little fingerpad action, I look into her crystalline, twinkling eyes and say softly, "Hey Sylvia. How's about I pay the check and then we go out to the old car and take a little drive up to Wheaton Regional Park? On this crisp fall night."

We're both leaning toward each other over the moo shi and orange beef. "Do you really feel that way about me, Sid?" Sylvia breathes. "Still?"

"Right now I do," I say.

Long, long moment. Long enough for me to about-face mentally and think, Sidney, tighten the screws here. You're waltzing into an unending tangle if you go do this. Man, it's been seven-plus months and you're still tripping over the *last* tangle. Which ensued from exactly three kisses.

And besides, it's a little tacky.

I don't get the chance to find out how my conscience

would have fielded that one, though, because Sylvia places my hand down next to the plum-sauce saucer, gives it a sisterly there-there pat, smiles so widely that it squeezes a tear out of the temple-side corner of each eye, and says, "No, Sid. Jesus has cleansed the lust demon from my heart." She clears her throat. "As I pray He will do for you."

It's such a relief, I almost like her. Thank you, Sylvia Goodwin, you've saved me from doing a shitty thing.

"Would you— would you pray now, with me, for that?" She clears her throat again. "Not that I wouldn't like to keep seeing you."

I smile at her and say, "Later for the prayer, okay? The dude's coming over with our fortune cookies."

"Fortune-telling is a snare of Satan," Sylvia remarks. She refuses to open hers.

We part with a firm Christian handclasp in the parking lot. "Sylvia," I say, giving her one of her own teasing finger-shakes, "I just bet I opened your cookie. 'Cause it said YOUR PATIENT AND FORGIVING NATURE EARNS FRIENDS' ADMIRATION. I'm all set to admire such a nature. Please think it over, you and your churchladies."

Sylvia says, "Please think over what I've said. And wrote. You must not allow yourself to be used by the powers of Darkness, Sid. Jesus has a baptism prepared for you. It's not too late."

"We agree to disagree. Been nice talking to you."

"You can call me."

Driving home I realize I've forgotten to smoke again.

The next day I give my reports over the phone to Colby Dunn and Ronda Loewenfels. "So there it is," I tell Colby. "My ass belongs to the Christian Right."

"Am I surprised?" says Colby. "No I am not. I talked to a lawyer, Sid."

"You what? With whose money?"

"Just talked, he's a friend. In his opinion we can make some powerful legal trouble for her."

I tell him to forget it. "I'm more interested in your Nashville opinions. Have you got 'em yet?"

Not yet, he says: we're playing phone tag. "They're It at the moment, Sid. They'll call back." Record the conversation, I tell him. I want to hear it.

Ronda Loewenfels is still being careful. "On behalf of We're Kidding! I want to thank you for trying to reason with this young woman, Sid. We're sending a representative to meet with her church group too."

"That's cool. But a waste of time."

"Well, no doubt. Perception. Appearances. We're perceived as proactive this way. Which reminds me: I don't suppose you *are* a Christian by any chance, Sid?"

"Ronda, I told you. Sylvia Goodwin is completely clueless. I'm not—"

"Understood, understood. I didn't mean her kind. I meant, if you were yourself a more *moderate* Christian—I don't know, an Episcopalian, better yet a Unitarian—we could craft a statement for you to the effect that *Super Seance* is perfectly in line with mainstream religious values and that you personally have no converse with the Devil or any of his, ah, minions. You know, like that?"

The last part, fine, I tell her: I have no truck with nonexistent creatures, not since I stopped eating mescaline. As for the first, I am, as they say, unchurched, and it would probably be better not to craft that particular statement.

Ronda chuckles, in that nice hoarse way of hers. "It was just a shot. Thanks for filling me in on your talk with Sylvia. Please know that We're Kidding! and *Super Seance* and myself personally remain one hundred percent behind you and your wonderful songs."

"Thank *you*, Ronda, because I did want to point out, Ronda, that even if for some reason I were *off* the program, this group would still be protesting, you agree? It just so happened that I drew their fire—Sylvia Goodwin's fire—but now they've got you in their sights and c'est la vie. You agree?"

"Indeed we do." Another chuckle. "Her fire. Let it be a lesson to you, Sid. Stop sleeping with those loose cannons."

"I didn't. We soul-kissed, like I said. And she tattled to Jesus, and now *he* wants to."

"Well, from the unsynagogued to the unchurched, hang in there."

The next week is a typical Sid Wicker week: a couple of community-event gigs, a couple of private kiddie birthday parties, old Sid Wicker singing the childhood favorites. I *like* children, I keep telling myself. They like *me*. They just make me a little tired. Colby claims to be still playing phone-tag with Nashville. I tell him to play harder. I have wondered from time to time if Colby fears I will desert him for a Nashville agent, should Nashville show enthusiasm for my new songs. That fear is not ungrounded.

I give Ronda Loewenfels a ring to ask how the representative made out with Sylvia's church group. Not so well, says Ronda. A basic difference on what's at stake, after all: We're Kidding! considers Gypsy Genevieve the Seance Lady, Wee Willie Ouija, et al. to be harmless amusement, whereas the Apostles True Covenant Church considers them to be slaves of Satan. Not much wiggle room.

I have not seen or heard from Sylvia. This makes me nervous. If she's given up trying to persuade me to do a Saul-to-Paul, then I guess here come the weapons of the spirit and Katie bar the door.

The day before the Dollar-Brite grand opening, it dawns on Colby and Ronda and Dollar-Brite's PR folk, more or less simultaneously judging from the flurry of phone calls and texts and emails, that October thirty-first is Halloween. "As you no doubt know, Sid, many Christians regard Halloween as a hostile pagan experience for their children," Ronda tells me.

Is it too late to change the date? I ask her.

Much too late. The Dollar-Brite PR folk feel real bad about it, though. They blame themselves. "They've definitely blotted their copybook on this one." Terrific, I say. Fuck 'em, Colby says. "Where is our backbone? Our spine? I mean, Sid, who knows kids better? Sid Wicker, who kids love, or some bunch of religious crazies? Have you ever heard of a kid being turned into a Satanist by Halloween?" Not the point, Colby, I tell him. You're using reason. This is spiritual warfare, not reasonable dialogue. He mutters about creationists and climate-deniers and clinic-bombers and claims not to know what his own country is coming to these days. "Spine! We must show spine!" So you'll be at the opening? Actually, no, he says; gotta see some movers and shakers up in NYC. Wrong, I tell him. You will *be* there. I want moral support. I want you to hold my coat if I have to fight any Christian soldiers.

The thirty-first dawns cloudy, and by one o'clock, as I pull up in front of the spanking new Dollar-Brite at Glenmont Square Shopping Plaza, we're into a serious and nape-chilling rain. Endlessly it comes splattering down. Will it keep my public home? No way, for as I take my guitar-and-case from the backseat and hop through the puddles toward the entrance, I see many moms, many dads even, and of course a swarm of their heirs and progeny running about in front of the doors, slowly entering, their entrance made slower than usual by the other sight I see: a coterie of organized protesters not exactly blocking the doors but arrayed in a semicircle around them. Signs, of course, some held on sticks, some dangling from twine around necks.

SAY NO TO SEANCE

NEW AGE = SATAN'S AGE

DOLLAR-BRITE SUPPORTS THE OCCULT
SHOULD *YOU* SUPPORT *THEM*?

THE DEVIL ♥ HALLOWEEN

A number of children are wearing their Halloween costumes, and I see a photographer (whose spiffy-looking equipment spells "media") snap a photo of a fey pre-K boy in a black-and-silver skeleton suit, the skull-mask pulled up on top of his towhead, gazing in wonder at a dripping church-lady who's smiling pityingly down at him. Her sign, which I fervently hope he's too young to read, says: SUPER SEANCE, DOLLAR-BRITE, SID WICKER = THE DEVIL'S TOOLS. But goddamn it, his parents aren't too young to read it, nor are the readers of whatever rag or blog or stream the photographer represents.

I have begun to be pissed off. I am wet and angry and, truth be told, a touch hung over. Were Colby here (and he better get here), were Ronda Loewenfels here, I would for a penny tell them just how I feel, which boils down to: I want to sing songs for *adults*, defined as non-church-crazed people who drink and smoke and screw, because this is the soul of country music and I am a country music artist, thank you very much—yet I seem to have awakened from some terrible enchantment at the age of thirty-eight (okay, Ronda, I fibbed) to find myself holding down a big-time humiliating niche in the world of popular music: the Bard of Gopher-Guts, the schmuck who is earning royalties from a composition entitled "The Squeak Squeak Song." Who let this happen to me? Are you listening, Jesus? We're Kidding? *You're* kidding!

Neither Colby nor Ronda nor Jesus is in evidence but Sylvia Goodwin will do, in fact will do splendidly, target-wise. But as I stand behind a pillar just outside the semi-circle of protesters, cradling my instrument, my O's cap turned right-side-round with the brim over my eyes in the goofy hope that no one will recognize me yet, that perhaps I'll be taken for some other bearded person with a guitar who just happened to show up at a Dollar-Brite grand opening, I do not see Sylvia either. I check out each protester's face: no. What is the deal here? I thought I was her prayer project. Have she and Jesus gone off to talk about someone else? She lets her posse do the dirty work on poor old Sid? Damn.

I decide that a straight, hard stride through the throng is the best bet. Difficult, though, to stride through small children. They don't dig how to get out of the way, and my new image as the Devil's plaything won't be improved if I trample 'em underfoot. I end up threading a path, holding my sodden guitar-and-case over their heads, trying not to meet anyone's eyes.

I'm just at the people-sensitive glass doors, which whoosh open for me, when I hear a female voice behind me say, "There he is! That's Sid Wicker!" I give a little wave, not looking back. A chant begins: "Sid Wicker, Wicked Sid / Don't forget what Jesus did! / Sid Wicker, Wicked Sid. . . ." I have for some reason become the center of attention. Just inside the store are many moms and dads and kids. I shrug, smile, make a kind of baffled gesture with my free hand. The looks I get back are by no means unfriendly. Intrigued, rather. I mean, here we have drama, a scene to enliven dull suburban lives: how will child entertainer Sid Wicker react to being branded with the number of the Beast?

Well, keep that smile going. Look like you've seen it all before. Crazy wet folk out there, right? Entitled to their viewpoint, of course. But hey. We're inside here, dry and sane and ready to have a good time. Right?

The Dollar-Brite people have set up a little Astroturfed dais over to the left, in front of the toy department. Chair, mic stand, mic, PA speakers. My audience is already about a hundred strong, I can see, all sitting on the floor, as is usual with the venues I play. Many more curious looks as I step to the edge of the cross-legged crowd and survey the scene. A guy in a flowery tie and one of those striped dress shirts with a white collar introduces himself to me as Joe something from Dollar-Brite PR.

"We sure have some excitement here today, don't we, Sid!" he remarks, smiling like a numbnuts and taking my coat. Which reminds me to ask him if he's seen a bald agent named Colby Dunn. Nope. "Now why don't you just get comfortable and then maybe greet some of these nice people. Mingle a little before you play for us."

Not today, I tell him. I'm not really in a mingling mood. Lemme just tune up and we'll get the ball rolling. Joe claps me on the back and says, "Looking forward to it! Looking forward to it! But see, Sid, your contract calls for you to mingle, greet, converse, and otherwise—"

Not today, I tell him. We're about to have a fight when

a real fight breaks out six feet to our left. Security guards are removing four protesters, two male, two female, who nonetheless manage to distribute many many pieces of bright yellow paper to the seated audience. These papers appear to be multiplying, à la the loaves and fishes. *Everybody*'s got one. A female protester gives me a staunch look and hands one to me as she's hustled away. I glance at it, seeing biblical quotes, quotes from Christian child psychologists, my name. I crumple it up and hand it to Joe.

"Joe," I say, "would it possible do you think for your security heavies to prevent these nice church people from entering the store during my performance?" Joe begins to explain how difficult it is to tell the church people from the ordinary customers if they're not carrying signs or chanting. He has a point, of course, but I'm in no mood to hear it. "Okay, screw it. But no mingling," I remind him again. "Is the PA on? No? Then crank it up. I'm ready to wail." I leave him mumbling about the contract and start walking through the crowd again.

"How you all doing today?" I call out as I walk. Oddly, this line gets a big laugh. Tension-breaker, maybe. Hey, fine, let's play it for yucks. "You all ready to sing some songs with the Devil?"

Major mistake. Dead silence. Joe goes stiff as a corpse, then lurches over to the edge of the dais, shaking his head until his jowls wiggle all over his white collar. I arrive, get my guitar out in record time, do a quick tune-check, and seat myself front and center. Joe is mouthing words at me. Man do I wish he'd go play with a toy or something. It was just a goddamn joke, okay? I begin to tell him this. "It was a goddamn—" Joe was wrong: the PA *is* on, and way too loud. GODDAMNDAMNDAMN goes my amplified voice. "—joke," I say sadly. JOKEJOKEJOKE. "*Well*, kids. Some fun, huh?" I hit a pretty E chord. "I'd like to perform a song from my CD entitled 'How Many Beans Make Three?'" A few people have the common goddamn decency to clap. Thank you very much, I tell them, and start the song.

It is not Sid Wicker's day. I am not getting that invaluable audience rapport, without which a singer might as well go hang himself. The kids, my public, who ought to be above it all, or beneath it all, seem a touch subdued. Disapproving. Disdainful would not be too strong. I know what's happening even as it's happening. You cannot fool a child. A child knows when tragedy strikes. A child reads subtext as it once drank mother's milk. The children at this Dollar-Brite today do not want to squeak. They are anxious about whatever vibes are vibrating back and forth and up and down all over the store, and they are not making any fine distinctions about who is responsible. In a word, they hate me.

The protesters have turned clever. They cause no disruption while I sing. They merely stand there watching me. Side by side. Not applauding. Hissing very faintly after every song, like a lit fuse. Their lack of applause is contagious.

I'd intended to do seven or eight numbers, but quit after the required five. I plug *Super Seance* at the end, as required. It's possible my plug lacks panache. At the word *seance* the hisses are heard. Louder, sounding more like snakes this time.

Thank you very much, I say again. Thank you for coming out on this dreary ol' rainy Saturday. Yeah, ol' Sid's caught a little cold, in fact. Feeling very poorly, and must regretfully leave now. Hope this doesn't prove a disappointment to you good people.

Evidently it doesn't—you might even say the good people are in a hurry to leave too—though Joe, who's watched me as if I was some ghastly thing from Hell throughout my performance, now has too many words to say about what are we going to do to defuse this negative situation, what about Dollar-Brite's family image, what about promoting expectations, what about—

"What about you let me get the fuck out of here and then you think of a way to explain to your superiors, of whom I'm sure there are many, how you let this Grand Opening go down the tubes due to inadequate security and brainless scheduling?" It gives him something to chew on as I slam my axe into its case and grab my coat and get ready to book.

I hop off the back of the dais. And here is Sylvia, all alone next to a rack of trikes. Wearing a chaste gray raincoat, a little plastic rainhat. Watching me.

"Well, well," I say, advancing on her. "We've *got* to stop meeting like this."

"Hello, Sid," she says. Looking me straight in the eye, I'll give her that.

"Are we satisfied now? Enjoying ourselves?" I ask her. "Helluva day's work, huh? Great protest action. Plus you got to attend Sid Wicker's all-time lousiest gig."

"I— We had to do it, Sid." Sylvia now begins to cry. "I want to say I'm sorry but I'm— I'm not. Not really."

"Yeah, I know. We must think of the poor empty vessels. Oh, and it was for *my* own good, too, right? Getting me all nice and humble and baptizable to go meet Jesus." Sylvia continues to cry, her arms held straight at her sides, sniffling and still looking right at me. "How come you skipped the best parts," I went on, "the Wicked Sid chants and all? Heck, when I didn't see you here I thought you'd decided to go taunt faggots instead, or some other fun thing."

"I know," Sylvia sniffles. "I saw you arrive and I just— I just couldn't— I was weak. Again."

I stand there with my guitar-and-case dragging down my arm. "Weak," I say. "Weak."

"Say there, Sid," says Colby Dunn. I turn around and there he is, grinning and fooling with his buttons. "*Gosh* I'm sorry I missed your performance. Pulled up not five minutes ago, rain, roads, uh, but what this fella Joe was just now telling me? I'm sure he was exaggerating—"

"No," I tell Colby. "It was Wicker's Last Stand. In more ways than one."

"Hello, honey," Colby says absently to Sylvia, who is patting her eyes with a pink tissue. "Now, Sidney, it couldn't've been *that* bad."

"Shut up," I tell him. "We have come to a parting of the ways. And don't you go saying sperm-of-the-moment to me because it isn't. I've been making this decision little by little for a good long time and now I'm printing it out. You reading, Colby? Nashville, Colby. I'm Nashville bound. No more gopher-guts."

"Uh," Colby says.

"Oh, *Sid*," Sylvia says.

I look at her. "And no more spiritual warfare. Feenee. Over. You win." I laugh. "You win, Sylvia Good-win. Ol' Sid Badloss is shaking the Devil's dust from his bootheels and riding off into the sunset to find him a new public."

"That's her?" Colby points at Sylvia. "She's the one responsible for this fiasco? Little lady," he says, still pointing, "I want you to know we are not without legal recourse."

"I said shut up," I tell him. "We will have no such recourse."

"Sid," Sylvia says in a small, mucus-thick voice, "you *are* walking toward Jesus, even if you don't believe it for a single moment."

I throw my O's cap to the floor. "Nashville!" I shout at her. "I am walking toward goddamn *Nashville*! Sylvia, Sylvia. . . ." I pick my cap up and stuff it in my back pocket, shaking my head. "You think poor little *Super Seance* is big-time evil? I urge you to visit Nashville. See some *real* sin! Yessir! And you know what? People down there actually have a good time on their way to Hell. They don't wuss around with crystal balls and ouija boards. 'Course," I point out, "they're adults."

"Now, Sid," says Colby. I yank my O's cap out of my pocket and hurl it at him. He fields it and looks at it.

"I will continue to pray for you, Sid," Sylvia tells me. The tissue is clutched in her fist and her voice sounds stronger.

"Be my guest," I tell her.

"You can call me."

"Ha. Maybe a text. To say Guess where *I* am."

Heading up the aisle and out toward the people-sensitive doors, I fire up a Marlboro—no mean feat with a guitar-and-case in one hand. Outside the sun is burning on a million parking-lot puddles and a strong breeze blows. Two dozen kids and moms still hang about, eating cotton candy that Dollar-Brite is giving away free. The protesters have some too, which strikes me as collaborationist but there you go.

"Look, Mommy! Sid Wicker's smoking a cigarette!"

I give my ex-public a wave and a big, big grin. A gust of wind blows rainwater off the roof and onto my capless head, drenching me, dousing my 'Boro and my grin. "Oh, nice work," I mutter, "you remembered the baptism," and head off to find some boxes for my move.

When I Snap My Fingers You Will Remember Everything

Cape Blackstone, Maryland, 1976. There is a small party taking place tonight at the beach house that Robinson Veazey, the famous American painter (which is to say that perhaps ten thousand of his fellow Americans have heard of him), rents for a month each summer.

Despite Robinson's warnings to be careful, the carpet is tracked with sand. Robinson, in any event, has already spilled his drink on it, which his old friend Peter Harnisch, the flautist, has pointed out to him, wiggling his fingers derisively at the stain. "Not so good for the fabric, Robinson." As an old friend, Peter can get away with it, but none of the other guests—two students, two poets, and a confectioner—would dare to refer to Robinson's clumsiness around gin.

"The hell with it—we're *talking*, Peter," Robinson says, flicking his cigarette ash into, or near to, the ashtray. Robinson's voice is a mentholated Brooklyn growl, and his big, blunt features, emerging like rocks from the surf of his gray-white beard, no longer put up any sort of fight against the amount of alcohol he drinks. They droop and erode, and his complexion is ruined. He has acne, like a teenager.

Peter laughs—a malicious and slightly overweight elf in his little beach shorts—says, "Oh, are 'we'?" and attempts to catch the eyes of the others, the point being that it is Robinson who has been talking, incessantly, repetitiously, about all his favorite subjects.

One of the students is thin and fair and wears his light brown hair tied back in a ponytail. His name is Gary Negretti, and he does not laugh with Peter Harnisch because he thinks it would be cruel, and because he's doing a lot of coursework with Robinson and doesn't want to make him angry, and also because he is interested in what Robinson has been saying. He isn't yet tired of Robinson's favorite subjects. Which are many: Robinson Veazey has taught guest courses in the English and philosophy departments, and he has published a temperamental, pugnacious book about the Idea of Beauty. Gary sometimes thinks of his teacher as an extremely eccentric, old-style jukebox, a little of this, a little of that, the tunes never updated, their labels blurred with spilled gin. But interesting.

Now Robinson says to Gary, "So where were we? Beethoven. Yeah, the Goya of music. Right, Gary?"

Gary Negretti agrees that this is definitely so. He's pretty sure that the Beethoven conversation was over at least an hour ago. "Both of them went deaf at roughly the same age," Robinson remarks, and squints through the haze—all seven men are heavy smokers—to reconnect with his audience, but he's obviously been thrown off pace. He takes a large, discontented gulp from his drink. "'Kay," he says. "Now, during the Renaissance. . . ."

Gary stubs out his cigarette, lights another, listens to the chatter of voices resume around him. But the room is hot and none of the three conversations taking place (two and a half, really; Robinson's contribution is as usual monologous) seems pursuable. Renaissance perspective, trompe l'oeil. Puns, anagrams, acrostics, "The Vane Sisters." The perils and pleasures of enjambment. Gary raises his glass to his lips and finds that there's only ice left. The flaws in the cogito. Pound versus Eliot. "You can have 'em both," one of the poets—the nonacademic one—mutters from a rickety couch set at right angles to Robinson's green foldout beach chair (which Robinson had insisted on bringing inside so he could "recline"— this accounts for a good deal of the sand). The poet's comment is not really meant as a challenge; Robinson rarely endures one. Oh, there are occasional bouts. Gary has watched Robinson's intellectual footwork carefully, over the two semesters he's known him. Could it be said that Robinson doesn't fight fair? Well, yes, sometimes; he kicks *ad hominem* sand, digresses craftily, throws quotes like rabbit punches. He will disappear if the going gets really tough. "That's when the tough get going: right out the door!" he will brag the next day, not the least shamefaced. Even a medical emergency isn't beyond him: Gary was present at a winter party at Robinson's Dupont Circle place when a Zen Buddhist sculptor in pigtails— who the hell invited *him*?—went toe to toe with his host on

Essential Form. With the sculptor ahead on points, Robinson suddenly gasped and groped for a tiny white pill. The whisper was passed from guest to guest: *angina*. End of party. . . .

Gary gets up out of his deck chair (unobtrusively, he hopes, though the floor tilts in a way that would be ominous if he were, for instance, about to lie down, for next come the spins, and then the whirls . . .) and goes into the kitchen for a very, very light drink: lots of Schweppes and crushed ice, perhaps just a jolt, or two, of gin. As he pours, the other student member of the gathering comes up behind him, a fellow fine arts major named, improbably, Marvin Bookvalid. ("Originally 'Buchenwald.' My father changed it. Wouldn't *you?*") Marvin has just graduated. He is a longtime protégé of Robinson Veazey. At every gathering where Robinson is to be found, Marvin is there too. He has taken every course Robinson offers. His equine, close-cropped head shows up in the background of college publicity photos of Robinson. Perhaps the word is devotee, not protégé. But tonight he has been aloof, self-contained, leaning on the edges of chair arms, legs crossed, seeming to be somewhere else. Gary doesn't care for Marvin, has always found him a somewhat creepy presence in the fine arts department, and at Robinson's. He is undeniably a talented painter, but his huge, shadowy canvases are so depressing that Gary secretly wonders if Marvin isn't, when you come right down to it, kidding. Can *any* twenty-two-year-old achieve that much *Weltschmerz?* "Enjoying yourself?" says Marvin in a faint voice. He opens the refrigerator and pours Coca-Cola into his glass.

"Yeah," says Gary. "Aren't you?" The kitchen receives almost no cross-ventilation, and is stunningly hot. Gary takes a gulp of his drink, then presses the cool-beaded glass against his forehead.

Marvin leans on the sink, makes a face, and reaches behind himself to remove a wet dishrag drooping over the edge. He tosses the rag onto the stack of dirty dishes in the sink and turns back to Gary. "You know something? In less than two months I'll be in Pasadena." He is referring to a prestigious graduate fellowship he has received. "I'll never see any of you people again," he says.

It's unclear to Gary how Marvin regards this prospect. "Yeah, too bad," Gary says neutrally. "I expect you'll keep in touch with Robinson."

"We'll write letters. And then we won't: they'll peter out. By mutual consent. You know something?" he asks again. "It's not worth it. It's just not worth the trouble."

"Writing letters?"

Marvin gives him a thin-lipped look. "Negretti," he says, "think twice before assuming the role of Robinson's favorite student. That's all I'll say."

Gary couldn't be more nonplussed. Is this really the loyal and reticent Marvin Bookvalid? And he's not even drunk. "Oh, nice talk," Gary says. "You accept the man's hospitality, to say nothing of the help he's given you. I mean, do you think you would've gotten within a *mile* of Pasadena without—"

"I have no idea," says Marvin. "And that's my point. Now I'll never know."

Gary puts his glass down, hard, on the kitchen table. "But that's the way it's *done*."

"Oh, come off it. Don't play innocent. You know what I'm talking about. It's started already, hasn't it? The phone calls. The notes. The invitations. And of course the catechism: 'Do you know Professor Spottswood? *He* said my book was "highly original." Whaddaya think of him? A helluva scholar, *isn't he, Marvin*? Can you believe that horseshit show at the Corcoran? Frauds, every one of 'em, *right, Marvin*?'" Marvin Bookvalid nods his head over and over, like a hand puppet. "Right, Robinson. Right, Robinson. Every single opinion you hold is right. Including, naturally, your opinion of my work. Which I have earned."

Gary has nothing to say. He's already received many late-night calls from the Dupont Circle apartment, Robinson's voice hobbled by drink and raspy with cigarette hacks. And the dinner invitations: once a week, sure, why not, but twice a week, three times a week? Let's go here, let's do that, let me tell you about this, let me show you that . . . And much praise for his coursework—which is earned, which is earned.

"Jesus, Bookvalid," says Gary. "Maybe he's lonely. Did you ever think of that?" Owen Jones, the nonacademic poet, enters the kitchen, frowning into his empty glass and rattling its cubes hopefully, as if they will generate more bourbon. He smoothes his extravagant sideburns and says to Gary, "*Il miglior fabbro*'s looking for you. Better hop to it." Gary shrugs, picks up his own glass—already, surprisingly, half-empty—and walks to the refrigerator. He opens the door and takes his time examining its contents (Schweppes, Schweppes, Schweppes, baking soda, an elaborate chocolate something in a bowl covered with cellophane on the bottom shelf), dawdling until his point is made. When Marvin and Owen turn away from him, he slams the door shut and hurries back into the main room.

The other poet, the academic one, is named Dennis Spottswood. (He is, as Marvin noted, one of the few Robinson Veazey fans on the faculty.) Spottswood has just agreed, after scraping vigorously at a nonexistent stain on his T–shirt, to recite something from his recent work. It is Peter Harnisch who has instigated this. Gary can tell that Peter's hoping for a clash between Spottswood and his nonacademic competitor, Owen Jones. It will also provide an interruption to Robinson's spieling. Peter stands up and, as if flagging down a cab, waves a hand at Robinson, deep into a lecture about hypnosis delivered to the seventh member of the gathering, the confectioner, who is Owen's boyfriend. (Gary finds it hateful that no one bothers to get the boyfriend's name right—since he's not there as an *equal*, you know—and is determined to learn before the night is over if it's Tony or Tommy.) Tony or Tommy is as slim and watchful as a doe, and he leans forward on the couch and stares at Robinson as the painter says, "And I suppose you've heard that stuff about how no one can be hypnotized to do something that's really against his will? Ha. Don't believe it."

"I *don't* believe it," says the confectioner.

Gary, standing above them, says, "Because it raises the question, doesn't it, of—"

"Oh, *there* you are," says Robinson, pointing his cigarette at Gary. "Exactly. Of the 'will,' so called. Much misunderstood term. Take the Thomistic stipulation for mortal sin, frinstance: 'full consent of the will.' Now—"

"I'm sorry," says the confectioner. "Take the what? I'm sorry," he says again.

"Take the— Look, what ya gotta understand is— *What*, Peter?"

"Dennis is going to recite a poem," says Peter, sinking down onto a hassock at Spottswood's feet and looking at him expectantly. Gary, back in the deck chair with his drink, can see the mischief in Peter's eye.

"Yeah?" says Robinson with a scowl.

Spottswood takes several backwards steps, and then several more to the left, like a tacking sloop, until he has docked against the screen of the veranda. He is a delicate, balding man with a bouquet of embarrassed gestures—fingertips rubbing against Adam's apple, palm swooping across the pink exposure of his scalp. Now he clears his throat and says to his host, whom he doesn't know all that well, "Oh, actually, I'd rather not, Robinson. I mean, I don't put these things *forward*, you know, it was only that Peter had brought it up—"

"Nah, what the hell, go ahead." Robinson pats the air reassuringly. "I *like* your poems. In fact, where's Marvin? I want Marvin to hear this."

Marvin Bookvalid is standing behind Robinson, canted

against the kitchen doorway. "Did I hear my name?" he asks the group.

"Dennis is about to recite one of his poems. Siddown and listen." Marvin drifts through the smoke, sits across from Gary, and gives him a small, personal smile. Owen Jones returns from the kitchen, carrying a drink of rich russet hue—could it be straight bourbon, Gary wonders? Robinson eyes him, takes a swallow of gin and tonic and then laughs explosively. "Oh, and of course we have Owen. You're Welsh, aren't you, Owen?"

Owen lights a cigarette, rolls his eyes, and says, "Of Welsh extraction. Do you want me to recite 'The force that through the green fuse drives the flower'?"

Robinson says, "The Welsh eat animal organs. Brains, testicles, whatnot. Racially, you need to learn restraint. Applies to poetry as well: green fuse, for Chrissake."

"It's a Celtic thing. You wouldn't understand," Owen replies mildly. He aims a jet of smoke at Robinson.

"Well, listen up. Could be a revelation for ya. Okay, everyone be quiet. Go ahead, Dennis."

Spottswood casts a tremulous and reproachful look down at Peter, still perched at his feet, and after clearing his throat again, recites a sonnet. Gary has spent the better part of the previous year catching up on poetry, at Robinson's urging, but still doesn't know what he likes. Well, he likes the fact that the sonnet is short—has to be, by God—and that Dennis Spottswood refuses to recite another one. The academic poet is smiling shyly, however, for Robinson has nodded at the group and said, "Damn good. Wasn't that good?" Everyone nods back. Peter is looking at Owen, but Owen does not curse or mutter in Welsh. He only raises his bourbon and says, simply, "Yes." Robinson says to Marvin, "Enjambment. See what I mean?" Marvin looks at Gary, like a runner passing the baton. "Mm-*hmm*," says Gary with a brisk nod. His bladder has been aching since the second quatrain.

Spottswood wipes his forehead with the bottom of his T–shirt, raising it like a tent flap to expose a sunburned patch of belly, and sits down on the couch next to Owen and Owen's boyfriend. The talk resumes. Gary heads for the bathroom, where he enjoys a timeless, shiver-inducing piss.

When he returns, they're back on hypnosis. The confectioner has somehow succeeded in getting the floor, and is concluding an anecdote—not well, judging from the expression on Robinson's face, and from the way Peter Harnisch is consulting his fingernails. But everyone in the room appears to have been listening. "So, not only did I not stop smoking, but I suffered these colossal migraines."

"All right, love," says Owen, rattling the ice in his glass. "Now, Robinson, about—"

"They kept up for months. And I twitched."

"Against your will," says Dennis Spottswood helpfully.

"At work, the powdered sugar would be everywhere. My boss didn't know what to *do* with me. I would get these spasms—"

Robinson makes a swatting motion. "You weren't successfully hypnotized, then," he declares. "Posthypnotic suggestion depends on trust. You didn't trust your hypnotist. That's the secret, ya see, the essential principle upon which—"

"Oh, but I did. He said I was one of the most suggestible clients he ever had. I said to him, If I'm so suggestible, Mister Expert, then why are my tortes suddenly a disgrace, *plus* I'm still sneaking into cold storage for a smoke every ten minutes?" Tony or Tommy looks first at Owen, then at the others, but only Gary meets his eyes. "He said he didn't know," the confectioner finishes unhappily.

"Well." Robinson drops him, watches Gary patting himself for a cigarette. "Did you get enough to eat?" he asks him.

Robinson had made an enormous and excellent soufflé for them all, hours ago, but Gary never has much appetite when he drinks. "Oh yeah," he assures Robinson. "It was great. I'm fine."

"I brought a dessert," says Tony or Tommy.

Robinson ignores him. "You're so goddamn thin," he says to Gary. "Next week, when I'm back in town, come over for dinner. Come on Tuesday. I'll make potato pancakes; you like those."

"Well, that's probably all right," says Gary, hoping Marvin Bookvalid isn't listening. "I need to look at my cal—"

"Make it definite. We can talk about those figure drawings you gave me. Damn good stuff there. One or two things I wanna show ya. But I'm impressed."

Tuesday will be fine, Gary agrees.

"Good. Speaking of figure drawings, has any of you ever read—"

"Oh! I think I forgot to put it in the refrigerator."

Robinson glares at the confectioner. "No one's hungry right now," he says.

Tony or Tommy stands up. "It's a mousse. I'd better check."

Peter Harnisch splutters with laughter. "Did you remove the antlers?" he gasps.

"A nice chocolate mousse, with mandarin orange glaze. I know you're teasing me," says Tony or Tommy. Robinson sighs loudly. Owen rattles his ice again. "I suppose we can have it later," Tony or Tommy whispers, and nods, agreeing with himself. "I'll just go see if it's in the fridge."

Dennis Spottswood breaks the silence that follows the confectioner's exit. "Have you ever been hypnotized, Robinson?" he asks.

Robinson grins, combs a hand through his beard, and replies, "I've *done* hypnotism, professionally. I used to have a stage show, a magic act. That was how I supported myself when I quit the Corcoran." At least half the guests have heard this one before, but the ensuing medley is welcome, under the circumstances: Robinson's adventures as a magician, segueing into the gullibility of scientists when confronted by alleged paranormal phenomena. When Robinson pauses to lift his glass, Peter says, "Robinson, why don't you hypnotize someone now? Do you know, in all the years we've known each other"—this grim number is invoked by Peter's gesture toward the horizons of space and time—"I've never actually seen you do it. Who knows what your victim might *reveal*?"

He sits up alertly, hands clasped.

Robinson bares his teeth. "Peter, don't be corny," he says. "And for your information, you *have* seen me do it. You just don't know what it looks like. It's not like the movies, ya know: the pocketwatch and chain, the mesmeric passes, all that Svengali stuff. Suggestibility and trust; that's all it is."

"Let's hypnotize you, love," says Owen to his boyfriend (who had returned during Robinson's monologue and given the group a reassuring nod, mouthing the words, *It's in the fridge*).

"No!" Tony or Tommy slaps Owen's thigh. "Haven't you heard a word I *said*? No one is ever doing that to me ever again."

"Your hypnotist was a fraud," says Robinson, making a semi-mesmeric pass at the confectioner, who flinches. "Look, I'll show you." ("Not *me*.") "If someone'll get me a refill?" Dennis Spottswood stands up quickly and takes Robinson's glass. "Lots of ice," Robinson calls after him.

It is late now, after midnight. Two electric fans blow air across Gary's face at intervals. Moth wings flutter and click against a nearby lampshade. "So," declares Robinson. "I need a subject. I'm certainly not going to hypnotize *you*, Peter." Gary doesn't quite see why this should be so, but Peter snickers and appears in complete agreement. "What about you, Marvin?" Robinson looks up at his protégé, who has been leaning against a bookshelf, lost in shadows.

"I pass, Robinson," says Marvin.

Robinson has put away close to two quarts of gin since morning, and is finally showing it. Like a fighter in the last rounds, his head bobs tiredly, and he hunches a bit, chin tucked in. "You pass," he says. "Whatsamatter?"

"Nothing. I'd just rather not."

"The li'l old lady from Pasadena," Robinson mumbles. Dennis Spottswood returns with the refill. Robinson grabs it awkwardly, seems not to know what to do with it, or with his cigarette, and all these fingers at the ends of his hands. He contrives to take a sloppy swallow, the cigarette having found its way, filter-first, into the ashtray. Gary is smiling when Robinson looks straight at him and says, "Gary. You're in a light trance at this very moment. Whaddaya think about *that*?"

Gary would have described his condition as a light stupor, brought on by too many jolts from the gin bottle, but shrugs and says, "You could be right." He sees Marvin shaking his head slowly.

"Sure," says Robinson. He picks up his cigarette and holds it in front of his chest, like a paintbrush. Gary stares at the delicate strokes of smoke curling up in front of Robinson's eyes, which are as penetrating as ever. "See, if we were really on stage," says Robinson, "I'd gradually lead you into all sorts of stupid, humiliating tricks—which would no doubt please one or two people here."

"Not *humiliating*, Robinson," protests Peter. "Just outrageous."

"But instead, I'm gonna show you what you're capable of, Gary."

And Tony or Tommy says, "You people think this is funny, but my hypnotist said—"

* * *

Gary opens his eyes. The conversation is lively but his mind has been elsewhere, it would seem. He tries to refocus. Robinson is talking about property duelists. What a peculiar term. Gary pictures a pair of irate landowners, back to back with pistols cocked, about to pace along some disputed boundary line before turning and firing. He takes a sip of his drink, certain that he must have missed something. "Cartesian dualism is hopeless, y'see." Robinson, his voice a sloshed slur, is waving an empty glass. "But *prop*erty dualism dozen possum elemental any's."

"Come again?" Owen, bored and scornful.

Robinson frowns at him. "I *said*," he says, and says it again, while Dennis Spottswood gives a simultaneous translation: "Doesn't posit any mental entities."

Oh, *dualists*. Gary laughs, and feels instantly paranoid, because everyone in the room falls silent and looks at him.

"Gary," Robinson says fondly. He grins around the circle of guests. "D'you 'member Dennis's poem?"

"Sure," says Gary guardedly.

"Nah, I mean really remember it, word for word."

"Oh. Well, no, I'm afraid not," says Gary, even more guardedly. Why is everybody staring at him? He looks apologetically at Spottswood, who makes an absolving gesture with both hands.

"Ha." Robinson pauses, and then, with some difficulty, snaps his fingers.

Fourteen iambic lines burst into bloom in Gary's mind.

He is intensely proud as he recites them, gazing round the room. His bladder starts to ache, his voice is loud.

After the final couplet, everyone (except Marvin Book-valid) applauds. Gary makes a bow from his deck chair. Then the bottom falls out of his self-satisfaction; he realizes that, in a profoundly upsetting sense, he has not intended to do any of this.

A cry from the couch: "Look, he's twitching! You see? It isn't funny. I *told* you what—"

"Shuddup, Tony," Robinson barks. ("Tommy," says the confectioner in a small voice, and takes Owen's hand.) "Everything's perfectly okay, Gary," says Robinson. "That was a li'l sample of posthypnotic suggestion."

"And very impressive, I must say," Spottswood declares, his pink face beaming. "Word-perfect, after hearing it once. I had no idea hypnotism was so *useful*. You couldn't have done that on your own, now could you?"

Peter Harnisch's eyes twinkle exuberantly. He's sitting cross-legged on the floor near a box of LPs. "Robinson programmed you to," he explains. "He said your subconscious had retained every word. Isn't that amazing?"

"*No*," says Gary. He feels, absurdly, like crying. He says to Robinson, "I don't think you should have done that. I mean, did I give you permission to do that?" His voice is high and strained. Robinson says nothing, his eyes pinning Gary's. "What else did you 'program' me to do?"

Peter says, "Come on, Gary, be a good sport. It was just the poem. You're not going to croak like a frog or try to strangle Marvin or anything." Peter's tone is both conciliatory and vaguely regretful.

Marvin is still leaning against the bookshelf. "Yes, Gary," he says earnestly. "Why don't you be a good sport."

Robinson holds up a hand. Everyone turns to him. He says, enunciating with care, "Let's all have dessert."

The hard, aching lump in Gary's throat is threatening to burst: into sobs, into whines. Turning to Spottswood, "Can I get a ride back with you?" he manages to say.

Spottswood runs a hand over his bald spot. He looks at Robinson. "Well, yes, if it's . . . agreeable."

Gary stands up. "Then let's go."

In the silence, the moths click against the lampshade.

"Oh, shit," says Robinson. There follows a loud, wretched wheeze. Robinson's face contorts, and he drops his glass.

Gary stays put as the others jump to their feet and surround the beach chair. "Are you all right?" "What should I—" "Jesus, he's— Owen, grab that cigarette, it's still lit."

"Fine, fine, leggo." Robinson's voice is hoarse.

Peter, kneeling: "Is it an attack, Robinson? Should I get your medicine? I'll get your medicine."

"You should go to bed right this minute," says the confectioner.

"Yeah. Lemme just— Gary?" Robinson looks up at him. "We were gonna go bike riding tomorrow." He coughs—it sounds like dry heaves—and inhales in several sharp gasps.

Gary sighs. "I know," he says, and sits back down. Peter and Spottswood are kneeling on either side of Robinson, staring at him. Peter has his hand on Robinson's shoulder. Robinson is doubled over, head nearly level with his knees.

"I'm fine," Robinson repeats. "You all just carry on. I'm gonna hit the sack." He stands up, in stages.

"Do you need help?" Spottswood asks. Robinson waves a hand at him and shuffles off down the hall, toward the back bedroom. A door snicks shut.

Gary looks around the room. Marvin Bookvalid is standing by the screen of the veranda, gazing out toward the ocean. A slight smile. Gary looks away. The others are still watching him, as if it's somehow his move. "I didn't mean to upset him," he says.

Peter hands Gary a drink. "Of course you didn't. My old friend will be fine tomorrow." He laughs. Gary remembers a certain pigtailed sculptor. "Let's put on some music."

On the couch, Tommy holds Owen's hand and says to Gary, "Well, I certainly hope you don't suffer any migraines."

With Robinson gone, the party degenerates. Peter puts on a Dolly Parton LP. Spottswood and Owen finally fall into a disagreement. Peter's head swings back and forth between them, observing each volley. "Ah, forget it," Owen finally bellows, and turns to Tommy. "And what are you being so silent about?" Tommy says calmly, "Don't be like this. You've had too much to drink."

Gary kills his in three swallows and lurches for the bathroom. He sees light shining beneath Robinson's door, and knocks softly. "Yeah?" comes Robinson's rasp. Gary pushes open the door. Robinson is lying on the bed, propped up against a disordered congeries of pillows, still dressed, clutching a cigarette. "Gary," he says, and the ash falls onto the sheet. His eyes are nearly shut. Gary stares at him and says, "I'm sorry I got mad at you." Robinson smiles angelically. "We'll go bike riding tomorrow, okay?" Gary whispers. The spins and the whirls have arrived. Robinson mumbles something; it sounds approximately like *Focus into the will*. The cigarette follows the ash, and Gary watches as Robinson fumbles to retrieve it, groping at the wrinkled sheet, at himself, slapping the tiny orange coal until it goes out.

Gary shuts the door, and next finds himself outside, stumbling over a dune, sand filling his shoes. He pisses in the direction of the ocean, turns around and sees Marvin Bookvalid emerge from the cottage with Spottswood and get in Spottswood's car. "That's right!" he shouts. "Go away! Go home!" The surf is much too loud for his words to be audible. After a while he sits down, then crawls through the sand toward the cottage, finally passing out beneath its raised flooring. His last thought is, Tommy, not Tony. He's glad to know. He must never forget.

Screamer

We didn't fight, my wife and I. It wasn't our style, and anyway the marriage was in too much trouble for that.

If you'd bugged our house, the result would not have been very titillating. Silences, sighs. The sound of someone picking up around the living room: newspapers being rustled, books going back on the shelves with efficient little sliding noises. Doors shut meaningfully. The occasional disingenuous question rooted in grievances stretching back for months. Answers that were really answers to other questions too humiliating to ask. Where am I supposed to put the can opener *this* time? Why don't you admire and cherish me any longer? Because I made a mistake, don't ask me what or when. In the silverware drawer, where it belongs. *Okay*?

I was the one to move out. Barbara stayed put, and I rented a one-bedroom apartment in a different suburb on the other side of Washington, in a little complex of red brick three-story buildings. We didn't have any children to worry about, only the dog, and even he didn't require discussion. I wasn't going to keep a Lab in an apartment. As for possessions, all I wanted was a comfortable chair and my desk and computer and a few tables and lamps. There was a big, soot-covered cardboard box full of things from my childhood, shoved away in a corner of our basement, that I should have taken with me too. But I hadn't opened it in years, and didn't want to now, and Barbara said nothing when I left it.

My new resident manager was a genial, spaced-out senior citizen named Mrs. Austin, who wanted me to call her Helen. I couldn't do it—I wasn't raised to call elderly ladies by their first name—but I didn't want to offend her, so I ended up not calling her anything. "Uh, hi there," I'd say on the phone. "It's Ned Marsh in apartment 119? I seem to be having a problem with the venetian blinds in my living room. They're sort of stuck." "Oh, my goodness. Well, I can't imagine how— All right, dear, I'll send George over in the morning." And her husband, a chain-smoker with a lot of white hair on his arms, would come over as promised—or sometimes it would be two mornings later, or three—knocking gently and calling out "Austin here!" as if I'd be spooked to get an unannounced visitor. The venetian blinds seemed to take a lot out of him. When he got done he looked like he was ready for a nap.

I had no complaints about my apartment: definitely a find, considering the neighborhood and the price. I was freelancing ("Data Processing Professional," my business cards read—in other words, I was a keyboard jock) and couldn't afford to splurge. It was on the ground floor. No central AC, but I liked hot weather and preferred fans and open windows. The living room had what I wanted: space and light. There was space to move around, to pace while I discussed things out loud with myself—especially after getting one of Barbara's letters—to dance a little, to do push-ups without moving aside any furniture. My dog might have been okay here. I thought about asking Barbara for him. I missed his tail-thumping and his goofy, clear gaze.

There were two sets of windows at opposite ends of the living room, and they gave me light both morning and evening. Out one set was the street, and a few trees. Out the other I could see, straight ahead, a little courtyard formed by the other buildings of the complex. In the middle of the courtyard someone had put up a chain-link fence, waist high, in a square about twenty feet across. Inside the square were a lot of torn-up turf and gravel and upended cinderblocks. God knows what the plan had been, originally. I imagined old Austin Here sinking the posts for the fence, starting to tear up that turf, clenching a Camel between his dentures and wheezing as he hauled in wheelbarrows loaded with cinderblocks. Maybe a small playground for the children of the tenants? The apartment complex didn't seem to have many children—another plus, as far as I was concerned—and maybe that was why he'd abandoned the project. The view didn't bother me at all. I would pause every now and then during my pacing or dancing or pushing-up; I would take a moment to look straight ahead out my window. The gray, broken-cornered cinderblocks were fenced in as if they were precious. I thought of them as an anti-monument, proof that some things just weren't meant to work out

* * *

I got home early one evening from delivering some work to a client. I hung up my windbreaker—it was April, but still chilly—and went into the kitchen and put on some water for tea. The refrigerator came to life with a sound like a fighter plane taking off. I walked back out to the living room and turned on the high-intensity light over my favorite armchair and picked up a book. Reading long novels was the only thing I enjoyed thoroughly, in those first months of leaving Barbara. The river of words and sentences and paragraphs and chapters flowed over me, higher and higher, imaginary scenes washing away the memories of her. I was learning to forget. Our marriage was like a country I carried around in my mind, with its own history of governance and rebellions, some flag-waving, some days of mourning. All of that had to be flooded away now. Eventually, it would only be an empty place on a map, and then not even that: at the moment of divorce, each of us would carve out what we thought was ours and annex it back, make it part of an older land. I was being divorced on grounds of desertion and mental cruelty. The words meant nothing, my attorney told me; mere formulaic gibberish. But it didn't bode well, and some of the legal maneuvering gave me that they're-out-to-get-me feeling. I would hang up the phone after talking to my attorney and blink the sweat out of my eyes.

That April evening I opened my book with relief. Then the peace was disturbed. Jesus Christ, I thought, someone is being murdered in the courtyard. A woman was screaming something hysterically at the top of her lungs. I couldn't make out what she was saying, but I heard the fury, the way her throat was raw from screaming out so much rage. My stomach balled up and my heart started to race. A deeper, less frantic voice, male, was talking loudly in the middle of her tirade too.

What were they fighting about? The words were indistinct, especially his. As for hers, I could pick out frequent obscenities, and a kind of rise and fall of accusation that would have been recognizable no matter if they'd been speaking Bengali, or Latin. I placed my book face-down on the floor, walked to the windows, and looked out into the courtyard, expecting to see a gawking crowd gathered around these two gladiators. But the courtyard was empty.

I looked to the right. The building was constructed in a U shape, and my apartment was at one of the bends in the U. Across the bend were the windows of another apartment, at right angles to mine. That apartment had been empty since I'd moved in. The venetian blinds were always up. I'd peeked in once on my way to the laundry room entrance in a different part of the U. Bare floors, cobwebs in the corners, a broken light globe on the ceiling. Now I saw that the blinds of the other apartment were down. A light was shining between the slats. I turned the stiff handle that opened my window. A wet breeze blew in. Now I heard the voices more clearly. "GET YOUR FUCKIN ASS OUTTA HERE!" the woman screamed. Rumble, rumble, went the man's voice. "I SAID *GET* YOUR GODDAMN ASS OUTTA HERE!" Rumble, rumble. And now I heard a child say something in a whiny, upset tone. "YOU

SHUT THE FUCK UP!" screamed the woman.

I cranked my window shut. My heart was still racing. Then I heard the hiss of the kettle, and I walked into the kitchen and turned off the burner. Slowly I selected a teabag, and put it into a mug, and poured the water in. What if it kept up? Night and day? I could call Mrs. Austin. She could send over Austin Here. No, this was no venetian blind. I didn't see old George being very eager to fix this one. Probably it wouldn't keep up, though. They had just moved in; moving is stressful, God knows; they were having a fight, and it was a bad one, but I hadn't heard any thumps or crunches. It was only words. She was verbally clobbering him, and probably whatever he was saying back wasn't too sweet either. That was a shame, but there wasn't much I could do about it. I imagined going out into the hallway, turning left at the bend in the U, and walking down the corridor until I came to their door. Would it have a name pasted into the little rectangular slot yet? Doubtful. I imagined knocking on their door, adding my knocks to the cacophony going on inside. The door would open; *he* would open it, I felt sure, with a nervous look. And I'd say, Excuse me, hi, welcome, I'm one of your new neighbors, your argument is disturbing me. And she would come charging to the door and tell me to get my goddamn ass out of there. And I would, my heart in my throat.

I took my tea into the living room. It was still going on. Her voice was like a flock of nasty ragged birds flying into my apartment, beating their wings and diving at me. COCK-SUCKER! MOTHERFUCKER! No one could scream like that all the time. This had to be a one-shot deal. I put the tea down and walked over to my stereo and turned the radio on. I pushed the volume up a little. I returned to my chair, picked up my book, and sipped tea and read, sort of, while the radio played Rachmaninoff's Second Piano Concerto. The music, full of aching and turbulence, would build and break open for a fierce piano cadenza, and when the piano quieted down my neighbors would do their own version.

Finally, near the end of the third movement, they stopped. I said my first prayer in my new apartment: Please God, don't make me live with that. And I turned off the radio.

They kept it up. Not night and day—that would have been intolerable. But at least twice a week I'd be tuning out with a novel, or doing a few leg-lifts, or pleading on the phone to my attorney, and suddenly here it came. Without warning, she'd start to scream. There was never any escalation. She always started off at full blast, like a siren. I would stop whatever I was doing, thinking Christ, not again. My stomach and heart never seemed to get used to it. My first impulse—unthinking, instinctive, an echo from a long time ago—was always to listen closely, to try to understand what she was screaming about. But then I would catch myself trying to figure it out, and the blood would roar at my temples, deafening me. The classical radio station and I became close companions.

Barbara's emails arrived every few days. As well reasoned as term papers, here were all the explanations for why our marriage hadn't worked. I was *a*, I was *b*, I was *c*. See footnote 2. She saw everything in a new light now, she told me. All the good times had been deceptive, each and every moment of love. It turned out we were one big mistake. I would finish an email and delete it, shaking my head, unable to see the discreditable things her new light revealed to her. I thought of what I might write back—denials, careful marshallings of contrary evidence, expostulations ("Hey, come on, we weren't *that* bad!")—but the words never made it onto the screen. What was the point of arguing? Even if our marriage had been fifty percent good, what difference did that make? Now it was a hundred percent over.

I never saw the screamer, or the man she screamed at, or the child. I knew all the other tenants by sight. I usually ran into them by the mailboxes or in the parking lot. But those three, I never saw. I would have noticed a new face. I didn't know if they were black or white, well-dressed or on the skids. Their apartment number—I did walk by it once, just to see—was 122. After a couple of weeks they still didn't have any name pasted up on the door. Nor was there a name on the mailbox for apartment 122. They were just three voices who had terrible fights, as regular as thunderstorms. At the front door one day I ran into the woman who lived in apartment 111—it was on the same side of the U as me—and asked her if she ever heard the screaming. She said yes, sometimes, faintly. "It doesn't really bother me. Your apartment is closer, I guess." She told me she'd seen the husband once. "He was standing outside his own window, talking through the glass.

Maybe she locked him out." She smiled, as if it was no big deal. What did he look like? I couldn't help asking. My neighbor was a weightlifter—two hours a day, six days a week, she'd told me once—and said scornfully, "He's small. Pathetic looking. Kind of bald, hunched over." "Huh" was the only reply I could come up with, and we went, as the lawyers say, our separate ways.

One Wednesday night, about a month after my lovely new neighbors had moved in, Barbara came by. I poured us each a gin and tonic, and we settled down on the couch. The windows were open, and crickets were fizzing and rasping out in the courtyard. A big folder that said Run For Your Life! was sticking out of Barbara's purse (she was the County Chief Administrator for Parks and Recreation). We were meeting to talk about the separation agreement.

We'd taken a sip or two from our drinks when, clear as hell, the woman across the U screamed out, "COCKSUCK-ER!" Barbara jumped. The ice in her glass tinkled. This time I heard the child before the man made his rumble, rumble. The child sounded like it was crying, but the voice didn't parse into words. It was just a complaining sound. "WHY DO I HAVE TO TELL YOU AGAIN!" the woman screamed. Now we heard his rumbling counterpoint. "My God, Ned," said Barbara. She stared at me.

"Aren't they a treat," I said.

We listened for a few more moments. More of the same.

Barbara said, "How often does this go on?"

I put my drink down on the coffee table and stretched, trying to get the tension out of my shoulders. "Just not quite often enough for me to do anything about it."

Barbara was frowning, her eyebrows angled down like a grave accent and an acute accent over her brown eyes. "Why don't you bang on the wall?"

"We don't have an adjoining wall, actually. It's coming from outside—over there." I pointed out the window.

Barbara looked sharply in the direction of my finger, as if she would be able to see the voices. "*I* DON'T NEED THIS!" the woman screamed. "MAYBE *YOU* NEED THIS SHIT, *I* DON'T NEED THIS!"

The child screamed too now. It wailed, "Mo-om!" Its mother told it to shut the fuck up.

Barbara said, "This is incredible." I watched the ice melting in her glass. I wanted to tell her to drink her drink, it was getting all watery. "You know which apartment it is?"

"I'm pretty sure I do, yes."

"Call the management!"

"It's not their cup of tea, believe me."

"So what's to stop *you* from walking down the hall and knocking on their door and complaining?" Barbara gave me a killing smile. "Besides your basic personality, that is."

I took a swallow of my G and T. As usual, my heart was pounding, as if the screaming were an emergency. "Barbara," I said, in a soft, reasonable voice, "you can hear what they're like. Do you think that woman is going to pay the slightest attention to some guy like me asking her to keep it down?"

We heard small running footsteps, and a door slamming. "STAY IN THERE!" The man began to rumble but was interrupted: "HE CAN PICK UP HIS OWN FUCKIN TOYS!" So the child was a boy. I didn't want to know. It was like finding out what they fought about.

I could feel the breath going in and out of me. Barbara finally sipped from her drink. "That poor child. What about that child?"

"Pretty lousy. I agree with you a hundred percent, Barbara. I'm just saying there's nothing I can do about it."

Barbara's eyes were blazing at me under their diacritics. "I think you have a responsibility," she said, clipping out the small, hard syllables. "They could be beating that boy."

I shook my head.

Her look softened a little. "You're not ten years old anymore, Ned. They're not your parents."

I said, "Barbara, leave my parents out of this. Anyway, they only yelled at each other. They never touched me."

Barbara said, "There's a county hotline for child abuse. We have to use it sometimes if a kid shows up at a rec center with bruises or burns. Would you please call it, Ned? Please?"

"That's ridiculous. I've never heard any physical fighting."

"Please? Not to report them, just to ask what you ought to do."

"Okay, sure. I'll call them tomorrow, okay?" The screaming was going on, all around and through our conversation. Pacing alleviated my tension a little, but not much.

"Okay," she said. "I think I understand how hard this is for you." Barbara had met my parents a few times before they died. I didn't answer. "Well, shall we go out for a drink, or a cup of coffee? I can bring all that stuff with me." She pointed to the folder.

"Yes, definitely," I said. "Let's get out of here."

I had no intention of phoning any hotlines, but the next day I was working at home and the screamer started off again. My windows were open to the May air, and her goddamn awful voice was echoing through my living room. "*WHADDAYOU DOING!*" No rumble, rumble, but I heard the little boy yell back at her. She screamed it again, as if her world was collapsing and it was his fault: "*WHADDAYOU DOING, I SAID! I DON'T FUCKIN NEED THIS!*" I stood there, biting my lip. Here was this screamer, disturbing my work, terrifying a little boy for the second day in a row. Usually the things that happened in my stomach and heart—the tightness, the pounding—felt like fear. But this time it felt a lot like anger, too. I was suddenly hot with hatred for her. Images came to me, of my fist slamming into that filthy mouth.

So I looked up the county hotline and dialed it. A man answered, which seemed wrong; I expected a stern, no-nonsense female. He asked me how he could help me.

I told him I had a concern about some neighbors who yelled at their little boy a lot.

"I see," he said. "It's good you called."

"I don't mean just ordinary yelling. The mother yells the most incredible obscenities at this child." I realized I was using Barbara's word, *incredible.*

"I hear you. Do you know how old the child is?"

"No idea. Younger than a teenager."

"Have you ever seen any signs of physical abuse? Bruises, limping, anything like that?"

"No, but the fact is I've never actually seen the boy." I felt ashamed to say it, as if it cast doubt on my story.

"Okay. Sounds of blows being struck?"

"In all honesty, no. It's what I would call severe verbal abuse. It's going on right now, in fact."

The man made a sympathetic noise. "It sounds deplorable, but here's the deal. We can send a county official in cases where there's evidence of physical or sexual abuse. In this case, we can't intervene. What you need to do is dial 911 the minute you hear anything that sounds like more than words. You understand? Then the police can follow up and look for signs of abuse on the boy."

"Okay," I said. I felt a little relieved, a little frustrated. And a lot justified. Barbara and her hotline—as if that could solve anything.

"We really appreciate you calling. And absolutely call back if you ever see the boy, and if there's ever any evidence of—"

"I know, physical abuse."

"And don't forget about 911. That's the other way."

"I won't," I said, and thanked him, and hung up.

"YOU LITTLE FUCKER!" the woman screamed. There are so many different kinds of screams. You can scream for help, scream in terror, you can scream in a powerful, controlled way. She screamed like a mental patient frothing at the mouth, ready to kill.

I sat with the phone in my lap, listening. Her screams were dark birds—I saw them more clearly than ever, their sharp beaks, their wings slicing the air. Her screams were a rotting odor, stinking up my living room. Her screams were gut punches, right in my solar plexus. I imagined the boy. He wouldn't cry, unless he just couldn't help it. He would find some corner of the apartment and stand there, making it his. He would keep his tears in his throat, and yell back if he was able. If there was a cat, he might pull its tail. I saw a lock of hair fall down onto his forehead, over his bright eyes. I saw her coming for him, a hand raised. The force of her swing would carry the blow like a storm wind, and bring it down wherever the storm took it. I shook my head, over and over. There were alternatives. I could dial 911 right now. I could go barreling down the hall and bang on the door of apartment 122. I could take off my clothes very calmly, hang them up, get into bed, and pull the covers up to my chin. I forced myself to keep listening. "DO LIKE I TELL YOU, GOD-DAMNIT!" Only words. This time. Calling the police would be crying wolf. They'd want my name, and when they arrived and found a mother yelling at her son they'd leave and probably not come again if I called back with something more dire. But perhaps that would scare her? Make her more cautious?

Oh sure, and man is a rational animal. Just like the sight of me at her door, trying to act tough—"Look here, lady, I've had about enough of this; if you don't cool it I'm going to. . . ." —would certainly soften her outlook. She'd start screaming at *me*. Yes, she would.

The phone was still in my lap. "TAKE THAT SHIT OUTTA HERE!" The boy yelled back, mimicking her, I thought, though I couldn't hear the words. "WHO THE FUCK YOU THINK YOU ARE!" she wanted to know.

My bed was inviting, but instead I turned on the radio, loud, and went back to my desk and tried to work.

Mere words or not, desertion and mental cruelty entitled Barbara to ask for money. I was trying to persuade her not to. You make more than me! I wrote, in a number of emails. Her replies were evasive. Mostly she continued to write about all the episodes and qualities and patterns she'd never understood before, but understood all too well now: I wouldn't have children, even though I knew how badly she wanted them, because I was afraid to be a father; I was uncommunicative because I was ashamed to express my feelings, and also—never mind the contradiction—because I was using silence to express my anger; I married her in the first place because I was "acting out" some goddamn thing or other. This sort of revisionism was very easy, it seemed to me. There was nothing that couldn't be described, if you tried hard enough, in terms of weaknesses and hidden motivations. I didn't try to answer these charges. If I had, I would have said, "Barbara, why can't you believe I married you because the curve of your lower lip made me want to kiss it incessantly, and because I loved you, and because I wanted, well, the comforts of home, just the two of us—is there something so wrong with that? It's just as real as this 'acting out' crap." I didn't write, though. I felt like she was describing some other couple's marriage. They were the words of a woman I didn't know. Her attorney, on the other hand, wrote the words of a prick, and sent them by registered mail.

Normal life—my new norm—went on. I accepted as many clients as I could, and worked at their offices whenever possible. I used my address book to call a few friends, and found out who was siding with whom. The teams were uneven, and sometimes I had to swallow hard and just not think about it. As the weather got warmer, the women striding along the streets began to draw my eyes. I asked my weight-lifter neighbor if she wanted to go out for a drink. We were standing by the mailboxes again. "I don't drink," she said.

"Oh, okay, no problem," I said. "I don't either, much."

"How you doing with those neighbors?" she asked, all business, as if she were inquiring about cockroaches or a leaky faucet.

"They're still . . . a major problem," I said; "you don't hear it?"

"Nope. Like I said," and she went off down the hall.

Three or four times a week now, the birds flew into my living room. When I heard the screaming start—"FUCK YOU! FUCK ALL THIS!" fuck, fuck, fuck, it was her favorite word—I would get up and shut the windows. But then the apartment got too hot. So I turned on a big floor fan, which functioned as a white-noise device, filling the air with a steady whirring sound, like a balm spread over a rash, and now only the sharpest spike of the screamer's fury, or an especially insistent wail from the boy, could come through. Rumble, rumble was a thing of the past; my fan took care of him.

But it didn't take care of me. Just knowing the fight was going on, and sometimes hearing a loud MOTHERFUCKER! over the noise of the rotating blades, still sent my stomach curling up like a woolly-bear caterpillar being poked with a stick. The emergency feeling wouldn't go away. Grow up, I said to myself.

A Washington swamp-night in June, and I was sweating even with my big fan on. Several G and Ts with maximum ice hadn't helped. I really wanted to open the windows but the screaming had started about twenty minutes before, so the windows were closed. I lay on my couch, wearing nothing but a pair of gym shorts, with the fan two feet from my face. I had a hefty novel open in front of me, its spine cutting a painful half inch into my abdomen, but the words weren't registering. Over the blades, here came a shriek: "OUT!" The blades whirred, and then again: "Da da na na something something OUT, YOU FUCKIN something ya ya ya. . . ." The blood slapped in my temples. Relax, grow up, I said to myself. *Fuck you*, came the answer, as angry as the screamer, hurtling out of my guts. My molars were clamped down like a vise. The phone rang, and I wanted to pick it up and throw it hard at the wall. I sat up and grabbed it, and my *hello* came out like *fuck you*, too.

"Ned?" It was Barbara.

"Can I call you back?" I said.

"I guess so. I may be going out. Is anything wrong?"

"I'm in a lousy mood. I just can't talk now." Sweat was dripping down my face.

"Is it about what I wrote? Or— well, I suppose you got my attorney's letter."

"Look, as a matter of fact, my lousy mood doesn't have anything to do with you, although now that you've 'supposed' it, yes, I got your goddamn lawyer's letter this afternoon, and for your information, he has once again fucked up our separation agreement."

Barbara was silent, and then she said, "Oh." Another silence. Finally: "Well, that's— I know you don't want to talk about it right now so—"

"He's a fucking jerk, you know that? Since you 'know' so much? This whole deal is getting completely out of hand because of your fucking cocksucker lawyer." I stopped and listened to myself. And then I noticed a shape outside my window. "I'll call you back," I said, and hung up.

There was one spotlight at either end of the courtyard. The shape had moved into the beam from the spot nearest me, and then disappeared. I walked over to the window. There was just enough light to see him standing outside the windows of apartment 122. He had his hands on his hips, staring, but the blinds were down: there was nothing to see. I wondered if he was staring at his own reflection in the glass. His bald spot gleamed.

I cranked open a window so I could hear better. The boy was yelling, and for once I could make out his words: "I don't *wanna*! I hate you!"

"WHO GIVES A FUCK WHAT YOU WANT!"

Then I heard what I seemed to have been waiting for forever. Something went BANG in their apartment, a loud thud.

I slammed a hand against my window, hard enough to make it rattle.

The man standing outside cupped his hands around his mouth and spoke through the screen, where one of his windows was open.

I called out to him, "Having some trouble there?" My voice sounded crazy and reckless and I loved the sound of it.

He whirled around. He was blond, and yes, small, and yes, *pathetic* was a good word too. He swallowed and said, "No," and then swallowed again. He hunched his head forward at me. I knew I would be just a shadow to him, backlit by my living room lamps.

Blood seemed to be quivering everywhere in my body, especially in my throat and hands. I wanted to laugh. So I did. I laughed and called out, "Sounds like trouble to me! Yes sir! Locked you out again, did she?"

He mumbled something and turned away from me, back to his window. Beyond the blinds, in that other world, the screamer was still screaming, and the boy was shouting hoarsely back at her. The blond man had his back to me and was talking again through the screen. He wanted to return into that world.

I strode across my living room, heading for my front door. The phone was ringing again, like an alarm going off. I reached a hand out in passing and shoved it off the coffee table.

Outside, my footsteps echoed up the stairwell as I ran past the mailboxes and out the main door of the building. The night was heavy with moisture and ragweed pollen. I sneezed, and felt like I had plunged underwater. The sweat ran off me as I rounded the corner of the building and entered the courtyard. He was still at the window. "FUCK OFF!" I heard her scream at him.

He saw me at his side and cringed away, his eyes narrowing. "Everything's okay," he said in that rumbling baritone. "Go back inside."

Again I had to laugh, feeling the heat and nerves all over and through me. "Come on, man!" I said. "You ready?" I dashed over to the chain-link square and vaulted over it. The gravel bit into my bare feet. I grabbed up a handful of it. "Watch out!" I called to him, and threw it before he could move out of the way. It pinged and chinked all over the wall and windows, and some of it must have stung him too. He winced and moved a hand to his head and gawped at me. I reached down and felt around until I found a bigger piece of gravel, a good-sized rock, really. "Watch it!" I called again, and this time he ducked off to the right, into the corner of the

U, during my wind-up. The rock hit the center windowpane dead on. The center panes were just like mine; they had no screens, since they couldn't be opened. The window starred and I saw cracks running all along it now, but it didn't shatter. The noise was like a handgun going off. I saw a few people come to their windows. I figured the Austins were probably watching too.

"Okay, here we go!" I said, and squatted down so I could get a good heft on the cinderblock at my feet. I lifted it up and tossed it over the fence. It thumped down onto the ground. I jumped over too, hoisted it up again, cradled it in my arms, and then ran with it, right at those center windowpanes. When I was a yard away, I hurled the cinderblock. The glass exploded. The venetian blinds came rattling down with the cinderblock in their midst, everything collapsing back into the apartment. The momentum of my approach carried me right up to the windowsill, and I had to stop myself with both palms on the rough concrete ledge or I'd have toppled right in too.

The screamer was silent now.

I leaned in, gasping for breath. She wasn't there. Maybe she was hiding in another room. Their living room was pretty bare. It wasn't as nice as mine. Now it was a disaster area.

The boy was there, though. He was about six or seven, wearing black jeans that were too long for him and a T–shirt. He was staring at me with his mouth open and his hands clasped in front of his crotch, standing right in the middle of the room. The blinds and the glass and the cinderblock were there on the bare floor in front of him. His forehead was bleeding.

We looked at each other.

"Don't be afraid," I said. "Jesus Christ."

But he screamed.

Would I Lie to You?

Early in the morning, the shadows still long, Audrey walked from the bus station out to the highway entrance, where there was a truck stop. Inside, three men sat at the restaurant counter, hunched over plates of eggs and hotcakes. They looked at the girl, stopped talking, and then resumed in lower voices. Audrey put her backpack on the stool beside her and ordered a coffee.

The man behind the counter asked, "Do you want hot water or regular for that coffee?" Audrey stared at him. He punched her lightly on the shoulder and said, "C'mon, kid. It's a joke." In her weariness it seemed actually funny, and she laughed behind her menu. Her shoulder was still sore from the previous evening.

"Anything else?" the counterman asked, and Audrey put the menu down and shook her head. She had three dollars left after the bus ticket.

She drank her coffee quickly, smoked a cigarette. Then she walked out to the northbound entrance ramp. The October day was warming up, and Audrey unzipped her suede windbreaker halfway down. She thought about lighting another cigarette, but a lot of drivers wouldn't stop for a smoker. Her shoulder throbbed. Birds called to each other in the trees lining the highway. Their chirps irritated her, and she scuffed her boots in the flinty gravel of the ramp's shoulder, making a scraping noise that cut across the sounds of nature. A starling hopped onto the gravel a few feet from her, bobbing its head like a mechanical toy.

Then the starling took flight. A small blue car was driving up the entrance ramp. Audrey saw that it was shiny, that it seemed in good repair, and that the only silhouette in the window was on the driver's side. Battered cars, cars with several men in them: trouble, bad rides. She put her thumb out, and the car rolled onto the shoulder in front of her. The driver leaned across the seat and opened the passenger door.

Audrey walked over and looked inside. He was thirty-five or forty—old—wearing a white dress shirt with the sleeves rolled up. His forearms were muscled, and she could see the definition of his biceps and shoulders through the contours of the shirt. He was smiling. His toast-brown hair was brushed back from his forehead, he wore gold-rimmed glasses that made him look studious despite his build, and his radio, or CD player, was playing "Strawberry Fields Forever."

Audrey held the door open but didn't get in. The driver said "Good morning," cheerily. His voice was high, perhaps foolish. He sounded to Audrey like a man pleased with himself because he was about to do a good deed, to be some kind of help to her.

"Hey," she said. "Where you headed?" He reminded her

of a man who had picked her up once, back in the winter, in an old van with one of those Christian-fish bumper stickers. He had also been cheerful, and concerned to help. He'd questioned her in a kind tone about her reasons for being alone, thumb out, on such a cruel day. Wasn't she a little young? Was she a runaway?

"I'm plenty old enough to be on my own. I'm having a vacation, okay with you?"

Did her parents know? Audrey had said that her parents were having a vacation too, as a matter of fact. Separate vacations on Christmas Eve? There'd been a change of plans, Audrey told him, not really knowing or caring what the words meant. It was just something to say.

He'd attempted, shyly, to engage her in prayer. "Let's not and say we did. Deal?" He'd agreed, but tried twice more before the ride was over. He had been a fool, but a good ride nonetheless, no trouble at all.

"North," said the driver.

He reached down and reduced the volume of the music. He was still smiling. "Where are *you* headed?" he asked.

"Huntstown," said Audrey. "Are you going that far?"

"No, gosh, sorry," he said. "But I can take you fifty miles or so, as far as University Park." He shrugged and looked down at his feet. "If you want."

Audrey decided he was probably okay. If he was another praying fool, she could deal with that. She was so tired, and she hated standing out here with the sunlight and the birds.

"Great," she said, and wriggled out of her backpack and got in. "Do you go to school there?" she asked, although he looked too old to be a student. She buckled her seat belt and kept her pack on her lap.

"Right." The driver was wearing his seat belt too. He put the car in gear and drove back onto the ramp.

"My boyfriend goes to MacAndrew College," said Audrey. "That's where I'm headed."

"Nice." He flicked on his turn signal and entered the highway. Once he got his speed up to sixty, he kept it there, and did not change lanes. He was a careful driver; Audrey relaxed.

He was watching the road, hardly glancing at her. After a mile or so he said, eyes still forward, "You can put your pack in the back seat if you want." He had a precise way of enunciating his words, as if he wanted to be sure he was understood.

"No, I'm fine," said Audrey. She liked to keep her possessions handy, especially her cell, in case her judgment of a ride turned out to be wrong.

After a few more moments, he said, "You're pretty young to be dating a college boy, aren't you?"

Audrey shot him a look, but he was smiling pleasantly at the road. "I knew him when he was in high school," she said. "He's only a sophomore."

"Are *you* still in high school?"

"Yeah— Well, no." When the driver said nothing, Audrey went on: "I just quit. I'm going up to stay with him. Permanently."

"Is that right," the driver said.

"I mean, he lives off-campus now and everything. He says it's a really nice apartment."

After a moment the driver said, "Are you a senior?"

"Junior. I was."

"Got it." He nodded. The windows were down, and Audrey's hair was getting blown around quite a bit, and the driver said, "Feel free to close that window if it's too much."

"I'm fine," she said. "Well, okay, I'll just roll mine up a little." She did so, and then asked, "Do you mind if I smoke?"

"Not at all," the driver said, and punched in the dashboard lighter for her with a quick and accurate jab of his thumb. Audrey nodded at him, took a cigarette from the pack in her jacket pocket, and lit it.

"Strawberry Fields Forever" had ended, "Penny Lane" had come and gone, and now "Baby You're a Rich Man" was playing. Her mother had this album.

"So you're what?" said the driver. "Sixteen?"

"And ten months."

"*Really*," he said, as if Audrey had made a perceptive remark. She took a closer look at him, out of the corners of her eyes, and caught him staring at her, no longer smiling. Her back teeth locked tightly together, and her knees, and she had to remind herself that there was no reason to be nervous. So what if he was a creep. He wouldn't be the first. She had a repertoire of put-downs that had proved successful on the few occasions when she'd needed them. The driver was watching the road now, and Audrey's gaze fell to his hands and arms.

He wore a ring with a red jewel on the middle finger of his right hand, which held the steering wheel steady. The ring looked cheap, a fake ruby.

Her teeth aching, she waited for the driver to hit on her, but they rode in silence for close to thirty minutes, and Audrey relaxed again. She flipped her cigarette out the window, lit another one a few minutes later (pushing the lighter in herself), flipped that one out when she'd done with it. She hadn't slept much on the bus, and now that the tension was gone, she had to force herself to stay awake.

She conjured up Dan's image and his voice. When she'd called him last night, standing out on Grozier Boulevard, he was surprised. Had he been pissed off too? Audrey went back over the conversation. It was more that he was pissed off at the situation, not at her. She didn't blame him; no one likes to be taken by surprise. "Look," he'd said, "I know they're crazy, that's a well-established fact, but you don't have any *money* or anything, you're still— you know, a minor. If you run off they'll call the cops." Audrey was able to convince him that the cops were the last people her parents would want to talk to, after what had happened. By the end of the call, he was back to being sweet to her. "Well, if *you're* sure, Audrey, then what the hay. Get on up here."

"It's definitely okay?"

"I promise you it's fine. My roommate's away for the weekend."

"For the weekend," she repeated, and Dan said he had to go now.

The driver made a little laughing noise. He was looking at her. He made the small laugh again. "You know what?" he said.

"What?"

"I'll admit something to you. When I saw you hitching, and I saw what a foxy girl you were, I admit I thought about hustling you."

His high, bland voice had a reminiscing tone to it, as if he were mentioning something long gone and far away. And his face was perfectly relaxed, smiling almost merrily. Audrey felt like smiling too, out of contempt for this creep and the words he used. *Foxy. Hustling.* She knew him for what he was. He would never have a girlfriend who could stand him for long. He *hung out* in bars at the university and bought women drinks and told them they looked *foxy*. Or else just stayed home with Internet porn.

"Thanks for not doing it," she said. "That would be a big mistake."

He nodded, and signaled for a lane change. "Sure. No offense. Any guy would think about it, seeing you. You're an absolute fox. Your hair, the way you wear it curled like that— fantastic."

"Huh," said Audrey.

"But, whoa, now I can *see* you're fifteen, and I'm basically twice your age, and that's that."

"Sixteen. And plus, I have a boyfriend," said Audrey.

"Right, you do. Not that I knew that, back there," said the driver. The Beatles CD ended, and he popped it out of the player and reached for another one from a little compartment next to the stick shift. "You like the Stones?"

"Why not," said Audrey. "You're really retro, huh?"

"Greatest Hits," the driver said earnestly, and put the CD in the player. "Ruby Tuesday" began to play, a song Audrey had always loved.

The driver pulled his visor down slightly. The sun glinted off his eyeglasses. "It's too bad," he said, looking straight ahead, "because what I had in mind wouldn't have involved you doing anything, absolutely nothing physical, and I was definitely prepared to reimburse you for your time."

So he was trouble after all. Audrey thought that maybe the thing to do was to freeze him out. She made herself cold, right down to her heart— she was already shivering, so it was easy. She ignored everything in the left half of her world and began looking out her passenger window. *Goodbye, Ruby Tuesday, who could hang a name on you?* the CD sang, and she froze it out too, even though she loved it.

The driver said nothing for a few minutes, and then he asked, "Aren't you curious to know what I was thinking about?"

Audrey stared out her window.

"Aren't you? Sure you are."

She shook her head slightly.

"Absolutely no involvement on your part, and an extremely generous reimbursement."

The articulation of this last phrase—the driver spoke to her as if she were a foreigner, or a stupid child—thawed her coldness into anger. Still refusing to look over at him, she said loudly, "I'm sure you think I'm desperate for ten or twenty bucks but I'd appreciate it if you'd just shut up. Or else let me out right here."

"One hundred dollars for three minutes of your time," he said in his precise voice.

Audrey jerked her head around to him. If he'd been breathing hard, or wetting his lips, or hunched more tightly around the steering wheel—but he was leaning back with one finger lightly holding the wheel, smiling with his lips closed, eyes on the road.

"One hun-dred dol-lars," she sneered, clipping off the syllables, trying to show him how obnoxious his voice was. "You think I believe that?" As soon as she'd spoken, her throat grew dry and she thought, *Jesus, what if I piss him off?*

But the driver showed no anger. He held up a finger—wait—then reached into his back pocket, still keeping his eyes on the road. Audrey had to admit he was a good driver. He pulled out his wallet, put it in his lap, and reached into it with a finger and a thumb. One by one he extracted five bills, five twenties, folded them, and tucked them into the ashtray, which Audrey had not used.

"Would I lie to you?" he said. "I'm perfectly serious, and as I was saying, it's a shame, because I *thought* about hustling you, I really did, but I can see you're too young. As I was saying, what I had in mind involves absolutely nothing physical from you—I mean, not you, since you're only a kid, but on the part of the person who would be involved in this—and would take literally three minutes." He put his wallet back into his pocket and said, "Oh well."

The edges of the bills flapped a little in the breeze. Audrey noticed the dashboard was very clean, as if the driver had given it a dusting before he left home in the morning.

"I really should know better," said the driver. "You're fifteen—"

"You know damn well I said *six*teen."

"*Six*teen, and there's a lot of things you wouldn't understand yet. About life, about men. I mean, that's not your fault, you're just young. Some men get a lot of pleasure out of some very silly, simple stuff."

"You think I don't know that?" The driver was silent. "Like what?"

"You really want to know?"

"Yes, I really want to know, if it's such a big deal."

"It's *not* a big deal," the driver said, his tone injured. "That's why I'm almost embarrassed to talk about it. You'll probably laugh." He looked in his rear-view mirror, then at Audrey. "You really want to know?"

"*Yes.*"

A truck passed them in the left lane, and the driver waited until the noise and smell had faded. Then he said, "I want you to— I would have wanted you to—"

Audrey knew the pause was theatrical, a put-on, but she couldn't help asking, "To what?"

"Well. To watch me," said the driver.

"Watch you. Watch you do what?"

"You know." The driver was still concentrating on the road, very relaxed. "No big deal," he said.

"While you're *driving*?"

He looked at her and gave her an exaggerated, kidding frown. "Of course not. Do I look like a jerk? Do you think I want to get us killed? No, I'll tell you, since you seem to want to know. Very simple. We pull into the Visitor Center at the University Park exit, right up ahead here, park way over at the side where there's never any other cars. You watch, you take the money, we say goodbye." His voice had picked up tempo a little, and Audrey could tell he had thought it all out before, probably done it all before, too. "I know this is ridiculous," he said, "because you're much too young, but I'll only add that if you were worried about your safety or something of that nature— well, it couldn't conceivably be a problem. It's broad daylight, and there'd be people nearby. Not *right* nearby, but plenty near enough. No harm could possibly come to you. And anyway, harming you is the furthest thing from my mind. I've told you exactly what I was thinking about. I'm not handing you a line. I've been completely honest with you."

"I don't believe you'd give anyone a hundred dollars for that. You'd probably grab the money and push them out of the car and, I don't know, take off or something." Audrey's voice had a little hitch in it; the beating of her heart was interfering with the evenness of the breath she needed to speak. "In fact, this whole thing is fucked up. I want you to let me out."

"Take the money right now," the driver said. "Put it in your pocket, put it where I couldn't get it without *handling* you, at which point you'd scream, so of course I wouldn't do it. But the thing is, I don't want to cheat you or get over on you. Please believe me. It's *worth* it to me. It really is. What can I say? It's just something that appeals to me."

The Stones were playing "Miss You." Audrey looked out the window and saw the sign for the University Park exit. She did not pick up the money. The driver signaled for the exit and steered the car onto the ramp. Ahead was the Visitor Center. Several cars were parked near the low fake-log-cabin building, but most of the parking lot was empty. The driver looked at Audrey—she was staring down at her backpack, but she could feel his head turn toward her—and drove slowly to the edge of the lot, where there were oak trees and a few deserted picnic tables. He backed into a space and cut the motor off. There was no more music. Audrey had a clear view of the Visitor Center and two or three people with soda cans walking out to their cars.

"Don't you trust me? Go ahead, take the money," he said. "Okay?"

Her heart and stomach were filled with a heavy, rhythmic pulsing. As she took the bills from the ashtray and put them in the pocket of her jeans, she realized that she could simply open the car door and run out, run to the Visitor Center with his hundred dollars in her pocket. She was afraid to do it. The driver swallowed, and unzipped his fly. He was wearing gray slacks.

The shade from the oak trees splashed onto the hood of the car in leaf-shaped puddles. A crisp breeze blew through the window and ruffled her curls. The ring's stone sent red spears of light darting across the dashboard. The ugly chant that had been playing when the driver killed the motor kept circling around in her head: *na na na na na na na, Lord I miss you.* Nothing new, she said to herself. Nothing was happening that she had not seen before, in cars as a matter of fact, with Dan before they had started to screw, and before that with other boys. And, twice, she and Dan had watched some of that Internet shit. Nothing new, she kept repeating to herself as she watched; it's no different from anything I've seen before. The whole damn world has seen this a million times before.

The driver said nothing, though his breathing was loud, and the crickets and birds made a racket outside the car. Audrey was sure three minutes had not elapsed—it was perhaps a minute at the most—when he said, "Listen, twenty dollars more, my word of honor, if you unbutton the top button, one button, of your jeans and lemme—let me see your underpants, just the very top." She shook her head no. He said it again: "My word of honor. Please." The words she would need to speak—*I can't do it, I don't want to*—spoke themselves in her mind. And in her mind the driver replied, *Don't you trust me?*

Audrey's throat was huge and achy as she shifted her backpack forward onto her knees and unbuttoned her jeans, exposing a tiny triangle of red synthetic fabric. "Thank you," the driver said, and all the breath went out of him with a groan. "Yes, watch now, watch," he whispered, and Audrey watched—she was afraid to look away—and then it was over. She swallowed down the ache in her throat. With shaky fingers she rebuttoned herself, looked around to see if they'd been observed, fumbled open her car door, and got out, clutching her backpack. "Wait, I promised," the driver said. He was wiping his hand with a wad of tissues. He took out his wallet and removed another bill, leaning across the car to hand it to her. His eyes begged her to take it, but she turned away from him and began walking. "Goodbye," she heard the driver say, and she walked rapidly toward the Visitor Center.

Once inside, she stayed by the window and watched the blue car drive off. She waited almost half an hour, just to be sure, and then used the restroom, bought a Coke, smoked several cigarettes, and finally felt ready to walk back up to the highway entrance ramp.

Her next ride was a lucky one: a husband and wife heading straight to Huntstown to visit their daughter at the college. They babbled back and forth to each other in the front seat while Audrey, knees drawn up in the back, began to freeze again. The back seat was full of shopping bags, groceries for the daughter. Audrey peeked into one and saw soup cans, bottles of fruit juice, and a big bag of corn chips. See? she would say to Dan. I do too have money. I saved it up. Take it, we can buy groceries and stuff. Or just take it. Okay? She pulled the zipper of her windbreaker all the way to her chin. She thought about having to find a job, make a living, and she held her backpack tightly. She thought about what she'd managed to fit into it—mostly clothes, her makeup and jewelry, her phone, a few photos, a few pictures she'd sketched—and tried to picture the drawer or the shelf where these possessions would be unpacked, in the apartment Dan shared with his roommate. She thought about the driver, who didn't lie, who kept his promises.

A Childhood

Yeager was only twenty-three, and he was getting married in June. It was hard to believe that the ceremony was five months off still; he felt like they'd been planning it forever. He was spending hours on the phone listening to Gail talk about it, using up all his minutes, and taking the train up from Washington to visit her at her parents' red brick Colonial house outside Philadelphia, where the four of them would huddle around the coffee table, planning, forecasting, anticipating contingencies. The Sheltons had money—it could even be said that they were wealthy—and the wedding would be handled on their terms. Yeager fantasized about calling it off, joked with Gail about eloping, but he knew that was crap. If you married money, you paid . . . well, a certain price. You had to act like a responsible adult. The marriage itself was more Gail's idea than his. He would have settled, happily, for a year's lease together somewhere, but no one did that with the Sheltons' daughter.

His own parents, who weren't in the Sheltons' league at all, had still managed to save up enough money to retire early, and the previous year had moved, much to Yeager's surprise, to Tempe, Arizona. It was an odd feeling, having them so far away from Washington, and from him. Yeager had returned to his hometown after college, to work in a K Street law office as a paralegal temp. On that salary, a basement efficiency on the wrong side of Capitol Hill was all he could afford. Yeager figured he'd wind up a lawyer himself—he felt he had the makings of a good one—but had so far punted the LSATs twice. Gail gave him to understand that the Sheltons would be glad, probably, to pay for law school, provided he was accepted somewhere classy. And if not, her father knew a lot of business people. Something would be arranged.

On the Wednesday night following his most recent trip to Philadelphia, the phone rang as Yeager sat at home in his apartment with a joint and a movie he'd streamed. The girl's voice asked him if he was the Mark Yeager who'd gone to Penn. When he said yes, she said, "I hope you don't mind my looking you up out of the blue like this. I *guess* you remember me. Erica Huysman?"

"Certainly," said Yeager, putting down the joint. He stopped the movie and asked her how she was, and told her it was nice to hear from her, but in reality he was puzzled. Erica Huysman had been an acquaintance of his senior year, another Main Line preppie like Gail, though the two girls weren't friends. Erica was part of a slightly duller crowd, a poli-sci crowd, and Yeager had never, as far as he could remember, been in her company alone. She was tall, with an attractive, deerlike gangliness, pretty in an overly blond-and-blue-eyed way, and she talked too much. Yeager had already been as good as engaged to Gail; as for Erica, he was fairly sure she hadn't been linked romantically with anyone in particular.

"Well, I've only just relocated here to D.C.," Erica now told him, "and I've started this cool job, and I thought I'd, you know, look up some old friends. And I remembered you saying you were going back to D.C. after graduation, so I just took a chance and found your number online."

"That's great," Yeager said, surprised and a little wary to learn that Erica Huysman thought of him as any kind of a friend. The weed made him detached. He knew the questions he should be asking—what job, where was she living, was she in touch with so-and-so—but his tongue was slow to form the words. Fortunately, it didn't matter. Erica was as garrulous as ever. For ten minutes, Yeager (now sprawled back on the couch, sucking quietly on the joint) had only to make affirmative noises as Erica filled him in. Did he remember Susan Conway and Phil Green? And Gerry Nunzio? Uh huh; that was the poli-sci crowd. Well, they were here in Washington too. "We got together a couple of times but I guess they're kind of busy." Her job was with a lobbying firm, specializing in senior citizen issues. "It's a huge office, and I really like the work, but it's a little impersonal too, if you know what I mean. The people, I mean. And of course a lot of them *are* senior citizens." Yeah, said Yeager, he knew what she meant.

Her dad was paying for her apartment—"Talk about guilty, after the divorce! Major guilt"—and Erica really liked it as well, though she hadn't especially gotten to know any of the other tenants. "We meet at the mailboxes, sometimes. You know how that is." In fact, Yeager had never given a moment's thought to whoever lived in his building, but said yeah.

Finally there was silence on the line. "So how long have you been down here?" Yeager asked.

"Oh, gosh," said Erica, laughing. "Not very long. It's been such a whirlwind. I don't know—four or five months? Five months."

Yeager had been thinking a few weeks, and felt like saying, *That long? Jesus, get a life.* "Really," he said. "Well, would you like to do something sometime? Have dinner or something?"

"That would be very nice," Erica said quickly. "That would be terrific."

Yeager was picturing her clearly now, after hearing so much of her voice. He could see her in crisp, ironed jeans with a loose college T–shirt tucked neatly into them, and he remembered how he used to think that she always wore loose shirts to disguise the fact that she had no tits to speak of. But she was very slim and had a nice ass, though she wore too much makeup—blush and eyeshadow and lipstick and all that crap—to suit his taste. Gail wore makeup too, but in such a way that you couldn't even tell. Yeager began to get a little aroused. It didn't happen often—in fact, never—that some girl called him up "out of the blue" and wanted to go out with him. And he realized too that Erica had not said a word about Gail, which would have been the normal, correct thing: to ask him whether he was still seeing her, and how she was and all that. Of course, he hadn't mentioned her either. As far as he was concerned, Gail wasn't an issue. He loved her. Sexual fidelity was a different subject entirely, one that remained open until they were man and wife. For all he knew, Gail felt the same way, though they had never discussed it.

After getting Erica's address and arranging to pick her up that Friday night, Yeager hung up the phone smiling. What with the weed and the sense of court being paid to him, he felt positively horny, and later, in bed, when he jerked off, he pictured Erica Huysman slowly shucking her jeans and staring at him with serious longing, completely silent.

Yeager knew that the Massachusetts Avenue address Erica had given him was somewhere around Embassy Row, an upscale part of town, but when he arrived there on Friday night he was taken aback by the opulence of the place. A doorman with a comic-opera uniform and a whistle around his neck held open the wide glass portal for him, then waited in non-judgmental stillness as he kicked some slush off his Nikes. Yeager made sure to kick it onto the black corrugated rubber mat, for the building's foyer was thick-carpeted and immaculate.

Erica's apartment was on the fifth floor. The doorman had called up, and she was waiting for Yeager when he turned the corner in the corridor. Her hair was shorter, with some kind of streaked effect dyed into it, but otherwise she seemed about the same. Yeager thought he caught a look of consternation as her eyes left his face and examined what he was wearing—a black leather jacket, black sweater, black jeans, and the Nikes were black too; Gail said black was his color—but she took both his hands and smiled, saying, "It's very nice to see you, Mark." Yeager gave her a kiss behind her left ear, smelling a sharp, oily fragrance that he associated, immediately and unpleasantly, with overdressed women of his mother's age, holding cocktail glasses and kissing him at parties. No one at Penn would have gotten away with wearing such a perfume, and he found that he disliked Erica Huysman's imitation of an adult.

Erica's clothes were also, Yeager felt, an obeisance to the wrong sumptuary laws: a white silk blouse with a lot of big decorative buttons, a knee-length gray pleated skirt, pearl necklace, high-heeled shoes with straps. Taking a closer look at her face and body, Yeager thought she looked even thinner than he remembered from college—especially the face, with its obdurate cheekbones and pure pale skin, artificially reddened. Erica was talking a mile a minute, and bustling into the dining area with Yeager's damp jacket, which she placed carefully across the back of an ornate wooden chair. The blouse was loose, the skirt fairly tight across her ass—yeah, same old Erica, perfume or no perfume, Yeager decided, nodding, raising his brows, smiling, as Erica showed him around the apartment, handed him a beer, talking all the while about her trip home from her job, which evidently had been marred by missed buses and nasty weather.

Yeager didn't have much of an eye, yet, for what money

could buy, but he was pretty sure the apartment was expensively decorated. That was the father's doing—major guilt, he remembered Erica saying—and the furnishings showed it: the whole layout was like something from a Fifties movie, something a rich husband would pony up for his little bride. Remind me not to let Gail's parents do that to us, he thought.

Now they were sitting at opposite ends of the big blue upholstered couch. Yeager told her he'd thought they could go to Thunder Burger on M Street, if that sounded okay. After the briefest of pauses, Erica said it sounded fine. Producing a joint from his shirt pocket, he asked her if she wanted to get high first. Erica laughed shrilly, with a touch of panic in the swift saccades of her eyes, and said she didn't really want to, right now. "But go ahead, if you feel like it." Yeager demurred, suggesting they save it till later. He couldn't remember if he'd ever gotten stoned with Erica (it would have been with a crowd of others, of course, in someone's dorm room) and found himself curious to know if it would settle her down some, or if—appalling thought—she'd start talking even faster, about God knew what.

The meal was a trial for him. He'd already finished his burger and was on his third beer while Erica was still toying with her salad. She took small bites whenever she paused in her monologue, and the monologue seemed to have no end. Why would she think he wanted to hear about her summer vacations in Maine as a teenager, or about her sister's fiancé's family, or the asshole her mother was going out with? Yeager decided she was the most boring person, bar none, he'd ever met. No wonder she hadn't made any friends down here. She had no general conversation, zero sense of humor. Nor had she asked him a single thing, really, about himself, just one or two questions about his work. When he'd replied, and begun to tell a story about one of the law firm's cases, Erica took the ball from him and he had to sit back and listen to some crap about her father, who was also a lawyer.

"He works so hard, and when he and Mom got divorced, that was what he kept saying to me and Kathleen: 'I worked so hard to give you girls a childhood you'd remember, and your mother was right there with me.' Right there with him! as if she was there in his office, helping him. Isn't that wild?" Was it? Yeager was lost, trying to figure out whose moral point of view he was supposed to be sympathizing with here, and Erica's tone of voice gave him no help: she rattled on about everything in the same high key, with broadened vowels that struck him as a pseudo–Bryn Mawr affectation, words tumbling after each other like the little balls in one of those colored-oil-and-water contraptions, endlessly rising to the surface only to fall again. Not that his confusion mattered, because Erica was off on a different subject by now, and Yeager tipped the last of his beer into his mouth, wondering if he was ever going to get laid.

Back at her apartment, Erica asked him if he wanted another beer, and turned on the television before she went into the kitchen to get it for him. Yeager settled back on the couch, paying no attention to the stupid sitcom on the tube. He was feeling pleased with his strategy, pleased that he'd bypassed all the disingenuous awkwardness of angling for an invitation to come upstairs with her. Instead, he'd simply cruised the blocks near her building until he found a parking place, then walked with her back to the opulent foyer and entered beside her, as if there were no question that they'd both want the evening to continue in this way. Erica's chatterboxing worked in his favor, too, since there were no uncomfortable pauses, no single moment for either of them to acknowledge the direction they were taking. It was almost, Yeager reflected, as if Erica hadn't noticed what was happening, she was so busy yacking. But surely that wasn't possible.

Turning on the TV was interesting, too. She'd have to sit next to him on the couch to watch it. Yeager gave her his best smile as she returned with his beer, already picturing her naked on the couch with him.

What actually transpired was embarrassing, though. Erica continued to talk, addressing her remarks to the television screen. After ten minutes, Yeager reached to his left and turned off the lamp. "Do you mind?" he said. "Oh," said Erica. "No." Then she was off again, giving him a little update on some of their Penn classmates. Yeager realized he was going to have to proceed as if she were a normal girl: just do all the things he would do if there were the usual hiatuses and silences and windows of opportunity. He took the joint from his pocket, lit it, took a hit, and passed it to Erica. She accepted it from him without pausing in her talk and held it. After a minute, Yeager gestured for its return and Erica gave it to him. This ritual repeated itself—Yeager smoking, passing the joint to her, Erica passing it back without raising it to her lips—until it was too small to be held. Yeager looked around, saw no ashtray, and wet the tips of his fingers to extinguish the roach, which he returned to his shirt pocket. Thoroughly buzzed now, and semidrunk on the beers, he realized he was in danger of retreating altogether inside himself. Erica's endless flow of words now appeared to him as a ribbon of silk spiraling out and out and around, cocooning her off from him. Yeager forced himself to fantasize about doing her; he winced slightly at the absurdity, sitting right next to the real live person yet requiring a fantasy to get aroused. But it worked, and there was even a perverse appeal about the whole situation. On and on and on Erica spun her innocent cocoon, her eyes fixed on the television screen, while silent Yeager felt the secret blood beating in his erection. He put his arm around Erica's shoulders and drew her to him. She returned his kiss and put one of her hands softly on his thigh. And then began talking again: back to the sister and the fiancé. It would have been funny if it wasn't so bizarre. Erica was invoking a man and a woman who were total strangers to him, two people he couldn't be presumed to have the slightest interest in, while here they sat, the two of them, two real people, making out. Yeager felt his inwardness return, the temptation to get lost in this train of thought. To combat it, he invoked his own, equally fantastic hallucination: Erica reduced to gusts of passion, coming like a maniac. This returned him to his immediate concern: how could you kiss a girl who wouldn't be quiet? Yeager decided to forget about kissing, and that too was arousing, to simply start feeling her up and unbuttoning her while she stared at the screen and talked and talked. Every now and then Erica turned to him and gave him a quick smile, as if to say *Oh, you men!*—certainly there was no protest in it—while he massaged her little tits and got his hand up under her skirt. Her cunt was wet, and this particular manifestation of desire had always worked magic on Yeager—it seemed the ultimate gift, or proof, a girl could give him. He clutched Erica's body, pulling her away from the television and crushing her against him. She stopped talking and sighed deeply. But then Yeager came in his pants, which hadn't happened to him since necking in middle school. Even as he kept Erica's flanks rubbing against his cock, blissed out on the stoned-orgasm sensation, he was calculating whether he could keep her from noticing. Probably the thing to do was to act as if he'd stopped making out with her because he was such a gentleman, and things were going too far and all that. So he gently removed Erica's body from his and returned her to her place beside him on the couch. After a quick, startled look, she began to talk again. Yeager reached out and put the tips of his fingers over her mouth. "Erica," he said, "I think I better go now. This is getting a little heavy and— you know, I had a really nice time and I don't want to spoil it."

"Oh? All right." She began to rebutton her blouse. "I don't mind if you stay a little longer."

"No, I should go." Yeager glanced down at his crotch, but

the dark fabric of his jeans showed nothing. "I didn't mean to get carried away like that." He reached over and patted her hand, then gave her a kiss on the top of her head. It was impossible, so soon after orgasm, to feel anything but a nearly desperate desire to go home, yet Yeager was at the same time alive to his disappointment, his awareness of having cheated himself, and he knew that, once he was back in his apartment, he would wish for another chance. Better to get that arranged now, before he left, so he wouldn't have to call her again and spend another half hour on the phone.

Erica had begun telling him about the New Year's Eve party she'd gone to. He interrupted her and suggested they watch a DVD together tomorrow evening. Now that their sexual destination was not in doubt, Yeager saw no point in wasting time on dinner and enduring another endless talk-session.

"Tomorrow?" said Erica. She had stood up when he did, and was smoothing down her skirt. "Listen, fella"—the words were mock-stern, Erica's expression coy—"I'm not always free on— But yes, I think tomorrow's okay."

Oops, thought Yeager, forgot about that one: you're not supposed to assume a girl doesn't have a date on Saturday night. "Only if you're sure it's okay," he said. "I know it's late notice but"—he gritted his teeth and said it—"I'd really like to see you again."

It was hard, of course, to get away, but by now Yeager knew that he just had to say and do exactly what he would say and do if Erica were a normal girl. Interrupt her talking whenever he had to, put on his jacket, give her another chaste kiss, say goodnight. She was telling him about her father again, how he used to play cards with the two sisters after their mother had gone to bed. She began to describe for Yeager the rules of a game called Casino. Yeager opened the door of the apartment and spoke over the description: "See you around eight, okay? Sleep well."

"Oh," said Erica, and gave him a smile so wide her eyes nearly disappeared. "Okay. I could make dinner for us?"

Yeager was walking down the corridor. He turned around, still walking, and said, "Hey, don't bother. Really. I'll probably go in to the office tomorrow and they usually spring for a pizza on Saturdays. 'Night, now."

Erica waved at him as he turned the bend toward the elevator.

Embarrassing as his incontinence was, Yeager could see the value of the evening as a kind of dry run—well, a wet run. It had clarified the requirements of his relationship with her. There would be no need, for instance, to bring over a movie with semi-erotic qualities. Clearly, Erica Huysman preferred sexuality to emerge without conscious acknowledgment or stimulation; any old film would do. A couple of condoms, on the other hand, were a must, and Yeager tucked them in the front pocket of his jeans so he wouldn't have to futz around with his wallet when the moment arrived.

Erica, he saw with approval, had dressed down for the occasion: her old college garb, bright blue jeans and an

Xtra-large T–shirt depicting a cartoon cat. He greeted her with a quick kiss on the lips; the perfume was the same, regrettably. It occurred to him that Erica was a cat person if there ever was one; boring, friendless people always had cats. He asked her about this, after complimenting the T–shirt.

Erica was in mid-monologue—something about bookstores, this time, and trying to find a special book for a senior citizen she liked who worked in her office. When Yeager overrode her words with his question, she looked down at the caricature and petted it. "Thank you," she said. "I did, but she died."

"Shit. I'm sorry."

"Gosh, I didn't offer you a beer," said Erica rapidly. "I went out and got some Heinekens, and oh, I also stopped at the Redbox and got us a couple of movies to choose from."

Yeager had tossed his DVDs on the couch when he removed his jacket; evidently Erica had not noticed. "Thanks; sure, I'll have a beer. I brought over a couple of films too, so now we've got choices galore."

"Oh, I didn't know you were going to. *I'm* sorry; we can watch what you brought."

"No, no, it doesn't matter," and they dithered around on that one for a while until Yeager, beer in hand, went over to the player and shoved in one of Erica's selections: predictably, a Hollywood comedy he'd never heard of.

Yeager knew it was crass, but driving over, he'd made a little bet with himself that he could get in Erica's pants within one hour of crossing her doorsill. And that—unless she turned out to be a fantastic lay, which was unlikely—would be that. Not long into the movie (twenty-two minutes and counting) he took out a joint and began to smoke it, this time not bothering to pass it to Erica, who said nothing about it. Indeed, she said almost nothing at all through the opening sequences of the movie, and Yeager found himself starting to get absorbed in the story, and to enjoy it, stupid though it was. But then something that happened to the protagonist reminded Erica of something that had happened to her, and she was off, telling him the story, and if he had actually given two shits he would have said, *Jesus, Erica, why do you bother to rent a movie if you're not going to watch it?*

Yeager let her go on while he finished the joint and returned the roach to his pocket. Then he put his arm around her and began to caress her shoulders and neck, nodding as she talked, keeping eye contact. The changing scenes on the television screen cast a succession of colors and lights on Erica's face, which itself did not change. The weed was sparking a riot of thoughts, nearly dividing him between the self that leaned forward to kiss her throat and the self that told him (*him*: yet a third self) that Erica had to keep controlling the words, spinning her cocoon, because if she allowed herself to fall silent, some dreadful and unbearable speech would burst out and . . . Yeager lost the thought. It was the weirdest seduction of his life. He went through all the standard stages while Erica continued to talk. The T–shirt came off, and the bra, revealing her tiny breasts with their pink, soft nipples. When it came to the jeans, Yeager was worried that he'd have to interrupt the flow to lean over and remove her shoes, or else ask Erica to do so, but when he looked, he saw that she'd already gotten them off somehow. So he was able to scoot the jeans down and off her legs (Erica obligingly lifted her ass) and then jam his fingers inside her frilled panties. With his other hand he found the remote control unit and stopped the movie.

What to do about his own clothes? He settled for lowering his pants and underwear to his ankles. With his free hand, he removed one of the rubbers. He required both hands, though, to tear open the foil package. Erica's words seemed to fall even more rapidly from her lips during the thirty seconds in which he was not touching her, in which he took out the condom and fitted it on himself. Yeager decided she really had a beautiful body, so tall and long and awkward. He reached over, eased the panties off, and drew Erica onto his lap, on her knees, facing him, and entered her. Unbelievably, she did not stop talking, though her breathing was pronounced and the words poured out in uneven, jagged phrases. Up until that moment, just like the night before, he'd found their mutual isolation arousing, but to have actual sex with a girl who wouldn't shut up while his johnson was inside her—that was the limit. Yeager embraced her and kissed her furiously, bringing a blessed silence to the living room of the Massachusetts Avenue apartment, and also causing him a second night's embarrassment, for he was unable to control himself and within a few seconds it was all over.

* * *

Four months later, Yeager concluded a telephone call with Gail (the wedding arrangements had achieved a peak of rococo complexity, and they spoke nearly every day now) and stood at the small, high window of his basement apartment, looking up at the heterogeneous bustle of Capitol Hill. The May evening was as perfect as an evening could be, its still air washing the street and cars and buildings until they seemed bathed in Impressionist pastels. He was expecting Gail to call him back directly; she needed to phone her mother to check on a detail of the reception plans, which she would then relay to Yeager. But when the phone rang and without looking at the number he said, "Hey sweetie," Erica Huysman's voice replied, coolly, by identifying herself and asking him how he was.

He'd screened all her calls, back in January, and February, returning none of them, and after leaving perhaps half a dozen messages she'd stopped trying to reach him. Now Yeager shut his eyes and made a comical wince; he would have given a great deal to avoid this. "I'm doing well," he said. "Very well. How about you?"

Erica laughed. "Oh, fine," she said. "Just— you know, about the same. I was sort of sitting around going through a few things and I thought I'd give you a call, even though"— her voice took on that coy, minatory sternness—"you never called *me* back, fella, which I certainly wondered about. But you're forgiven. I'm sure you were—"

"Yeah, very busy." Yeager decided to take the plunge at once. "It's been a pretty hectic time. Gail and I— You remember

Gail? We're getting married next month."

"Really." There was a pause, and Yeager could almost hear the wheels turning as Erica rolled with that one. Then she said, "I didn't realize you were still seeing her."

"Oh sure," Yeager said. "We've been engaged for over a year."

"I see." If there was any recompense to be had from this miserable conversation, Yeager reflected, it lay in the silence he was finally exacting from Erica Huysman. This one stretched on, and at last Erica said, "You didn't tell me that, back when we were together."

Together? Jesus. "You didn't ask," said Yeager.

"Well, you asked me *out*."

"Look, if it was a concern of yours, you should have pursued it. It wasn't a concern of mine; that's why I didn't say anything about it."

Erica did not reply. From his window, craning his neck, Yeager could just make out the dome of the Capitol, transfigured by ochre rays of sunset. The silence was filled with voices and laughter from the street, and some dewy, flowery fragrance, as if the city concealed a secret bower of blossoms at its heart. Finally Erica said, "I guess we had a misunderstanding, then."

"I guess so." Here was a reasonable place to conclude the conversation, to put paid to the entire fucked-up episode—he could say, *Well, gotta run; take care of yourself*—but he couldn't help feeling sorry for her, a little. Calling a guy up *again*, after all those unanswered messages—a guy, furthermore, who'd turned in an absolutely rotten sexual performance—only to get dumped. Yeager, sighing, offered Erica a chance to become herself: "So, what's new? How have you been?" He walked over to his couch and sat down, leaning back, prepared to listen for as long as it took.

But Erica only said, "Goodbye, Mark," and hung up.

Yeager took the phone from his ear, looked at it, then shrugged and dropped it on the couch. Despite himself, he smiled. He had to admire her for that, though getting hung up on was not something he appreciated, as a rule. But her response was, after all, appropriate. It had been an honest phone call, on both their parts; neither of them were pretending to be something they weren't. He hadn't thought Erica capable of such honesty, nor of expressing it with so few words. Perhaps she had grown up in the last several months, had achieved some awareness of herself and her cluelessness about other people, and had vowed to amend it. Perhaps she was in therapy—yeah, talk-therapy, Yeager thought, smiling again. If he was partially responsible for that, he supposed he could take some comfort in the result.

Erica's face and voice came to him from time to time during the next few weeks, once in the silence following sex with Gail, and Yeager had to struggle to find something he could start talking about to make the image go away. He wasn't sure what bothered him more, the silence itself, like a reversal, a negative, of Erica's yacking, or the memory of his poor performance falling like a dream over this perfectly real and satisfactory session with Gail. And once, disgustedly, he thought of Erica when Gail, sitting beside him at the Sheltons' kitchen table, spoke with deference but at much too great a length about what schools Yeager would apply to after the honeymoon; Yeager stopped her words with a frowning kiss. Worst, though, was the moment when he stood at the altar with his bride beside him, and heard Gail say *I do*. Immediately he pictured the other girl, and found himself wondering if a grown-up Erica would be able to confine her reply to those two syllables, or would she become a child again, and chatter on, careless even of the sacrament now being enacted? It was a funny and therefore horrible thought, given the circumstances: The last thing Yeager wanted to do was to burst out laughing in the middle of his own wedding.

Me and Martin and Our Wives

After the ceremony I stand in line outside the church, frying in the sun, and finally get to give him a hug. "Congratulations," I whisper, squeezing hard. I let him loose, touch my breast pocket, and say, "There go my sunglasses."

"Yeah, I heard 'em crack," my old friend Martin says, eyes already moving worriedly to the next in line. He's as abstracted as a half-wit, and hardly seems to have noticed who he's hugging. I'm just another guest.

"What's the matter?" my wife Nan asks me a few minutes later, as we walk down the flagstone steps to the parking lot.

My disappointment is too intricate for words, and besides, I'm nervous about Nan. This is the first time we've seen each other in almost a year.

"I broke my goddamn sunglasses," I say, squinting dramatically. It's tempting to blame this on Martin, and I open my mouth to do so, but the words as I begin to formulate them are ridiculous, so I remain silent.

* * *

All the relatives, and especially Julie's relatives, thought it was outrageous for Martin to want to play at his own wedding reception. He wouldn't budge, though. He gave in on a lot of other things—the endless guest list, the engraved invitations, being "counseled" by the minister in the moral complexities of Christian marriage—but he wouldn't give in on that.

I approve, naturally, since I did the same thing when I got married, eight years ago. Martin and I were in a band together then, too, just like now, and we played a bunch of somewhat nasty New Wave originals for my wedding reception, instead of the polkas and waltzes and slow-dances all the guests were expecting. They were polite about it, from what I can remember, though it's hard to remember much, what with all the cocaine and tequila. A tape exists, which Martin has listened to and assures me is gruesome.

Our current band, a four-piece, plays nothing but Sixties music—the Bashful Kidneys, we're called. Not a tough gig. We play the songs we grew up playing anyway, and are paid a surprising amount of money to perform them at motel lounges and high school reunions and other not very serious venues. Fortieth birthday parties. Wedding receptions. We're fine for wedding receptions, very listenable. Even the Class of '92 seems to dig us; we went over big at a high school prom a couple of months ago. It's a part-time job. We're all too old to try to make a living at it, pushing forty ourselves. Every one of us wanted to when we were younger, though. I was the last to give up, but now I work for a living too.

Since he would be rather busy, getting married and all,

the band gave Martin the afternoon off from loading in. We're being big about this, we reminded him at rehearsal. Take your time, take your time. We'll get everything set up. Just come over and be ready to play, motherfucker.

It is very hot, loading in. The bass player, Steven, and I do most of it. Nan has gone for a walk.

The reception hall is attached to the church, which is located in a guano-spattered cul-de-sac behind a shopping center. Old, heavy rafter beams inside; linoleum; wood and stucco walls—oh, the echoes will be awful. Caterers are spreading tablecloths over rickety bridge tables.

Steven and I have been in bands together for only ten years or so, and are thus recent colleagues compared to me and Martin. I think about this as I grab a handful of mic stands and drag them into the hall. I certainly don't have an older friend than Martin. I think of the two of us, both fourteen, trudging through the snow up to the Burger King after school, and him reciting from memory the lyrics to "I Am the Walrus," complete with *goo goo goo joob*s. The record had just come out, and neither of us had ever heard anything like it before. Our English teacher had instructed us to learn a poem by heart. It made perfect sense to me that Martin would memorize those incredible words. I wanted to do so myself. Instead, I picked "A Day in the Life." Miss Ryan wouldn't let us recite them. She gave us a lecture, in front of the whole class, on why they weren't poetry.

I used to buy the sheet music to all the records we

loved and bring it over to his house. We would prop it up on the broken piano in the basement and play through it, me sight-reading like a good classical piano student (not yet having learned how to use my ears), him strumming along cacophonously on his new electric guitar (not yet having learned how to tune it). At first I played the melody with my right hand, just like the ignorant arrangement in the sheet music. It sounded like death. Then I got the hang of playing chords instead, and we began to sing.

"The niiiight . . . they *drove* old Dixie *down*," we mourned. Martin's ponytailed mother came downstairs with two Cokes and congratulated us for playing a meaningful American song for a change. I fingered one of the bad keys, listening to it go *sproing!* Martin and I looked at each other like conspirators, secret British agents. We accepted our Cokes and switched to the Beatles songbook for the rest of the afternoon.

Years later, the night Lennon was murdered, I called him, drunk, in tears. He had the same radio station on; I could hear it in the background as we tried to talk. I snorted and honked into a tissue, but Martin's grief had dried him right up. After each of my soggy laments, I would hear a croak: "I know. I know."

Do you? I wanted to shout. Do you really? Shock, Jim Beam, and resentment made me want to doubt him. Martin had by now settled easily enough—too easily, as far as I was concerned—into a government job, with music coming second. I hadn't settled into anything, not yet, and continued to draw unemployment and survive on cheese and crackers while seeing my face on the cover of *Rolling Stone*, or something even classier. I had grasped the thorn; but how else to pluck the sweet rose of fame? I wanted Martin too to feel the prick of adversity. We still played in bands together, but for him it was diversion, while I hung all my hopes on it, every ear-numbing, smoke-filled night, waiting for the big break. We often bickered, often separated. Yet when that babbling freak shot the Walrus, I knew who I had to call. Both of us were living alone that December.

Steven unwinds a mic cord and says, "He looked like he was going to pass out, standing up there grinning at the minister. Talk about stage fright."

"I thought he'd forget the words," I agree.

"Do you know the guy who was best man?"

"He's an old high school friend," I reply, but it's a delicate point and I say no more, pretending to be out of breath from lugging Martin's huge amp onto the stage.

A delicate point: I was not Martin's best man. They had a formal dress-up wedding, with ushers and bridesmaids and a tiny knock-kneed ring bearer. The best man was Barry Zane, also a very old friend of his. I scarcely know him, though we all went to school together. Somehow the circles of our friendships never intersected. Barry has played on every one of Martin's bowling teams, for instance, and I don't bowl.

Well, Martin hadn't been my best man either. We were in the midst of another squabble. A month before my wedding, I told him I could no longer play music with him if he didn't start showing up on time for rehearsals. I knew he was incapable of doing this. His reply wasn't satisfactory—something about working a lot of overtime—and I said, "You're fired." He looked at me stonily. Martin has large dark eyes. Our band was not doing well, and I was unhappy, and drinking too much. The thorn had grown sharper, the rose no sweeter, and no nearer.

Nan and I married ourselves, according to Quaker custom, in the only state in the Union that permits this practice. We aren't Quakers; the point was to disdain ceremony. We took two witnesses—a friend of mine and a friend of hers—both sets of parents, my eighty-six-year-old great-aunt whom I'm fond of, and the marriage license, and hauled the whole show across the state line to Gettysburg, Pennsylvania. We led everyone into Gettysburg Park, past plaques and maps detailing the various events of the great battle, sat them down on a fallen log in a sun-dappled clearing near the site of Pickett's Charge, and declared ourselves married. Our parents looked unhappily at each other and toasted us in the champagne they'd brought, picking gnats out of the glasses and flicking them away. My mother examined her shiny black pumps, which I'd told her three times not to wear, and tssked at the dirt and leaves adhering to them, while Nan's egg-bald dad kept waving a white handkerchief over his dome to keep the mosquitoes off; it fluttered back and forth, back and forth, like a request for parley. My great-aunt had a splendid time, however. "Children, this is so *refreshing*," she told us repeatedly, burping.

Then we threw a big reception at the Townshend Mansion

back home, but no nonsense with garters or bouquets or first dances. Just a big old party featuring my very own band.

So Martin couldn't have been my best man anyway, because I had no best man. But he was also not the friend I brought along across the state line. I had just fired him from the band; how could I invite him to Gettysburg? Yet I asked him back in the band to play at my reception. It was too late to get another guitar player, I told him. I knew he would say yes.

Eight years later, I shove my electric piano onto the stage and think, *You could have said, Come to Gettysburg: it's too late to get another best friend.*

My wife now enters the church hall, heels clicking on the linoleum. (Yes, the echo is awful.) She stops in the middle of the room, stares at the stage set-up. Her expression is not precisely wistful, but she doesn't look as if she hates the sight of it either.

Her hair has gone so gray, so early. The color is like snow on winter leaves.

We've been separated for over a year, and her appearance with me at the church surprised most of my friends. But she likes Martin, and didn't want to pass up the wedding. After a series of telephone discussions, she and I decided to go as a couple. It would be easier on us, and less awkward for our friends, and this is what we have told everyone.

We haven't told them that we're also considering getting back together. Long letters have been exchanged. I'm squarely in favor of it; she's wavering, I think. It's been a drawn-out, horrible separation, from my point of view, and I want her back. I'm tired of pretending that the decision to split was mutual. I have a steady job now, I'm willing to settle down.

I hop off the stage and walk shyly over to Nan and touch her wintry hair. She has been agreeable and distant all afternoon, as if we were already fondly divorced, and this concerns me. "Hello there," I say.

"It's scorching out," she says.

I refuse to discuss the weather. I say, "I'm glad you're here." She doesn't respond, and I backtrack. "I mean, you've hardly ever heard this band play. I'm curious to know what you think. It's just a part-time thing, of course."

She looks at me. "Just Fridays, Saturdays and Sundays, right?" Looks away, at the cluttered stage.

I feel the need to get back up there, get the cords taped down (where *is* the duct tape? doesn't Martin usually bring that in his guitar case?), do a sound check. This awful wood-and-stucco room is going to reverberate like a great big barrel.

"Well, save me a chair."

Nan says, "Certainly. We're here as a couple." I listen hard for irony or regret, but can't detect any.

When the hall is three-quarters full, Martin and his new wife arrive to applause. We've got everything waiting for him, except his guitar. He'd insisted on bringing that with him, so Mr. and Mrs. Anderson's entrance is a little kooky: Martin, face flushed, hair askew, still in his gray tux, totes Julie on one arm and his Fender on the other. Laughter, cheers. Even her relatives think it's funny.

Martin is very happy, I can see (although I can also see that he's hyperventilating with nervousness). He keeps glancing at Julie like it's Halloween and they're a couple of kids all dressed up in masquerade, out to fool the grown-ups and make off with a sack of candy.

He grins and snickers, makes witty retorts to the volley of remarks thrown at him by his friends. He manages to be decorous to all the relatives. It's a great entrance, better than I could have done, or did do, when I showed up drunk at the Townshend Mansion.

Martin and I sat in my new apartment last spring, a week after he and Julie had mailed the wedding invitations. It all happened so fast, this courtship. I don't know Julie at all. She is quiet, young. A good fifteen years younger than Martin. A research assistant at the government office where he works. She has a halo of curling chestnut hair, inviting hackneyed pre-Raphaelite comparisons. She is, she has . . . but I don't know her at all.

Martin declined another beer and got up to empty the ashtray I always put out for him so he doesn't have to ask if he can smoke. His smoking is suicidal—he has high blood pressure and a family history of heart disease.

We had been talking about nothing special for hours. Now he lit another Pall Mall, blew smoke carefully out the window. I could see a mosquito turn in midair and flee the cloud. "I like the smell," I told him for the thousandth time, but he continued to blow it away from me.

He stroked my cat, who adores him. He was silent, and then said, "I feel like my tongue is being cut out."

"What do you mean?" It wasn't Martin's style to be so direct and dramatic, and I was taken aback. He shook his head.

"Is it something about Julie?"

"I don't know. I feel like I have a lot to express, and I don't know how to do it anymore." A worm of satisfaction stirred inside me. Now you know, my friend. I pictured my old friend Martin with blood pouring from his mute mouth.

My cat meowed, and settled on his lap. He took a deep drag from his cigarette, stared out the window, then released all the smoke with a sigh. "I want the band to play at our reception."

"There you go," I said. "That's the spirit. We had fun at mine."

He looked at me, eyes hurting, and I regretted my lie: in fact, it had been a miserable time, me drunk and frightened and belligerent. I'd been a mess the entire month before Gettysburg. Firing him from the band. Feeling his reproachful dark eyes on me as Nan's relatives handed me wedding cake and told me how much they liked the way we played.

He stubbed his cigarette out, laughed, and dusted off an old joke: "You never should have got married at Gettysburg, man. Your marriage was doomed to be a fucking battlefield."

Martin is a Civil War enthusiast, and I asked him whether, in his opinion, Meade's decision not to attack Lee's retreating army was a mistake.

Various relatives and co-workers of Martin's insist on com-
mandeering the microphone throughout the evening. They
want to toast him, tease him, make speeches. As the champagne goes down, these orations become increasingly daft.

But in between all that, we get some playing done. The
room bounces the music back to us in a dense, undifferentiat-
ed roar. The guests must be feeling sandbagged by it.

Martin's head isn't here. I've played on stages with him
for twenty years and I can tell in a minute whether he's into it
or not. And he's not—the distractions and obligations of the
day are impossible for him to overcome. His face wears the
same half-witted, anxious expression I saw when I hugged
him outside the church. Yet how can I blame him? It's his
wedding day, for God's sake. Of course he's distracted. He's
not thinking about music. Today it doesn't matter to him how
long he and I have been playing these songs together. But if it
doesn't matter, then they're just a bunch of songs. The lyrics
are silly and the emotions trite. You have to love them to re-
deem them. Yet how can I blame him? Do I blame him? Yes.
Best man Barry Zane dances past with his wife and thrusts
his fist in the air. "Right on, Airplane! Right on, Doors!" His
face is red from champagne. Now he makes a peace sign, two
fingers raised over his wife's head like tiny antennae. "Power
to the purple! Right arm!"

He's imitating an imitation of something that never existed in the first place. This angers me so much that I feel hot, and

for a few bars the instrument beneath my fingers is baffling, alien, an unyielding contraption of black-and-white plastic. Everyone else in the band is paying attention, fortunately, or we'd be sounding pathetic. Steven is in good form, pumping out the Motown bass lines, tossing gentle fills into the ballads.

He and I team up to sing a pretty good "Tracks of My Tears."

Our drummer is on medication again—the poor bastard is a legal junkie due to a terminal bone disease—and playing like there's no tomorrow, which for him is an all-too-realistic possibility. Having a relapse improves his chops. It's what he lives for, this business of performing, hearing the applause. *His* head is into it, I think resentfully, though I realize the comparison is hardly apt.

After every number, someone, an uncle or a new in-law or a federal computer programmer, comes up to Martin, tugging his pants leg from the dance floor, complimenting the band or just wanting a cheerful word with him. He hams it up, seems to turn gratefully away from the rest of us. Our set is not, to put it mildly, streamlined.

I lean on my piano during one of these hiatuses. The lights are in my eyes (we bought some new gels for them—a mistake—and everyone's skin glows a nauseous sallow color, like modeling clay) but I'm sure I see Nan and Julie talking. They've never met before. Nan is laughing; she looks comfortable, like a marriage veteran. Julie's face is so childlike, and the bridal gown and veil emphasize this. Nan is quite a few years older than me. Does that make her old enough to be

Julie's mother? I calculate. Yes, it does. Easily. Well for Christ's sake.

I'm trying to decide how to ask Nan to come home with me. The cat, perhaps. I could invoke the cat, describe how much it misses her. It's quite true. Our cat has pined and lost weight. It won't go outside anymore.

Each time I think of Nan my lungs get too big for my chest, and my head hurts. I have my distractions too, Martin. But I'm hitting the keys like I mean it.

Nan looks good in her blue cotton dress and high heels. Earlier, at the church, she'd squeezed my arm and whispered, "I like you without your beard." My stomach dropped. It was dreadful to realize that this was the first time she'd seen me without it. I'd shaved it off months and months ago.

With one more set to go, we take a break. A DJ begins to play current top 40, too loud. The other Kidneys, minus me and Martin, go out to the parking lot to get high. I haven't done that in years, now that I don't drink either, and Martin can't get away—he's been dragooned by Julie's relatives to sit with them and eat wedding cake.

I stand in the middle of the hall, wondering where Nan is. Julie walks over to me and holds out her hand. I shake it, feeling foolish, then kiss her cheek like an uncle. "How are you holding up?" I ask her.

"Oh my God." She looks around the chattering hall and laughs helplessly. "It's just too much. I'm having a wonderful time but I can't wait for it to be over."

"That sounds about normal. What time is your plane?" They are honeymooning in St. Thomas.

"Three a.m. My God. I can't believe he booked it for the same night as . . . all this. I don't know why I let him do it. It seemed like it made sense at the time. Just leave here, go home and change, and then head for the airport. We must have been out of our minds."

"You'll make it," I say. "How's your husband doing?"

Julie blushes. "That's so weird: 'my husband.' He's fine, I guess. You guys sound great."

"Thanks, but no. So now you're a musician's wife."

She nods. "God, I guess so. No, really, it's a blast. I love listening to him play."

"It wouldn't be such a blast if he was trying to do it full time. Believe me."

Julie doesn't know what to say to that. I assume that the idea of Martin as a full-time musician has never crossed her mind. "Yeah, Nan was telling me some stories," she blurts, then blushes again and tries to laugh. "Oops, was that the wrong thing to say?"

"Not at all," I tell her. "It's no secret. The music business was not exactly friendly to our marriage."

"Hey, Julie!" a hoarse voice yells. "C'mere and eat some cake!" Julie excuses herself with a wave, and walks over to her relatives' table. I see Nan, seated near the back of the room, and head toward her, but am waylaid by Martin's mother, midway.

"It's so— Well, I'm at a loss for words," she tells me. I nod.

His mother is heavier, and her ponytail is gone. Now she wears her hair in a fluffy perm. "Tell me honestly," she says, "*honestly* now"—she's a bit loaded—"did you ever think he'd get married?"

"Of course," I say, surprised. Martin loves animals and children and I never thought for a moment he wouldn't raise a family.

"Well, I was starting to wonder," says Martin's mother. "He'd gotten. . . . "

When she hesitates, I wait for a moment and then suggest, "Older?"

Apparently we're on the same wavelength. She bobs her head vigorously.

"Come on, Mrs. Anderson," I say. "He was just waiting for the right girl."

She touches my arm. "And to see you all still up there together, after all this time. Lord—I remember when you and Martin used to play music in our basement. Do you remember? You played that horrible old piano we had, and we'd just gotten him an electric guitar. It wasn't a very good one, was it?"

"Not exactly. Plastic tuning pegs, if I recall. But it was a start." Her nostalgia so distressingly echoes my own that I make a can't-hear gesture, pointing at the DJ and then at my ears, and move on.

I sit down next to Nan, who is eating a salad, but I can't shake the sentimental images of myself and Martin at fourteen, peering at sheet music, trying to sing in harmony, trying to get the chords right. We were going to write a rock opera and avoid going to college. *That was a glorious and not unrealizable ambition*, I think pugnaciously. Whoever it is I'm arguing with doesn't answer.

I whisper to Nan, "You could come back with me after this?"

She puts her fork down and says, "Oh, no, I don't think so." But her fine gray eyes have instantly teared up, and I'm certain her answer is not definitive. Tactics: leave her alone for the nonce, let the seed be planted.

I stroke her arm—very tan; I wonder what beach she's been going to this summer—and say, "Well, it's just an idea." Busily: "Got to get back to the guys. Talk to you later."

Martin comes up to me right before we start the last set and says, "Do you remember 'You Never Can Tell'?"

"Sort of," I say. "Very appropriate choice." It's a Chuck Berry song, all about a wedding down in Louisiana. One of our previous bands used to play it.

"Let's do it last," Martin says. "Julie's parents asked me if we could play something from the Fifties."

"Sure," I say, thinking, Oh man, since when do you take requests? "Who's going to sing it?"

Martin laughs. "Fuck, didn't you use to?"

"I remember maybe half the words. Come on, you sang all the harmonies. You know as many of the words as I do."

"Well, we'll get through it," he says. "I'll start singing it, okay? You jump in if I can't remember."

"What about the other guys?"

"Steven knows the chords. The drums are just rock and roll. It'll fall together."

This is lame, and unprofessional, but it's his party. "Hey, Martin?" I say. He looks at me. He's loosened his tie, and his thinning hair strays off in several directions. "Nan and I may get back together."

"Yeah?" he says. His eyes roam the hall, looking for Julie. "That's great. I never really knew why you split up in the first place. You didn't talk much about it."

"Who knows," I say. "She's glad I'm not living in clubs anymore, I know that."

"I'll bet," says Martin.

"Martin?"

"Yeah?"

"Did I ever apologize about my wedding? You know, throwing you out of the band and then asking you back and all that?"

"That was a million years ago," says Martin. "Forget it." But I have his attention.

"Well, I *am* sorry. I don't know what was the matter with me."

"We were like on different rhythms." Martin takes a deep breath, and then smiles. "But now we're both over the hill, so what the fuck. I hope you and Nan work it out."

"Thanks," I say. "I hope you and Julie do too." Then I reflect on how that sounded, and bite my lip, wanting the words back. "Shit, I'm sorry. I didn't mean I thought there was anything to work out."

"No, that's a reasonable thing to say," says Martin earnestly. "Just because I'm getting married doesn't mean I know what I'm doing, right?" He laughs.

"Gettysburg," I say, and Martin laughs again and says, "Could be."

A lot of the guests have left when Martin announces over the mic, "Now we'd like to end with a little tune called 'C'est La Vie, Say the Old Folks, It Goes to Show You Never Can Tell'." Scattered hoots. His mother calls out, "'S right! You never can tell! Amen!"

Our drummer, his face haggard, counts it off. Martin starts the guitar figure, which is pinched from "Johnny B. Goode." Then he begins to sing, and I throw in the harmony.

It was a teenage wedding and the old folks wished 'em well
You could see that Pierre did truly love the Mademoiselle. . . .

We get through the first two verses all right, and Martin cries, "Go!" and looks at me. I start soloing. At the turnback I nod at him to take one, and go back to chording. His lead doesn't threaten Chuck Berry.

The third verse starts, Martin sings the first line, and then blanks. I happen to know what's next, and jump in. He looks tired and lost, puffy around the eyes. In between lines I move my mouth away from the mic and yell at him, "Sing, asshole!" I guess it refreshes his memory. Now he's singing harmony over me.

They had a hi-fi phono, boy did they let it blast
Seven hundred little records, all rock, rhythm 'n' jazz. . . .

And finally our eyes lock and we're watching each other's lips, singing more or less in tune. Trying to remember the words, wondering if we're going to get through it.

We do, of course—when have we not?—and receive a nice hand, especially from Nan and Julie. I bow toward them, think about leaving here with or without Nan, and lose my breath. I look over at Martin, and he too has made a little bow toward our wives, and his expression is at first gleeful, more of that trick-or-treat stuff. Then he stops smiling and slowly lifts his Fender off and puts it on its stand. He pulls out the patch cord and begins to wind it carefully into a loop. He walks over to his amp, flicks the power switch off. The tiny orange cue light fades out.

I stand up from behind my piano and say, "No encores tonight. You've got a plane to catch."

Martin nods.

"Are you worried about making the flight?"

Martin says, "Not really. I think we're just about done here."

Set List

"Lucky Me"

The eleven-year-old Nova, which I'd bought especially for the trip, had a horrible time pulling the U-Haul trailer, grinding and growling at 45 mph all the way from Philly down to D.C. When I got to Georgia Avenue and turned into the driveway of the house we'd rented, it was eight thirty in the evening, nearly dark. None of the other guys were there, so I sweated all my stuff out of the trailer myself, wrestling it upstairs to my attic room. It was the beginning of summer, and Washington was full of the usual swamp-heat and thunderstorms.

It took me almost another half hour to angle the car and trailer backwards out the driveway. At one point I thought I was going to have to give up; I just couldn't figure out how to reverse properly and get safely into the traffic on Georgia Avenue. Finally I did it, and drove to the U-Haul place. The attendant there started to uncouple the trailer as I watched. He turned to me and said, "Did you ever check this thing while you were driving, ace?" I said no. "You should've. It's hanging on by one pin. Another—" he squinted, figuring it out—"another ten miles, I'd give you, and off it comes. You're one lucky sonofabitch."

"Mice in Love"

The house was big and old and dilapidated, set back from Georgia Avenue in a grove of sweet-gum trees. We'd chosen it as a good place to rehearse. The basement was totally underground, and there weren't any houses nearby to be disturbed. The owner was a man not much older than us, but a good citizen, a teacher of some kind. He traded us the first month's rent for a complete inside paint job, which we accomplished that first weekend.

The previous occupant of my room had lined every surface—all four walls, the ceiling, even the floor—with tinfoil. R.J. and I ripped it all out while Benjamin and Skip ran their rollers along the walls of the stairwell. Then we painted my room, sloppily, ignoring the trim, getting white drops all over the nice wooden floor. We were drunk at this point.

The previous occupant had left behind a work of art, hanging on one of the bright silver walls. It was a painting in a frame, of a nineteenth-century woman playing the spinet, her back mostly turned, and the room full of curios and sofas and vases. Later, we added a whole cast of characters to it, cut out from magazines and whatnot: Bob Dylan accompanying the lady on guitar; Roger Daltrey whirling his mic towards a vase; our new president, Jimmy Carter, smiling like a beaver at the whole scene. Later still, I met the man who'd lived in that room before me—the owner of the painting. He came to audition on bass for a band I was putting together, long after the Georgia Avenue Band broke up. I had the picture hanging in the basement, still festooned with decorations. Our auditioning bass player was insane or high or both. He played badly; he wiggled and grinned and, at one uncomfortable juncture, offered to show us pictures of himself in a previous incarnation. Suddenly he caught sight of the painting. He fell to his knees before it, and gazed at it as if the whole room had become a shrine. "Where did you get that?" he cried. I explained, and he told me (the other guys in the band were getting impatient, wanting to move on to the next auditioner) how he'd been part of another group-house group that had lived in the Georgia Avenue house. Quite a coincidence: the tinfoil room had been his, and then mine. "Wasn't it great?" he said. I told him we'd taken the tinfoil down, sorry. "You did? But it was so great." This is your brain on drugs. I apologized for desecrating his painting, and asked him if he wanted it back. "No, *please*," he said, still on his knees. "It's yours. You've earned it. You've made it your own."

After we painted the house, we had our first rehearsal: big Benjamin on drums, Skip frowning down at his guitar, my best friend R.J. on bass and sometimes guitar, me on keyboards and sometimes bass. We began by screwing around with Sixties stuff, a little Beatles, a little Band, a little Motown. But nostalgia was not the point. We'd all agreed that the point was to make money, to play the current hits.

Reluctantly, we put down our instruments and huddled around a copy of *Billboard* to figure out what the hell the current hits were, and which of them we had a prayer of covering. It was Disco Summer II. Benjamin and R.J. were going to do most of the singing. R.J. clutched his balls and went, *Oo, oo, oo, oo, stayin alive!* Benjamin went over to his drums and showed us he could play the disco beat and go *oo* at the same time. Skip frowned and joined in, playing the stupid chords on the off-off-beats. R.J. and I looked at each other, and he passed me the wine bottle, and I took a good hit.

I was on the run from grad school and a woman I was desperately-in-love-with-but-it-hadn't-worked-out. Coming back here to D.C.—I'd known all these guys since I was small—was the only thing I could think to do. I'd told everyone I was leaving Philly because I had this great opportunity to put together a killer band back home. Maybe that would turn out to be true, but I knew the real reason was that I had to get away from that horrible motherfucker of a campus, and from Therese. I had to prove I could live without her. Prove it to whom? To her; if she saw I wasn't so desperately in love with her, maybe she'd decide to get back together with me.

We bashed through a funk thing called "Brick House" and stopped. It was not us, this song. The silence grew, and then we heard, deep in the silence, a rustling and scampering. It was coming from the walls. "Mice," said Benjamin; "we have mice, gentlemen." He hit his snare drum and the rustling stopped. Then it resumed.

"I'll buy some mouse killer tomorrow," I said, and I did, and all the rest of that summer we rehearsed to the stink of dead mice, rotting somewhere inside the walls.

"Stamina"

I was out of money, after the first week. My Nova needed to go into the shop, and I was surprising myself with the amount of beer and wine I needed in order to sleep each night through.

So I got a job at a record store that had just opened in a new shopping mall. The mall was extremely ritzy. It had a Bloomingdale's. Elizabeth Taylor—at the time married to the Governor of Virginia, or it may have been the Senator—used to come and shop there. Bloomingdale's would close the store to everyone else but her.

I was shy around strangers, and at first my fellow record store employees were just names and smiles. After a few days one of them, a guy about my age with a golden beard and a gentle, eager laugh, began to make friends with me. His name was Evan. He wanted to go to lunch with me all the time, and talk about classical music. I thought of what my mother had told me, when I went off to summer camp: Be careful of the ones who are anxious to make friends; they're always the outcasts. But so what. I liked Evan all right. We went outside the mall and smoked dope during lunch break, and he told me a little about himself. He had almost made it as a classical pianist. "But I don't have the stamina," he said, with a beautiful smile. He was living at home with his rich parents, trying to kick a heroin habit.

Once I went over to his parents' place with him. They were out. The living room looked like a museum; I expected to see plush ropes warning me away from the upholstered settees and the floor-to-ceiling china cabinet. Evan sat down at a black Baldwin baby grand and played some Ives for me. I could never understand Ives, but Evan played the piece as if he knew what he was doing, and something communicated itself to me. He had great technique, that was for sure. Afterwards we helped ourselves to ice cream and Boston cream pie from his parents' refrigerator, and lounged around in the air conditioning, hating to go out into the swamp-weather. Evan lay back with his dirty loafers up on a couch, his eyelids drooping, and the sleeve of his shirt fell open a little, and I could see the yellow bruises on his arm where he'd been skin-popping. I didn't say anything. Later in the summer I met his parents, who were old and sweet and treated Evan like he was God. "To have a talented child. . . ." his mother whispered to me when Evan left to use the bathroom. "You can't imagine." I thought I could, but maybe not: when I looked at her, there was nothing but pride and love in her face.

"Stained Glass Nightmare"

I started to get postcards from Therese. She was in West Virginia for the summer, learning to make stained glass windows. The cards were friendly, with no hidden messages that I could detect. Nonetheless I read a lot into them. Mainly I wondered obsessively about who she was seeing. I couldn't imagine heading off to an adventure in West Virginia without having a romance with somebody. Even though I was going to bed—falling to my mattress—drunk every night, I still woke up twitching in the small hours from terrible dreams about Therese in the arms of another.

"What Room This?"

We'd only been in the Georgia Avenue house for a month when its owner came by to tell us he'd sold it. Soon the new owner came by too—the first of many such visits of inspection. She was Japanese, very petite, with her jet-black hair done up in a high and threatening bouffant. Her name was Naso. Accompanying her was . . . Veitch. "This Veitch," Naso said, as if that explained everything. Veitch looked like a decrepit Viking, tall, stooped, and ugly as sin. He said nothing, but glowered at each of us in turn as if we disgusted him.

Naso spoke rudimentary English, and the imperative was the tense she had learned best. "Go look there," she said to Veitch, and he glowered and went and looked where she pointed. "Go bring that," and he went to the car and brought in a screen for a window. His face was red with broken veins, and his hands trembled. I didn't like to think about drunks, since I knew I was in danger of becoming one, but clearly Veitch was a drunk. We learned later that he and Naso ran a liquor store in Northeast. That's where we'd bring the cash for the rent each month. He sat behind the counter and never said a word, just hated us with his eyes.

Naso hated us too, but it seemed less personal. She hated the idea of tenants, we decided. Our lease was for six months, and she couldn't throw us out. Furthermore, she was obvious-ly appalled at the sort of tenants we were: young, long-haired, musicians, sloppy, didn't cut the grass, etc. On her first visit, she and Veitch walked into every room of the house. R.J. and I were the only ones home, so we trailed along. She crossed a threshold and stopped dead. "What room this?" The question was put suspiciously, as if the room had no business being there, or was up to no good. That's the dining room, I said. She put her hands on her hips and took it in. Then we fol-lowed her to the next room. "What room this?" Pointing to the stove, R.J. said gravely, "We call this the *kitchen*." Up the stairs. "What room this?" This would be a bedroom, I said, indicating my mattress.

In the basement, after we'd identified it, Naso stared at Veitch and said, "Bad smell!" Veitch sneered. "Dead mice," R.J. and I said simultaneously—we'd fallen into her telegraph-ic style. Naso shut her eyes and shuddered.

When the tour was over, she and Veitch went outside to examine the property. R.J. and I looked at each other and stayed in the living room. "What lawn this?" I said. Back and forth across the property our new landlady paced, hands on hips, with Veitch hulking behind her.

Five years later, R.J. called me up and read me a story out of the newspaper. Naso had been arrested for attempt-ing to block the advance of a team of wreckers, set on tearing down the Georgia Avenue house. The county had bought her out because the property was to be used as part of the new Metrorail station. Naso had refused and refused (I could hear her: "What Metro this?") and finally she just planted herself in the path of the bulldozers, which did no good whatsoever, although the story, as R.J. read it to me, was sympathetic to her. There was no mention of Veitch.

"Root Boy Slim Blues"

A community café said we could play for the door. Whatever we took in was ours. It was our first job. Benjamin's brother agreed to be the doorman, and make sure everyone who came in paid a cover. What should the cover be? We decided two dollars was about right.

Our repertoire was really motley: half the stuff was our version of current hits, the other half was whatever we already knew how to play, older songs. The hits sounded so god-awful I was humiliated to be playing them. Only about twenty people came to the café to listen and they obviously despised these hits too. Our older songs went over much better, because we had some soul, and it was audible. I liked playing bass the best, just plunking away, way down below everyone else, hitting the downbeats with Benjamin's kick-drum, driving the music home. We played "Look Out Cleveland" by The Band. I sang some harmony with Benjamin and R.J. Our eyes met, and we all grinned. Yeah, it was a gift, playing this great song, singing something we loved to sing. By now it was clear we stood to make maybe thirty dollars. Benjamin's brother was drunk and had been letting people in for pocket change, but I didn't care, and for a few good moments, in this song and one or two others, none of the other guys cared either. I could tell. We were doing what we loved, and money has nothing to say to that, nor does skill, for that matter. We made all kinds of mistakes but the mistakes were much less important than the feeling. The great pianist Artur Schnabel believed this too, according to Evan, who was there, laughing and droopy-eyed, all alone at a table in the back.

When we were done, around one a.m., a huge, filthy, wobbling guy from the audience leapt across the monitors and demanded to sing. He revealed himself as Root Boy Slim, a D.C.-area fixture who, incredibly enough, would in sub-sequent years become nationally famous before dying. Root Boy wrote his own blues songs, quite nasty ones, and growled them out like a pit bull. He was always drunk; that was his gimmick. The other guys in my band knew of him, but since I'd been up in Philly I was unaware of his rep. I didn't want to let him sing, but Skip said, "Oh yeah, this is Root Boy Slim, let's back him up." Christ, all right, I said, and Root Boy told us to play 12-bar blues, we picked a key, and he sang "Boo-gie Till You Puke." And then he did: he vomited all over our equipment, broke a bottle of Thunderbird he'd been holding, and staggered out into the swamp-night. The seven people left in the café dug it a lot. I was outraged about the mess, but I could see the point, and the attraction. This too was soul, a soul distorted and shamed, but soul. Far better to sing your blues and puke onstage than to be Billy Joel or Kansas or the fucking Bee Gees.

"I Never Saw the Scars"

A new clerk was hired by the record store in mid-July, and I convinced myself, inside of two days, that I was in love with her. Older than me by seven or eight years (like Therese), Rae seemed sure of herself, with a clever, ironic way about her, and she dressed much better than most of us at the store. Rae was first-generation American. Her father, who was from Spain, was some kind of elder in the Catholic Charismatic movement. Her gig at the store was classical music. Evan really liked her too, and followed her around like a puppy, talking about Brendel and Schnabel and other men who played the piano much better than I ever would.

I asked Rae out to dinner, to an expensive restaurant in Georgetown. She had a glass of wine, while I got drunk, but I stayed very polite and courtly. Since I loved her, there was no rush; we didn't have to sleep together anytime soon. I gave her a courtly goodnight kiss at the door of her apartment in D.C., and the next day we smiled moonily at each other, helping customers. That went on for a couple of weeks—dinner dates, conversations about books, little Spanish lessons—and finally she asked me in and we became lovers. She wouldn't let me see her naked. She told me a terrible story: how her husband had been killed in a car accident, and she herself badly injured. The scars—all over her thighs and back, she said—made her feel ugly. I told her I didn't care, it didn't matter, but I never saw the scars. It was out of the question for her.

Then a postcard came from Therese, mentioning that she

would be coming back through the D.C. area in late August, and would I like her to visit me. Yes! I wrote back, and now I was no longer in love with Rae. All my courtliness was gone.

"WE6-1212"

The Georgia Avenue Band started to pick up a few more bookings. We played a high school reunion, a college mixer for a frat house, an Irish bar in Arlington. We rehearsed very hard, but it was such a desperate and unlikely task—to sound like polished 1977 hits when we had no technique for that, no love, no interest. Sometimes, down in the basement with the smell of rotting mice, we would take off on something, some riff or rhythm that had nothing to do with any song, and lift it right off the ground, loud, hard, but flying. I was always playing bass when we did that, and I felt on the brink of discovery, as if there was a new way of creating music that shot holes through disco and bypassed Heavy Metal and went *forward*, not backward to the Sixties.

At the frat house, we were doing a dumb Steve Miller song and R.J. forgot the words. He then displayed an aspect of his talent hitherto untapped. As the rest of us watched him anxiously, he began to improvise: weird, ruminative couplets about buying a Tastykake lemon pie at the 7-Eleven, putting five dollars of gas in his car, making a late-night phone call to the weather number. None of it made any sense, but the lines rhymed and they fit the meter, and by the end of the song I was throwing in little comments—"That's the way it was, mama . . .", "Listen to the man now . . ."—and Benjamin went

nuts on the tom-toms, and I wished we had a tape record-
er running. When R.J. stopped singing we double-timed the
tempo and just flailed away, trying to get to the heart of our
troubles, to break past the frat-house walls, to make it sound—
this dawned on me as I dripped sweat onto the frets—like *the
basement*. To be who we were, a basement band. Those darn
Philistine college kids didn't appreciate it. We weren't sounding like our demo tape. We probably weren't sounding like
much of anything, truth be told. One of them actually threw a
beer bottle at us. It exploded on the wall, right behind Skip's
guitar amp, and Skip took his Fender off and snapped off the
amp switch and said, "Okay, that's the limit," and walked out.
We were a trio for the remainder of the set.

There was an argument at the end of the night about
whether we would be paid. The frat boss claimed we were
fucked up and hadn't played at full strength—what was the
deal with the guitar player walking out? Benjamin explained
that it was all part of the act, I nodded, R.J. smirked, and somehow we got our money.

"Soon, Soon, Soon"

I went to the record store manager one day and said I had
to have a raise, I couldn't make it on minimum wage anymore. He said he would have to think about it. The next day
he called me into his office and said, "We've decided to let you
go." Oh.

I filed for unemployment, and learned that the record
store was contesting my claim, maintaining I'd quit. Rae had

been in the office when the manager fired me, so I told the case officer at the unemployment bureau to talk to her, that maybe she would back my story. I realized that was a pretty long shot, since she was mad at me for breaking up with her, but somehow I didn't think she would flat-out perjure herself, whereas it didn't surprise me at all that the manager would. He was just a company kiss-ass.

And she came through—she backed me up. I got on the dole, some ridiculous sum, thirty-five dollars a week or thereabouts. They sent me a list of other benefits I was eligible for, and I saw that one of them was free psychotherapy at the county mental health clinic. I wasn't sleeping or eating, the alcohol never completely left my bloodstream, and the thought of Therese coming soon, soon, soon, made me nauseated whenever I considered it, which was a hundred times a day. So why not? I made an appointment.

Dr. Dewey was, it developed, some kind of aversion therapist. He heard me out and said, "Okay, whenever you think about this Therese chick, I want you to imagine her with a big picture of Mickey Mouse hanging from her nose." Bastard jerk asshole, I thought, and never saw him again.

"There"

I kept in touch with Evan, and one day he called and told me that he and Rae were now together. That's great, I said, though I had my doubts. He'd seemed much too worshipful toward her, and also I really didn't know how she would deal with his drug battles. Rae acted as if she knew nothing about the Sixties and Seventies. I had, in addition, a doubt or two about Evan's sexual interest in women, not that there'd been anything overt the other way.

"Come down to her place, okay? On Saturday? We've invited a bunch of people over. Bring anyone you want."

I persuaded R.J. to come with me—to drive, so I could drink as much as I wanted. Rae's little apartment was as I remembered it, and looked even smaller with all the people crowded into it. Rae's friends were quite well dressed and conversable, in their thirties or even older. Evan's buddies wore whatever they felt like, and were very hip but not especially communicative, and first one guy, and then another, drifted out of the bathroom looking hipper than he'd looked before he went in. Each faction talked mostly with itself. Evan was wearing a loose cotton Mexican shirt, and his face looked freshly scrubbed, his beard trimmed. He was beaming at everyone, touching Rae whenever possible, hopping around the room getting drinks and chips for people. But sometimes he would pause in the midst of all that activity, and his eyelids came down, and I could see he was high on something, probably some kind of chemical cocktail that pulled him in several directions at once.

R.J., somewhat to my surprise, settled in with Rae's people and got involved talking about Shakespeare. I kept forgetting he'd been an English major, and still had hopes of getting advanced degrees and teaching (assuming we didn't become famous musicians). I got Evan to show me where the vodka was kept; I remembered Rae's vodka from my previous stays at the apartment, but its repository was a blank, along with so many other details of my doings when the sun went down. With a drunk's jealous concern for his stash, I disguised my libation so no one else would seek out the vodka, spiking a Coke can and going back to replenish it through the poptop whenever necessary. The party was making me nervous, all these people not mixing, and the music was too fey, lots of lutes and harpsichords, and I started hating Rae a little for the way she would not respond when Evan touched her or caught her eye across the room or said something to her. *Saturday Night Live* appeared on the television, and several of us, including Rae, sat on the floor to watch. Evan went into the bathroom, and didn't come out until the opening monologue was long over. He sat next to Rae, then slowly sank to the carpet and put his head in her lap, closing his eyes. His color was terrible, greenish and wet. Rae began to ignore the TV and to talk animatedly with one of her friends, a graying man in a sports coat who kept leaning toward her and pushing a strand of hair out of her face. I saw her look down at Evan's head in her lap and say something to her friend, and they both laughed. Then she picked up Evan's head as if it were a cat and placed it on the floor, and scooted over closer to the man. I shook Evan's shoulder and said, too loudly, "Wake up!" But he dreamed on. When *Saturday Night Live* was over, Rae asked me if I could take Evan home. "Why don't you let him crash here?" I said. "He's completely out of it."

"I really don't think so," said Rae. "Would you mind?" Jesus, I said, okay. R.J. and I pulled him to his feet and put one of his arms around each of our shoulders and hauled him out the door. As we arranged him in the backseat, Evan sat up suddenly and said, "Are we there?"

I couldn't see taking him to his parents—we would certainly wake them up, trying to get him to bed—so R.J. and I ended up guiding him to the couch in our living room. In the morning he was gone. I called him later in the afternoon to see how he was. "Fine," he said. "I don't blame her." I do, I said. "No, I was useless. I'm— I had too much to drink." And what else? I wanted to ask, but the understanding between me and Evan was that he didn't shoot dope anymore, and I didn't want to challenge him. Don't drink so much, I told him. You can't handle it. Look at me—*I* know how to drink, and I can't handle it either.

"Virginia Is a Long Way Gone"

Therese was due in less than a week. To forget about T-Day, I went to a party with Skip down in Reston, Virginia. Like most musicians, I hated to dance, but soon enough I was drunk, and willing to flop around to whatever was on the stereo. In some ways the party was a Sixties throwback. Nobody seemed particularly coupled up, and the dancing was being done en masse, with an emphasis on interpretive gestures rather than disco slave-moves. I found myself dancing with, or at, or near, a girl with long black hair and a long, shroud-like, black-and-gold dress. At one point she twirled herself around, the dress lifted, and I saw she had a cat's face painted or tattooed on each shin. The music was not Sixties, though, it was strange to me, but I eventually connected it with some names I'd been reading about, new British bands. The guitars clanged, Cockney voices howled, and everything moved at a fast tempo. It was amateurish and wonderful. But the strange thing was that I felt like we'd already invented it, down in the basement at Georgia Avenue, and I had a sudden, sodden vision: it was happening in basements across America, across Britain, across the entire world of young musicians, everyone was so desperate for a way out that they abandoned all pretense of talent, of art, and just *played really loud* until someone noticed.

The girl and I stumbled outside, into the muggy darkness. We were all over each other, and when she suggested that I come home with her, I didn't think twice. I went back in to tell Skip. He frowned and said, "So I guess you'll get back somehow, then? Tomorrow?" He said some other stuff too but I just said sure, sure.

She drove us to her townhouse, a long drive even deeper down into Virginia. It was a big place, and very opulently furnished. I did start to be a little curious about who this person was, and what she did for a living. Her bed was in a huge loft overlooking the living room. The sex, for me, never seemed to end. I had found that being drunk generally led to one of two kinds of sex: either I came right away, boorishly, and passed out, or else I became cut off from my body, and kept going and going, but didn't feel anything, and was free to reflect and ponder and dream while the action went on so far below me. This was what happened with me and China Cat Sunflower. It lasted a long time, but she was no more transported than I was. In the light of the candles she'd placed beside the bed, I could see a distant, placid expression on her face, one I was powerless to change.

When I woke up it was past noon, and the band had a rehearsal at two. China Cat was gone from the bed. I could hear her moving about below, in the kitchen. My hangover was the full-body version: fluttery stomach, delicate limbs, Sahara thirst, a headache that attaches itself to every movement of your eyeballs. I pulled on my clothes, which smelled, and went downstairs. After refusing food or coffee (I wouldn't have refused a beer, but China Cat didn't offer one, and she was very much a stranger again, or still, so I didn't ask), I mentioned that I had to get back to Wheaton. "All right," she said. She was wearing a long safari shirt and nothing else. The cat faces had disappeared from her legs.

"You're not heading in that general direction by any chance."

"I'm afraid not."

"Is there a Metro stop this far south?"

"No."

"Buses?"

"I don't know."

"Are we near a main road?"

"Not very."

I stared at her, trying to understand her through my hangover. She was being perfectly pleasant. It was just clear that she felt no obligation to me or my needs, and my problems were my problems. I struggled to find a way to resent this, but the whole premise of our being together was that we meant nothing to each other, so what was there to resent? Okay, obviously I'd have to ride my thumb. I stood up. "Goodbye, then," I said, and added, pro forma, "Could I call you sometime?"

She reached into the left breast pocket of the safari shirt and handed me a business card. It said "China Cat Sunflower," and then the phone number. Nothing else. "Thanks," I said. "Let me write down my number for you." She smiled and pointed to a pencil on the table. I wrote my number on a napkin. "And your name," she said. "Oh, right," I said, and wrote that down too. "Goodbye," I said again, she nodded politely, and I throbbed out the door.

The hitching on a Sunday afternoon was dreadful. I was two hours late for rehearsal, and the guys were mad at me. Skip had already told them I'd gone off with a stranger the previous night. "Man, I tried to warn you about her," said Skip. "You acted like you didn't hear a word I was saying."

"I didn't," I said. "What do you mean, warn me? What did you say?"

"I said she was this heiress who never tells anyone her real name and—"

"So?"

"Let me finish. And she claims to be a witch, and worships Satan."

"That's bullshit," I said. "I definitely saw no signs of Satan worship."

"Stamina Part Two"

Evan was found in his car, in a parking lot, with the spike in his arm. Rae called me from the record store and told me. Much to my surprise, I began to cry. "Do you think he— did it to himself?" Rae said in a small voice.

"Of course not," I said. "He OD'd. Evan was just stupid. I mean, about drugs."

"Do you want to go to the funeral? I have the—"

"No," I said, "no, please. Man, his parents. No."

"The First Hundred Songs"

Suddenly it was T-Day. The other guys were at their day jobs. I hung around on the porch for a while, looking at my watch every five minutes, looking for her red van to pull up the driveway, and then I went downstairs to the basement. The mouse corpses were really smelling. I was dying for a beer, but if I had one I wouldn't be able to stop, and that would be a very stupid move, an Evan-like move. I'd even foregone my morning joint. I needed my wits about me when I saw Therese's face.

By the sick glow of the 40-watt overhead bulb, I examined the keys of my electric piano. I sat down and flicked on the power switch. Maybe I should write a song, I thought. I had never considered being a songwriter before. I played a few chords, in a minor key. Then I played some in E major. Well, what was there to write about?

What *wasn't* there? I had enough material for a hundred

songs. The next hundred would come a lot harder—the dead mice needed to be dealt with, you could say—but when Therese arrived, she had to holler down the stairs for me, because I was busy working.

THE OTHER SIDE

A Dream That Paul Is Dead

Henry, Warren, and I collaborated on the report. This being 1969, Miss Eke permitted us to present it to our English class.

We sat at a rectangular table, facing the ninth grade like a Senate subcommittee. Henry began.

"Here are the clues to be found in the songs:

At the end of 'Strawberry Fields Forever,' a voice, probably John's, says: *I buried Paul.*

The muttering voice, probably John's, at the end of 'Blackbird,' played backwards, says: *Paul is dead — miss him, miss him.*

The many voices throughout the fadeout of 'I Am the Walrus' all speak of death: *Is he dead? Sit you down, father, rest you. Oh, untimely death!*

The walrus is an Icelandic death symbol. John declares, in the eponymous song: *I am the walrus.* However, the subtitle of the song is: '"No you're not!" said Little Nicola'; and in his subsequent song, 'Glass Onion,' John forthrightly asserts: *The walrus was Paul*.

John's song, 'A Day in the Life,' refers to Paul's death in the car accident: *He blew his mind out in a car*. The orchestral crescendos depict a car spinning out of control and crashing.

Perhaps most importantly, the entire 'Revolution 9' track is a disguised musique-concrète recounting of Paul's death. You can hear the car wreck, the flames, the anguished whimpering. (Which Beatle took on the grisly task of imitating the dying Paul? We suspect John.) A voice speaks of going to a dentist for a new set of teeth. This is a reference to Paul's lookalike, who must be furnished with dentures so all medical records will match, preparatory to taking Paul's place. The repeated refrain, *Number 9, Number 9*, when played backwards, becomes: *Turn me on, dead man*. And in 'A Day in the Life,' John had sung: *I'd love to turn you on. . . .*"

"Thank you," said Miss Eke. The ninth grade applauded gently. "Questions: Were you aware that the spoken lines at the end of 'I Am the Walrus' are quotations from Shakespeare's *King Lear*?"

"No, Miss Eke, I was not," Henry said, smudging his glasses determinedly. "The fact remains that they were carefully chosen to speak of death."

"Agreed," Miss Eke said. "What do you make of John's implication in so many of these clues?"

Henry said, "There is something in John that loves the grave, I think."

"Agreed," Miss Eke said. "Had it occurred to you that the phrase 'Blackbird played backwards' contains a very interesting and complex rhyme?"

"No, Miss Eke, it had not." Henry frowned. "It had occurred to me that the phrase is something of a tongue twister."

"That too," Miss Eke said.

"The rhyming is accidental, though."

"Better to say, in this context, aleatoric. Congratulations." I saw pencils in motion as the ninth grade wrote the word *aleatoric* in their notebooks for later definition. "Lastly: Art and its interpretations are of course eternal, but depend on their physical substrates. Could you explain to the class how to play a record backwards?"

Henry brightened. "Sure. There's a way on just about every record player to turn the power on without bringing the arm over the record and starting the turntable. Do that, and then turn the turntable the wrong way with your finger. Get it going at what looks like about the right speed and then put the needle where you want it." The ninth grade took notes. "Don't tell your parents because I'm pretty sure it messes up the needle."

"That was very succinct. Thank you. Please continue." Miss Eke smiled her famous inverted smile. The corners of her mouth tugged down instead of up, creating an effect charming beyond the bounds of good taste, and we all smiled dewily back.

I spoke next, consulting a green spiral-bound notebook that resembled one I had lost in a snowbank the previous winter, shortly after the White Album was released. I had been keeping—until I encountered the snowbank—a kind of timetable of my parents' separate comings and goings; various symbols designated departures with front door slammed versus eased shut, returns following nights spent entirely apart, etc. It seemed important to keep track. But the notebook before me was a new one, coincidentally green.

"Here are the clues to be found in the album covers:

The cover of *Abbey Road* is a little death tableau. We see Paul walking out of step with the others, dressed in black, barefoot. Being buried barefoot is an Italian custom. John is a holy man, dressed in white. Ringo is an undertaker, dressed in a nice suit. George is a gravedigger, dressed in denims. The license plate of the Volkswagen in the background says '28IF'; that is, Paul would be 28 IF he had lived.

The back cover of *Abbey Road* also offers clues. The holes near the word *Beatles* are another Icelandic death symbol. Paul's face, contorted in his death throes, is depicted subliminally in a woman's elbow.

A hand held over the head is another death symbol, not Icelandic. A hand is held over Paul's head in several of the photos in the *Magical Mystery Tour* album.

Other clues from that album: the photo of Paul seated at a desk shows a nameplate on the desk which reads 'I Was You.'

In the dress-up photos, the other three Beatles are wearing red carnations; Paul's is black. Paul's salute finds his arm cocked to his head at a strange angle; this is a death symbol.

The *Sgt. Pepper* cover depicts a funeral, obviously Paul's. Paul's pose resembles a corpse laid out for military burial, with his clarinet held like a rifle. A hand is reaching out from the crowd, directly above his head (cf. *Magical Mystery Tour* photos).

The middle photo shows Paul wearing a badge with the letters *O.P.D.* This stands for Officially Pronounced Dead.

On the back cover, Paul alone stands with his back to the camera."

"Thank you," said Miss Eke. A few members of the ninth grade applauded very gently. "Questions: In what year was Paul born?"

"1942," I replied. "On June 16th."

"Bloomsday. If you say so," said Miss Eke. "Therefore, how do you account for the fact that Paul would be only 27, not 28, if he had lived?"

I was prepared for this. Did she take us for simpletons? "It's easily explained, Miss Eke. The original plan called for the Beatles to release an *entirely different* album in the fall of this year. It was to be entitled *Get Back, Don't Let Me Down, and 12 Others*. *Abbey Road*'s release was planned for the summer of 1970, when Paul would have been 28. However, as you may know from hearing various bootlegged tracks on the radio,

Get Back, Don't Let Me Down, and 12 Others is by no means ready for the public, whereas *Abbey Road* was finished more quickly than expected, and very successfully. Thus the decision was made to substitute the one for the other, despite the resulting damage to the 28IF clue."

"I see," said Miss Eke. "And why did they not save the album jacket with the 28IF clue for their 1970 release, *Get Back, Don't Let*, etc.?"

"Because," I replied, "that jacket shows the Beatles crossing Abbey Road. It has to enclose the record called *Abbey Road*."

"Agreed," said Miss Eke. "But why not call the 1969 release something else, and save the title *Abbey Road* for the 1970 release, so that the *Abbey Road* jacket could enclose it, rendering the 28IF clue accurate?"

"Miss Eke," I said, "I admit this is conjectural, but I strongly believe that, for the Beatles, the names of these records are not merely 'labels stuck on and tapped with the side of the fist.' The title *Abbey Road* 'shines through the record like a watermark.' It is inextricably a part of what the music offers."

I heard someone in the back row of the class yawn heavily. Miss Eke tugged her lips down. "Excellent. I trust that your report includes the source of those, ah, transparent quotes." I nodded, somewhat in shock, my mind racing to decide if her adjective was coincidental or intentional. My quotes were taken from a novel not yet written by Vivian Bloodmark entitled *Transparent Things* (McGraw-Hill, 1972). Miss Eke went on,

"Has it occurred to you that Paul may be walking out of step with the others because he alone is left-handed? Let us imagine" (intentional, I decided, and was able to refocus) "that the photograph was posed by asking each Beatle to take one step forward from a standing position. Each would lead with his strongest foot, and, as you may know, footedness is correlated with handedness."

"*But*," I pounced, "you have not examined the text carefully enough. Here's the flaw in your interpretation: Paul is out of step to the tune of a *right* foot, not a left."

"Ah," breathed Miss Eke. "Thank you for pointing that out to me." But her look told me that she had known it all along; it had been a trick question. I was certain to get an A for this report. "Haven't you mistaken an English horn for a clarinet?"

Here was an unexpected poser. "I'm not sure, Miss Eke," I mumbled. "I'd need to research it." Well, an A minus.

"Do so. Lastly, a matter of terminology: oughtn't you to have made clear, perhaps in a prefatory disclaimer, that your use of the name *Paul* is actually a sort of shorthand, which, expanded, means the putative Paul, or the Paul so-called, or Paul's double, or whoever is in fact the subject of those various allegedly postmortem photographs?"

"Yes, Miss Eke," I said. "I took that to be understood."

"Very well," said Miss Eke. "I know you did. And that leads us nicely into your presentation, doesn't it, Warren?"

Pale Warren nodded. Softly he began. "I will present two theories. One describes how Paul's death has been covered up through the employment of a double. The other suggests that Paul has indeed disappeared, but is not dead. Rather, he is hidden from us, but poised to return."

The ninth grade writhed in exasperation. Warren's report was murmurous, measured. It began to put me to sleep. My earlier tension was gone. I felt drowsy, and this class, these theories, even the Beatles themselves, all seemed like a languorous dream. I had stayed up too late the night before, although I'd been very tired; circumstances had demanded it. . . . I could not attend to each sentence, but in any case I knew the drift. Warren's first theory argued that one of the "lookalike/soundalike" winners from the various contests held in 1964 and 1965 had been located and persuaded to impersonate Paul after the car crash. I found his supporting evidence thin, although I accepted that some sort of impersonation must be taking place. The lookalike-contest explanation seemed plausible, but hardly necessitated.

I was even less in sympathy with his *Tod und Verklärung* theory, as I privately thought of it. Warren believed, or maintained that he believed, that either 1) Paul's "death" was faked, and he is actually alive and well on an uncharted island, along with other not-dead stars like Brian Jones and Jimi Hendrix, there to await the millennium? a better world? the revolution?—it was unclear to me; or 2) Paul did "die," in some sense, but has been transported? resurrected? transfigured? sent on holiday? to an uncharted island, along with . . . etc. (Mindful of Miss Eke's comment on my use of the name *Paul*, Warren was careful to explain that, in the light of his second theory, such terms as "car crash," "death," "dead," etc., were to be bracketed, so to speak. "Put in putation marks," offered Miss Eke with a smile. "Thank you," said Warren. A girl in the second row named Marcia Kleks said, "Can't we just listen to the records?") The photos on pages 5, 10, and 12–13 of the *Magical Mystery Tour* album show a desolate landscape with rather uncanny architectural features. These photos were supposedly taken on the Island of the Undead Rock Stars.

Warren ended his report and I sat up straight. Miss Eke thanked him. No one failed not to applaud. "I have no questions for you, Warren. This level of theory does not admit of questions, any more than a dream can be asked to justify itself, but I sense you know that, and are comfortable with it."

Warren nodded once. "I am." He stared palely out at the ninth grade, who were doodling, whispering, and snoozing.

"Very well," said Miss Eke. "Our time is almost up, but I would like to ask each of you this: based on your examination of the materials available to you—the records, the jackets, your lives—are you in fact convinced that Paul is dead? (This term to include island residency, Warren.) Can other explanations be offered?"

Henry said, "Miss Eke, I don't actually believe that Paul is dead, or that any of these clues, in putation marks, really exist. No one put them there, either as signposts to a real event, or as a hoax. The entire affair is an example of what can be read into a text, once a particular conclusion is *a priori* decided upon. One could just as easily declare that Ringo was dead, and find the clues to support it."

"Well put," said Miss Eke. "For next week, please report on the evidence of Ringo's death." Henry groaned, and took off his glasses.

Warren said, "Poor Henry. He looks but doesn't see. Paul is taken from us, gone, dead—it doesn't matter how you phrase it. But this is transitory. His true meaning, and ultimate return, we still await."

"Why," asked Miss Eke, "did the other Beatles choose to present us with clues to these events, rather than simply keeping silent altogether about Paul's transformation? (Will that word do?)"

"(It will, nicely.) Benevolence. It's done for us, their audience. We need to know, but gently. We need to re-enact a similar movement in our lives: to live, to die, to appear to live on, to transcend, to be more than alive. The clues are love, speaking to us in the Beatles' history."

"Intricate, but not unfamiliar," remarked Miss Eke. There was a silence as she looked at me.

"I disagree with Henry," I said, "and agree with Warren to the extent that I believe the clues were deliberately placed, and refer to an actual event. Beyond that, however, lies meaningless mysticism. The event is unambiguous: Paul is dead. He is not transformed, and he is not coming back. He was killed in a car accident."

"Same question, then, to you," said Miss Eke. "Why were the clues placed? Why would the Beatles flirt with the undoing of their own cover-up?"

"The imp of the perverse," I replied, feeling my spine

shiver. "Horrible knowledge that insists on voicing itself."

"Then why cover up Paul's death in the first place?"

"They feared for their future as Beatles if the public knew they were minus a member. These three famous, frightened children" (ripples spiraling up and down the vertebrae) "believed they had the power to cover up death. No doubt it was John's idea. But they hadn't reckoned with the imp."

Miss Eke looked at me solemnly, then at the clock. "We have a minute. May I give you *my* interpretation?"

We all nodded. The ninth grade came to attention, pencils at the ready.

Miss Eke said, "All the clues were deliberately placed, to lead strongly to the supposition that Paul is dead, and less strongly to your lookalike-contest and mysterious-island theories, Warren. In short, we have indeed uncovered intentionality. But I think Paul is really alive, that these events we've been clued in to never happened. It wouldn't surprise me to learn that Paul himself authored the whole thing."

"Why?" Henry and I both asked her. Warren seemed in the grip of a trance.

"Art," said Miss Eke. Thirty pencils wrote *Art*, producing a light buzzing sound, ending abruptly on the crossbar of the T. "Class dismissed. And thank you again, boys."

I walked out into the rustling autumn afternoon. The dream was over, and now my feet dragged through the leaves as I headed slowly home. "Paul is dead, Paul is dead!" Marcia Kleks taunted me, and dumped my books as she raced by on her Schwinn.

My mother and father were ominously silent over dinner, but later, as I lay in bed almost asleep, I heard their voices, short taps of anger at first, and then more sustained volleys. I came wide awake, my stomach in knots. I listened but as usual couldn't make out what they were arguing about. I tiptoed out of my room until I came to the bend in the hall. Around the corner was the corridor to the living room, where they sat, or perhaps were standing now, facing each other's accusations and defenses. I crouched down, slowly made myself comfortable on the carpet (though I was chilly in my pajamas), and began to listen. Gradually I was able to put together enough clues, and a story emerged, new in its details this time, yet always essentially the same. It was going to be another long night. Art, I thought. Fat chance. It's all real.

Oh J let me up out of this

The Twenty-First Rule

His father and he arrived at a small, furtive doorway, somewhere on F Street, on a block crowded with liquor stores, pawnshops, and storefront churches. They entered; inside, the lights were achingly bright, illuminating row after row of magazines and paperbacks, all arranged face out along the shelves. Before Jim could really X-rate the scenes displayed along every rank and file of the store's black-and-white checkerboard linoleum floor, or flinch from the browsers staring at him out of their solemn isolation, a black man in a tight-fitting white T–shirt charged down on the two of them from an elevated booth, barking to Jim's father, "Get him out! Get him out!" Jim felt his father's hand on his shoulder, steering him toward the door, and he was happy to go: he knew he'd entered a forbidden world, Adults Only, and felt wilted with humiliation. Behind him he heard his father remonstrating with the store's watchdog: "Don't you think you ought to *indicate* what sort of bookstore you are, in your listing? I mean to say, 'Collectibles,' after all: I had every reason to assume that—" but all the man would say was, "Get him out!" Then he muttered, "You can come back in without him." "Certainly not," Jim's father replied, and the glass-and-wire-mesh door closed behind them with a scornful pneumatic wheeze.

"Well," his father said as they retreated to the car, "disgusting place." Jim said nothing. His father made a patting motion near Jim's shoulder and said, "A little early in the day to speak about these matters, but. Bear in mind, for the future. Romance: that's the ticket, with women. Not that— that sort of thing." Jim nodded. His father adjusted his glasses, and sighed. "What would you say to a movie?" "Can we go to Bargain Books instead?" Jim asked, his throat tight. They got in the car. "Certainly," his father said, and turned the ignition key briskly, like a punctuation mark.

Meanwhile, and in general, Jim's mother attacked a jigsaw puzzle the way we all do: start with the straight-edged pieces, then fill in the middle; look for matching details; save the monochrome sky-bits for last. My story contains a puzzle too, a wrongdoer to be identified, though at this late date her name hardly matters—if it mattered then. Like all mysteries, it's food for thought, but *a steady diet of such fare is unwholesome*, especially for growing boys. What else, in the way of ingredients and nutritional information? This story offers reliable reports concerning several nearly forgotten writers of detective fiction, one of whom, fair warning, is invented for the occasion. The *Cratylus* is an additive, utilized only to dye the herring red. My young protagonist is not meant, was never meant, to harvest the abundant clues I've planted, but if the reader feels challenged to pluck, trim, and arrange them,

I promise that the Fifteenth Rule has been, however eccentrically, enforced: "The truth of the problem must at all times be apparent—provided the reader is shrewd enough to see it."

Here we have the Starlings. Jim: twelve years old, with a passion for Golden Age detective stories. His father: also a reader, of biographies, of baseball reminiscences, of tales about time travel. His mother: jigsaw puzzles for her, and the *New York Times* crossword and Double-Acrostic, and contract bridge. The arguments of the two adult Starlings seemed to swell, crest, and break under the influence of some lunar force. When the tide was out, they coexisted amicably enough, to melodious Broadway show music on the record player and his mother's occasional requests for assistance: "'A Vane sister,' spelled capital V-a-n-e? Seven letters? No? How about 'Merlin, for one'? Six letters?" "Wizard!" "Uh uh, doesn't key. . . ." Then the tide rushed in once more, usually after sundown, and different problems were propounded: "Some little chippy, I suppose? Or is it more than one?" "You don't know what you're talking about. I detest promiscuity." "Oh, an affair of the *heart*, then. I *see*." (According to the Twelfth Rule, as Jim knew, "There must be but one culprit; the entire indignation of the reader must be permitted to concentrate on a single black nature.") "Tell me her name! I want to know her name!" The needle scraped across the grooves.

That Jim's father relished spending long hours with the boy, away from her: this we can assume, I think. So nearly every weekend they used to go to secondhand bookstores,

puttering off in his pint-sized, peacock-blue Dauphin. Usually they headed for Washington's familiar shops—Bargain
Books, Lowdermilk's, the Salvation Army Bookstore down on
D Street—but occasionally Jim's father would lift the Yellow
Pages from the top of the refrigerator and "have a look-see"
at the listings for *Books—Used and Rare.* These attempts at
diversity could backfire, as I've tried to suggest.

Jim's taste in murder mysteries was severe: only the
fair-play tales about the great serial detectives would do. He
wanted to open each book and walk into a world of logic
and ingenuity, crimes without passion, resolutions without
loose ends. He enjoyed matching wits with the author, and
never entered a revelatory chapter before preparing his own
theory of the crime, yet would shrug in disappointment if
his solution turned out to be correct. How much better to be
confounded, to watch a bigger and brighter bunny emerge
from the top hat!

He made a point of researching the bibliographies of his
favorite authors so he'd know exactly where he stood in his
hunt for their complete works. Some of these Golden Agers
had written lamentably few books before dying or otherwise
collapsing their literary tents. Clayton Rawson, for instance,
creator of The Great Merlini—a professional magician who
solved murder cases as a somewhat supererogatory pas-
time—had managed to produce only four novels. The fourth,
No Coffin for the Corpse (Little, Brown, 1942), was hard to come
by. One frosty, white-skied day, Jim discovered a signed first
edition at the Salvation Army Bookstore.

What a fine-looking volume it was: matte black, title embossed in yellow, and it boasted for a frontispiece a marvelous, grim, blueprint-like illustration captioned, "Residence of Dudley T. Wolff, Esq." The ceiling was cut away for the reader to ponder the floorplan, presumably for clues to the mystery's solution—and to espy two corpses, one male, one female (Lawyer Wolff and wife?), lying helplessly before a fireplace, which was depicted complete with tiny, absurdly literal andirons.

All hardbacks at the Salvation Army sold for twenty-five cents. Jim stared at the inscription (it was a presentation copy: "To Robin—Fondest regards—Clayt"), unable to believe what he saw, then ran to get his father, whom he found browsing in the poetry section, for some reason: head canted to read the spines, a small, hopeful smile on his lips, his glasses gleaming in the Salvation Army's inferior fluorescence. He wore his standard secondhand-bookstore outfit: a battered olive-green army jacket over white shirt, tie, and cufflinks. Jim held the book out to him, open at the flyleaf, stammered, and pointed. His father read the inscription and nodded. He whispered to Jim that they must be certain to bring quite a few purchases to the front counter ("as camouflage"); he would keep up a conversation with the clerk and, with luck, the fellow would not notice Clayt's fondest regards when they passed in front of his cash register. (An unnecessary stratagem, I feel certain. The Salvation Army book clerks were ex-winos, now steeped in Jesus, and had no interest in the commerce that took place in the enterprises of their redemptors.)

They gathered their camouflage, approached the register, and Jim's father began an affable monologue about the demolition taking place across the street, where yet another rooming house was going under the ball. The clerk—I can see him, frighteningly thin, wispy-haired, with pale wet eyes behind pale-rimmed plastic eyeglasses, one hinge patched with Scotch tape—bobbed his knobby Adam's apple in agreement and rang up several Agatha Christies, an anthology of "Locked Rooms and Impossible Situations," a volume each by Byron and Dickinson, and *No Coffin for the Corpse*, without comment or surcharge. Out on the sidewalk, Jim wanted to shriek and skip. A snowflake landed on his left eyelash, and he blinked. "Well, Jim, we got away with it, didn't we?" His father's voice was full of pleasure, which at first pleased Jim too, until he recalled a recent nighttime eavesdropping session. *You think you got away with it, don't you!* He clutched his books and nodded, ashamed.

If Rawson had written too little, several others among Jim's favorites were mind-bogglingly prolific, and the pursuit of their complete works was an endless and keen obsession. Ellery Queen. S.S. Van Dine. John Dickson Carr (also Carter Dickson, a pseudonymous bonus). Van Dine; let me say something about Van Dine; he commanded a special, eerie place in Jim's search. All of his "Philo Vance" mysteries were issued, once a year like hardy annuals, between 1926 and 1939, at which point he—actually a mentally unstable art critic named Willard Huntington Wright—died. Van Dine must have given inaccurate information to his publishers about forthcoming titles. In the various novels Jim had acquired, after the list of "Also by. . . ." would appear, in bolder, expectant type, "In Preparation." And more often than not, the title that followed would be strange, unknown, not listed in the bibliography in the *Modern Writers of Mystery* compendium (Howard Haycraft, Ed.) that Jim had memorized. Did they or did they not exist? I remember two of these supposed productions very well: *The Powwow Murder Case* and *The Autumn Murder Case*. (One should mention—and if I don't, might it not be forgotten? isn't it entirely possible that I am the last human being on earth who knows this fact?—that Van Dine always filled in his formula, The _____ Murder Case, with a six-letter word, mimicking, according to a chatty dust-jacket biography, the number of letters in his *actual last name*, Wright.)

Over several years, Jim hunted down the entire Van Dine corpus. *The Casino Murder Case* showed up at the Salvation Army, minus a dust jacket but still sparkling. *The Winter Murder Case* was a "letter-perfect first draft of some 30,000 words, highly readable" (in his publisher's optimistic appraisal), left unfleshed at the time of Van Dine's, of Wright's, death; its posthumous publication included as an appendix the master's stern "Twenty Rules for Writing Detective Stories"; Jim found it misfiled under W at Biblo & Tannen's, a Fourth Avenue store they visited whenever they went to New York to see Jim's parents' parents. When Lowdermilk's (haughty clerks, imitation Oriental carpets, eccentric and undependable hours of operation) yielded *The Dragon Murder Case*, his

final missing Van Dine, his excitement was so effervescent
that he exploded into a loud, shrill, quite promising topic sentence—"Do you realize what this *means*?"—and would have
answered the question at length, but his father shushed him,
glaring; I think he felt a little intimidated at Lowdermilk's and
wanted them to be on their best behavior. Or perhaps, for him,
that weekend was marked by another significant event, a cul-
mination quite separate from his son's, leaving him testy, or
hung over, or frightened. Jim didn't know, he didn't know.
Please. He didn't know. Recently he had awakened one night
to feel his mother's hand holding his, green radium-light from
the clockface glittering in her eyes. "Jim . . . Jimmy. . . do you
know who she is? Tell me. Tell me her name." It wasn't the
sort of case Philo Vance would have been any good at solving.

But even after Jim's Van Dine set was complete, the named
yet unwritten books hovered over him. The act of naming had
made them real. "Powwow," "Autumn": he pictured Indians
dancing around Philo Vance, making weird ululations with
palms patting open mouths; he saw red, gold, auburn leaves
piled up against a gloomy mansion, whose denizens would
soon be corpses or suspects. He wanted to believe that these
books did exist somewhere, that they had fallen between Haycraft's bibliographical cracks. A recurring dream found him
in the great dusty secondhand bookstore of the unconscious,
searching the "Mystery S–Z" shelves. There, pushed between
a well-preserved Collier reprint of *The Bishop Murder Case*
(bound in a pebbled gray leatheroid, with maroon-and-gold
spiderweb radiating out from the title, so much tastier, in fact,

than the black, bulky Scribner firsts) and twin copies of *The Scarab Murder Case*, spines identically fractured at the top vertebra, was a dark volume, title too faded to read. He removed it from the shelf, opened it to the title page, and found himself in possession of an unknown Van Dine. Which one, was never clear: his dream refused to concretize Van Dine's predictions. But in his exhilaration he ran through the looming shelves, looking for the way out, looking for his father.

Sometimes the dream turned to nightmare. Shouts, and thumps, and the sound of breakage echoed down the aisles, where no adults were to be found, however desperately he searched. Then, sometimes, the nightmare would recede, and his father was there—tall, smiling—and Jim thrust the book into his hands, pointed, and stammered, "Read it! Oh, look-see what I've found!"

Here the dream forked once more. Benignly, his father might puff dust from the book's deckled edge, open it, and nod. Jim would notice that his mother had appeared, all tension gone from her face as if puffed away by her husband's breath, to join him in inspecting *The _____ Murder Case*. Waking from this version, Jim could almost pronounce the missing six-letter word, so intense was the feeling of accomplishment and wonder, as if his discovery had widened the gyre of reality itself. Of course, the darker ending was more common, though it too began with an attempt to wipe clean the miraculous Van Dine. Jim's father removed a handkerchief from his back pocket and passed it over and over the black front cover. To Jim's disgust, a pasty stain was transferred from the handkerchief to the book. Then he realized that the sticky stuff was not what one might at first assume. The handkerchief had been put to another use, a use not unfamiliar just these last few months to pubescent Jim. The danger was that his mother would see, would begin to scream. To avoid this, Jim did the screaming himself, and it always surprised him how, upon jerking awake, his cries were no louder than cat-mews.

VanDine, and Willard Huntington Wright, had died almost thirty years before Jim began to read about Philo Vance. Others of his favorites were alive, however. One summer evening he met John Dickson Carr. On the bulletin board of their public library had appeared a notice that the "renowned Anglo-American author of over fifty ingenious detective stories" would give a talk the following week. Jim's father was happy to accompany him. They left the silent apartment (Jim only glanced at his mother, who sat, cigarette in hand, hand held to forehead, at a bridge table in the living room, staring down at a completed interlock of straight-edged frame pieces, her other hand sorting the scattered middle bits, with their bulging pseudopods, exiled outside the borders until the pattern could be made clear) and revved up the Dauphin. The little meeting room was crowded, and Jim stared wretchedly at the floor. He had entered the first year of what proved to be an enduring hell of shame concerning his acne; being seen (observed, inspected, scrutinized, rejected!) by anyone caused a more or less constant wincing and stooping, an attempt at complete invisibility. He had brought a copy of one of Carr's "Carter Dickson" efforts, *The Peacock Feather Murders*, for him to autograph.

Carr was a smallish, gaunt man, with a nervous smile that tick-tocked on and off, and much given to gesticulation. Jim was surprised to find him clean-shaven (his dust-jacket photographs always showed him sporting a modest mustache) and elderly (it was always the same photo, book after book). His accent, almost British, not quite American, confused Jim until he remembered that Carr was in fact born here, the son of a Pennsylvania Congressman, but had lived the bulk of his life in England, where nearly all his books were set.

I would be hard pressed to reconstruct his talk. The subject, I know, was the history of the detective story. *The Peacock Feather Murders* rested in Jim's lap, a blue-and-black stage on which his fingers twined and untwined themselves like an anxious ensemble. Jim's father chuckled as Carr retold the Poe story, "Thou Art the Man!", complete with burlesque of its undeniably ludicrous denouement—the dead man rising up to point a baleful finger at his murderer. Afterwards they lined up at the lectern and Jim, wishing his face were behind a mask, offered *The Peacock Feather Murders* for Carr's signature. Carr asked Jim's name, shook his hand, and thanked him for coming. Jim could think of nothing to say; in that moment he could not endow the small, courteous gentleman bending over the book, ballpoint in hand, with the Anglo-American intellect that had created "over fifty ingenious detective stories." The ballpoint gave out mid-inscription. Carr clucked, shook the pen in the air, then examined its tip. A young woman whom Jim had noticed hanging about to no apparent purpose now stepped forward, touched Carr's arm, and held out a replacement. Carr said, "Thank you, my dear," absently presented the dead Bic to Jim, and bent down once more.

Driving home, Jim's father said he had enjoyed the talk a great deal, and urged Jim to look people in the eye when he met them. It was something, he explained, that he had been meaning to mention for quite a while. And something else too: you mustn't be upset about these moods of your mother's. In the dark Dauphin, Jim gripped his prize ("To Jim Starling," in gradually fading black; "with all best wishes," in fresh blue). I think you've overheard certain accusations. I want you to know they aren't true. "I haven't heard anything," Jim said. This so-called evidence. "Can we uh." I beg your pardon? "Go to that new bookstore in Bethesda this weekend?" Oh. Certainly.

Jim also met, in a sense, Ellery Queen. (I think a respite is in order, after that last scene; I feel sure Jim would agree.) In 1929, two young New Yorkers named Danny Nathan and Manny Lepofsky changed their names to Frederic Dannay and Manfred B. Lee. (Why? one wonders. But no, this is meant to be a respite; ignore the Jewish question.) Taking a further step into unreality, they conjointly adopted the pen name "Ellery Queen" and wrote *The Roman Hat Mystery*, which was speedily published and much admired. Their serial detective, an effete, pince-nez'd young bibliophile, was also named Ellery Queen. And all of their titles, until World War Two shattered the Golden Age, obeyed the formula: The [Nationality][Ordinary Object] Mystery. *Roman Hat* was followed by *French Powder, Egyptian Cross, Chinese Orange*, and *Spanish Cape*.

Postwar tastes changed, so "Ellery Queen" commenced to write more up-to-date, though equally ratiocinative, Ellery Queen stories. Bookish Ellery was provided with a succession of love interests—Jim thought they were a bore—and novel followed novel until 1971, when Manfred B. Lee died. Ellery Queen's final opus, published that same year, was called *A Fine and Private Place* (tastes in titles had changed too since 1929, arguably for the worse). After reading it, Jim was seized with the certainty that there was *another, equally necessitated* solution to the mystery, besides the one unearthed by Ellery Queen (still a bibliophile, still on the effete side, minus his pince-nez, and still youthful, though if he'd aged along with his universe he'd be pushing eighty).

Jim had begun to write almost every evening—the typewriter made a useful racket. He favored enthusiastic pastiches of authors whose styles were not, *ipso facto*, inimitable. He decided that he would write a letter to "Ellery Queen" (Jim knew he was a dyad, or had been, and wondered whether Dannay alone would continue the pen name), in care of his publisher, in which he would enclose a new ending to *AFAPP*, composed in the Queen style, revealing his alternate solution.

AFAPP is not one of the better Queen productions. Its insufficiently twisty plot deploys a flock of clues involving nines. That is, the victim, named Nino (get it?) Importunato, is done in with nine blows to the head; nine sarcastic notes are sent to the police; nine days, weeks, months elapse between the sundry activities of the perpetrator; etc. In the original, published solution, these clues are revealed to have been *planted by the murderer* as camouflage to conceal *one, essential* clue, which points inexorably (thou art the man!) at him— and which also "contains" a nine, but only incidentally, so to speak. Thus, the meaningless proliferation of nines would throw the investigation onto the wrong track. Now, one of the suspects is named Peter Ennis. Pause. Examine the surname. *Impossible, impossible* that this was inadvertent! Yet the anagram is never revealed, and Peter Ennis is not the murderer. In Jim's solution, therefore, this inexplicably unexplained fact is the basis for establishing Ennis's guilt.

Every night for a week, he hurried to finish his homework, then labored until bedtime on his letter/chapter for Dannay. His father would walk past his room, knock on the open door (they were a polite family, at least until Jim was in bed and thought to be asleep), and ask him what he was doing. "Writing." "For school?" "Mmm." "Miss Falcon's class?" (pretty Miss Falcon, his English teacher). "Mmp." "Very good. I met her at PTA. Very intelligent woman." Finally it was finished, a dead-clever Queenian revelation chapter complete with "Challenge to the Reader," a device Queen had abandoned in the 1930s but whose revival Jim thought Dannay might appreciate. He composed a brief cover letter expressing his regard for the Queen oeuvre, along with appropriately modest phrases about his enclosed contribution to it. He then made the terrible mistake of rereading his chapter.

Precious, jejune, unbearable! It was as if an image of his acne-ridden face had surfaced on every page. In an agony of self-consciousness, he destroyed it. Instead he typed out a hasty, conventional letter that outlined his Ennis theory, and mailed it to Dannay via Simon and Schuster, hating himself.

A few weeks later (a time filled with dreams of the strangest transformations, dreams infiltrated by half-awakenings to shouted stories and counterstories and then redreamed as, well, for instance, a quick and bloody naval maneuver, a surprise massacre of retreating forces, all the seamen mopped up in the act of withdrawal) he received a letter from Larchmont, New York. On the back of the envelope was a brisk "EQ" scrawled in red felt-tip pen. The note, signed by Frederic Dannay (with another "EQ" dashed off beneath his signature), thanked Jim for his "provocative" letter. "I attempted to phone you so that we could discuss your most interesting theory, but I find that you are not listed at the address given in your letter. Will you be kind enough, then, to call me (reversing the charges, to be sure) so that I may have the pleasure of speaking with you?" And he enclosed his telephone number.

For days Jim carried this letter everywhere, tucked in a textbook or folded tight into the tiny pocket-above-the-pocket of his jeans. With each rereading, a small but efficient whirlwind of anxiety blew through him. He wanted very much to tell his father but was afraid that he would be forbidden to call Dannay—or worse, that his father would insist on taking part in the conversation. Finally he decided he would make the call on a Thursday night, when his mother went to her bridge game and his father regularly worked late.

He sat at the glass-topped kitchen table, drumming the

moist fingertips of one hand on the reverberant surface, while with the other he throttled the phone receiver, and asked the operator to place a collect call to Larchmont, New York. A subdued tenor voice answered after only one ring. "Mr. Dannay?" "Speaking." Jim bumbled and stuttered, and finally explained who he was.

Dannay's response opened the curtain on the secret Jim had thought so well concealed: "Ah? You sound— That is, may I ask how old you are?" Jim told him, adding a year. He could hear Dannay breathing, and then: "Well. Your letter certainly led me to believe you were an adult. That explains—" "Yes, why I don't have a phone listing, but. . . ." His interruption foundered, and an endless silence piled up on Dannay's phone bill. Then Ellery Queen said, "In any event, that was a very fine letter you wrote me, young man. I suppose you're old enough to understand what I intended to say to you." He went on to explain that Peter Ennis's name had been chosen to suggest the word *penis*, since the Ennis character was a virile sort who had cuckolded the soon-to-be-murdered Nino Importunato. Dannay also noted that *Importunato* was meant to evoke *impotent*. "I suppose you understand the term?"

"Oh, certainly," Jim croaked. His face red, he hunched over the kitchen table, over the trapdoor, over the oubliette that led back out, into the world. What did this have to do with clues, with fair play, with anagrammatic ingenuity? Paralyzed, Jim was unable to ask Dannay the question which to this day remains unanswered: Leaving aside the penile pun on "P. Ennis," *had he or had he not been aware when writing AFAPP that "Ennis" was an anagram for "nines"*? One of the axioms of fair play was, is, that no clue goes unexplained, including those not needed for the correct solution. They must still be accounted for, just as every piece of a jigsaw puzzle, even the boring sky-bits, must be fitted into place. Coincidence and superfluity are forbidden. Ennis! the man's *name*, his very being, fits the *deductive* pattern—to hell with penises!—to perfection, yet it is left unremarked. The puzzle's answer excludes an apparently essential datum, like a piece of long division whose quotient coughs up a bulky, unchewable remainder. It won't divide evenly, yet it must, it should!

The conversation was concluded. Jim mumbled his thanks, and Dannay encouraged him to write again if he enjoyed the next novel. Jim said he would. Dannay wished him well. But there was no next novel. Dannay never published another word; I suppose the loss of his partner left him, poor monad, unable to conjure "Ellery Queen." He rejoined Manfred B. Lee a few years later, in that fine and private place, but none I think do there embrace.

Now, as to "X," and *The Thirteenth Hour*: Jim came upon it by accident at Bargain Books, scanning the Mystery shelves at random. His father was outside, making a phone call, he said. It had been a good visit, and while Jim browsed he contentedly caressed one of his last missing John Dickson Carrs. (We might as well picture it pinned like a rare specimen: "*The Problem of the Green Capsule*, 1939, captured w/ dust jacket, ex libris, Bargain Books, February 5, 19—".) A bright scarlet letter caught his eye, jumping off a fat spine. He unshelved the book and read the front flap: "Readers, we can tell you nothing about the mysterious X. He has instructed us to send what we confidently predict will be a cavalcade of royalty checks to a solicitor in Swan Cove, Dorsetshire. This gentleman (whose identity we know, of course, but who also has requested anonymity) will assure us only that he is X's trusted amanuensis, and that no further word concerning that worthy's pedigree or activities shall ever pass his lips. We believe him!" Jim turned to the copyright page: 1937, perfect. Backflipping once, he saw, opposite the title page: "In Preparation: *The Fourteenth Trump*." Terrific, a series. He added *The Thirteenth Hour* to his small stack of purchases, glanced again at the Vs just in case a miracle had occurred, and walked to the front of the store to find his father. After a moment the door's sleigh bells jingled, and his father came in, hands deep into the pockets of his army jacket. He said to Jim, "Sorry I took so long." "It doesn't matter," Jim said quickly, and handed him the books.

Despite all that hokey Thirties dust-jacket puffery, Jim thought, and I do too, that the mystery of *The Thirteenth Hour*'s authorship was real. To the best of my knowledge, X has never been solved for. In preparing to write this piece, I consulted a recent reference work (*Twentieth-Century Detective Fiction*, Nora Abbey and D. Frederick Jones, Eds.) and learned that X was the only entry under "X," that *The Fourteenth Trump* was never played, and that Nora and Fred knew no more about X than Jim did. (They dismissed the whole business as "undoubtedly that long-ago season's most effective publishing stunt.") I also discovered, sadly, that they didn't think much of *The Thirteenth Hour*. They synopsized it as follows: "Despite its peculiarly angled perspective, X's sole opus is in most respects a fairly traditional example of *entre-les-deux-guerres* English mystery construction. During a snowbound house party at Three Oaks Hall, host Sir Hawley Belmoth's wife, Melissa, is found bludgeoned to death in her bed. As sole inheritor of Lady Belmoth's fortune, Sir Hawley is the prime suspect. A bloodstained handkerchief is found concealed in his dressing gown; various incriminating letters surface. Suspicion is also cast on pretty Nancy Chatfoil, a young schoolteacher hired by Sir Hawley to catalogue his library, and of course on the obligatory houseguests. One of them, amateur detective cum Idealist philosopher Sebastian Rook, steps in to conduct the investigation, quoting Bradley, Collingwood, and the *Cratylus* at a length modern-day readers will no longer find amusing or even endurable. Then—"

But I would prefer to do this myself. Jim and his father arrived home. Heading off to his room with *The Problem of the Green Capsule* and *The Thirteenth Hour*, Jim heard his mother say, behind him, "What are *you* looking so miserable about?" Jim increased his pace, almost trotting down the hallway, and shut the door of his room. His father's reply was inaudible.

The alternation of argument and truce between his parents had lately seemed to quicken. Nearly every night the tide came crashing onto the rocks, disturbing various life forms. Jim was eager to hole up with something good, and this "X" business was intriguing, but first there was the problematic green capsule. Jim began the book at once, curled in his

Naugahyde armchair, was interrupted by the silent triangle of dinnertime, and finished it before falling asleep. Not bad. Sufficient, definitely, to encapsulate the bedroom.

He took *The Thirteenth Hour* with him to school the next day. His English class was set free to "study" in the library, and while Miss Falcon went whispering and bending from student to student, Jim concealed X behind his tall, fat Nine-teenth-Century American Literature anthology, faking occa-sional non-notes in his notebook. The first chapter was good. A snowstorm such as Sussex has rarely seen came howling down upon Three Oaks Hall, that freezing February night in. . . . His attention was diverted when he realized that Miss Fal-con had circled too close for comfort, had in fact perched next door, her soft scholia now intelligible ("I think you're right, Lisa, it *is* a poem about privacy"), and so he hastily collapsed X's world ("but also about *shared* privacy between 'a pair of us'"), pushed it beneath his notebook ("'I'm Nobody!' she says, but then, you see, she *also* asks"), poised his pen ("'Are you—Nobody—Too?', doesn't she?"), and found a plausi-ble place for his gaze to rest on the shiny anthology page—where are we? Nobody, Somebody, "to tell one's name," right, okay—a curious adjacency, it struck him, of anonymities, X and Emily. Miss Falcon gave Lisa a smile, stood up, glanced at Jim, but moved off toward a table of gigglers, and Jim eased *The Thirteenth Hour* out of hiding again.

School ended. He walked home, kicking clots of slush aside and tugging the earflaps of his cap down against the February wind. In the apartment he waved at his mother, vacuuming, headed for his room, and settled into his armchair. The second chapter was good too, but starting to get a little weird. Evening came, his mother clattered pans and his father did not arrive home at six.

What Nora and Fred miss is the deliberate doubleness of X's vision. That "peculiarly angled perspective". . . X is aware, and wants his readers to be, of the conventions and punchlines of the ink-and-paper world he has populated. Winks and nudges abound. Several of the characters are themselves enthusiastic readers of detective stories. The servants, always faceless and ignored during the Golden Age (the Eleventh Rule specifies a *dramatis personae* of "decidedly worthwhile" characters, and offers a helpful list of those who are not: "butlers, footmen, valets, gamekeepers, cooks, and the like"), are here further reduced to a series of lower-class linguistic tics, over which the "obligatory house-guests" literally stumble ("Mrs. Dudshoot lost her way in the vast upper corridors of the manse. She descended by an unfamiliar dark staircase, tripped over a glottal stop, and nearly pitched down the steps. . . ."). Herr Vogel is called a "German philanthropist" but appears to be impersonating Ludwig Wittgenstein in a bad, mantic, mystic mood. And Sebastian Rook himself, that self-doubting sleuth, uses the *Cratylus* and other Platonic dialogues to prod his own interlocutors into a contemplation of higher, more human mysteries, of the very sort I would have supposed a detective story was meant to avoid.

Well, but did any of this register with Jim, sniffing roast chicken and glancing every now and then at his watch? No.

Yet he was aware, as chapter followed chapter, that X and his characters communicated a knowingness, an implied collusion with the mind behind the eyes that scanned the pages, which this particular young mind had never before encountered. It was as if X, smiling self-consciously, had managed to thrust Three Oaks Hall into another dimension (skipping our familiar Third, going from page-flat Two to Four), making the worlds of the other Golden Agers appear boringly, and falsely, "real." At every gloomy turning of its corridors, Three Oaks Hall seemed to contain a mirror in which Sir Hawley and Rook and Herr Vogel and the rest all saw themselves reflected, along with the eyes peering over their shoulders. . . . At any rate, Jim found it refreshing, though he worried that X might not be relied upon to plant his clues according to the rules.

Chapter followed chapter. In the absence of the police (downed phone lines, drifts blocking all roads), Sebastian Rook is prevailed upon by Melissa Belmoth's visiting brother, Malcolm, no friend to Sir Hawley, to investigate. Rook first issues a Socratic caveat, a lesson allegedly learned from earlier forays into detection ("After much study I found myself more puzzled than I was when I began"), and then uncovers motives aplenty—greed, jealousy, the hint of madness—among the usual host- and/or hostess-hating house party gathered by happenstance (bad luck for the victim, good luck for the reader!), and all presented in the simplistic manner required by the genre—though the smile of Cheshire X seems to hover above these absurdities. A cry is heard in the night by Mrs. Dudshoot (but not, interestingly, by her husband Ivan, always a light sleeper); Rook establishes the impossibility of any sub-zero arrivals or departures through the lashings of the snowstorm; and then there is the gaudily bloodstained handkerchief which Rook finds in Sir Hawley's dressing gown pocket, and which the likable lexicographer refuses to account for, while maintaining his innocence of any crime.

At seven Jim's mother called him to eat, and in silence the two of them consumed the dry, shrunken-skinned roast chicken. It began to snow, in light crystalline bursts against the apartment windows. Brother Malcolm, Rook learns, also stands to inherit. A whiff of blackmail emanates from disingenuous young Nancy Chatfoil. A small seed found gripped in the corpse's rigid fist: it comes from the bottom of the empty birdcage which Ivan Dudshoot has taken with him to Three Oaks, I forget precisely why. At just before eight o'clock the phone rang, and Jim's head, ringing in sympathy, leaped off his palm. He heard his mother's voice, then the click of the receiver being replaced. If Jim's father was not all right, she would come and say something, so when she did not, Jim resumed reading.

Viewed from Level One of the Least-Likely-Suspect Principle, Sir Hawley, being the obvious culprit, must be innocent. But shifting to Level Two, Sir Hawley, being the obvious culprit, is therefore the "least likely suspect" for readers who doggedly remain on Level One, and so may be guilty after all. Jim followed this delicate interplay with no difficulty, feeling all the while convinced that Sir Hawley, on any level, was a blameless victim, somehow preyed upon, framed, blackmailed, forced into a gallant defense. Returning to Level One, the least likely suspect here, he decided, was Mrs. Dudshoot, who had no motive, no attributes, not even a Christian name.

The snow appeared to have stopped. He went out into the kitchen and cut a brownie from the foil-wrapped tin next to the refrigerator. In the living room he saw his mother fit one, then another, piece into her puzzle, smoke curling above her head. Jim walked out and stood behind her, brownie in hand. It was still too early to ask where his father was, so he stared at the puzzle for a few moments: coming along nicely, a rural something or other; oak trees, a stream flowing down and out of the picture, lots of majestic hills and pacific sky-bits still to come. Jim thought he could see where one dragon-shaped piece was meant to attach, and reached a hand out for it, but his mother picked it up first and placed it in a quite different spot, extending the tree line another few hundred yards. Jim pretended he had been reaching out so as to free his cuff from his wrist so as to look at his watch: nearly nine. His mother put her cigarette to her lips and inhaled; then she enshrouded the countryside in mist. Jim returned to his room, chewing.

By ten thirty he was three-quarters of the way through *The Thirteenth Hour*. Some trickery with clocks is afoot (a good title is a clue in itself): Rook asks to see Herr Vogel's wristwatch, compares it with the tolling grandfather in the main hallway, and nods. The letters which Rook discovers, minus envelopes, tucked into a copy of *The Complete*

Dialogues, Bollingen Edition, are in Sir Hawley's hand, without salutation, but obviously written to a secret paramour, and full of the fear of discovery. Rook, whose quote-mania is extreme though hardly unendurable, quotes meaningfully: ". . . now a nightingale / Carols, yearns—circling high above / The flames of illicit love. . . ." Jim could isolate, consciously, little. Caroling, yearning—no thanks! He initiated a fleeting, altogether ludicrous consideration of *names*. Pause. Quotes meaningfully.

There were three chapters left. Jim could see from their titles as given in the table of contents ("The Face of the Perpetrator," "Sebastian Rook Explains," and "Thaw Comes to Three Oaks") that these chapters would obey the classic formula: antepenultimate chapter = denouement, often culminating with murderer's name revealed in final paragraph; penultimate chapter = detective reconstructs logic of solution, receives plaudits; ultimate chapter = five- or six-page envoi to the surviving characters, including resolution of love interest, if any (often best skipped). It was time for him to formulate his theory.

He heard his father's key in the front door. Without putting down the book, Jim walked to his own door and shut it. He sat down and closed his eyes, calling up the image of Three Oaks Hall. On Level One, then— Soon the voices came through the barrier: accusations and denials, no doubt, though only one word in four was audible. The world of Three Oaks seemed to slip from his grasp, despite the impending climax. According to Rook, the point of each Platonic dialogue is *aporia*, a state

of confusion meant to provoke insight on a new level, a previ-
ously untried path of investigation. The voices beckoned. Jim
placed his bookmark (a postcard from the Holmes Museum
at 221B Baker Street, which a traveling uncle had sent him)
in *The Thirteenth Hour*, set it down on his desk, and walked to
the door. He opened it and moved silently down the carpeted
hallway. Here, concealed by a right-angled bend, he was able
to listen. *I you she*. Jim considered the bend. It was no barrier
at all. The choice to investigate remained with him. He could
walk into the living room and begin his questioning.

We know that Jim did nothing of the sort, not for many
years. That night (which is many nights in one, a contrivance
as artificial as *The Thirteenth Hour*) he returned quietly to his
room, to consider once again the mystery at Three Oaks, the
wrong mystery. His father, necktie awry, came in to see him a
little later (a pot clattered down into the stainless steel sink,
far, far away), and found him curled toward the powerful
reading lamp, moistening a finger to turn the page. Jim looked
up, his vision fractured by the bright beam cast from bulb to
book. Beyond it was his dim father, who reached out a hand
and squeezed Jim's shoulder. Neither Starling smiled. "Everything all right?" "Sure." "All right then. . . ." Jim's father said.
Jim sensed he would say more, and forestalled him with a dis-
missive "Of course it is," and brought his eyes back down to
the page, and his father withdrew his hand. Jim found himself
heading for the assembled suspects, in step with Sebastian
Rook, and it is not necessary to follow him any further, although the solution is nicely handled. Why pursue a pointless

identity, an answer that leaves everything unexplained? You may find it worthwhile to fill it in, at leisure. The final sky-bit, the last piece snugged into place, might not be so boring after all: the curved slash of brown across the blue is now seen to link with another, similar slash on the adjacent piece, and the predator takes wing.

Twenty Visions of
Poor Alice Rosenbaum

One. Alice is sixteen, living with her family in the Crimea. Her mind teems with stories. The new Communist government announces a "week of poverty." Three soldiers burst into the Rosenbaums' wretched cottage. "You have too much!" the lieutenant thunders. His beard trembles. Fronz Rosenbaum motions to his daughters, Alice and Nora, to leave, to go to their bedroom and shut the door. Little Nora obeys. Alice refuses. She wants to see. She stiffens with hatred, she wants to remember. The lieutenant looks about him. But what is there to take? These Jews have so little. The other two soldiers mutter, appear shamefaced. Then—"What's in those boxes?" demands the lieutenant, pointing his broken-nailed finger at a stack of lavender cardboard cartons resting in a corner next to Fronz's walking stick. Alice is a few feet away from them, and can smell their sweet and hopeful fragrance. "Soap, Comrade Lieutenant," says Fronz. "I have kept these boxes of soap from my shop— that is," he stammers, "the shop which, in my ignorance, I believed I 'owned,' before our glorious Revolution." The lieutenant nods curtly to his minions. They heft the soap cartons, sniff them, tuck them beneath uniformed arms. The lieutenant jerks his head, and all three depart. Alice feels her hatred ignite. The soap, she knows, will be distributed to Party members, who are the State. To sacrifice for the State is to lose what is yours to men who will cynically profit from the power they have over you. But even if it were not so? Even if the soap were given to those who have no soap? Is another's need a moral claim? Alice's soul burns high. No. And forever no. This was *our* soap. Her father's walking stick leans in the soapless corner. Above it, on the mantelpiece, the useless menorah.

Two. Alice in Hollywood! She has escaped Soviet Russia, she has learned (after a fashion) English. Left behind is the tyranny of the Collective, whose philosophical justifications Alice has mouthed and mastered, inwardly seething, thanks to four years at the University of Petrograd. The State expected this girl to trumpet, despite her racial handicap, the truths of historical materialism, but instead Alice has emerged with her own truth. Not Marxism (that shabby hypocrisy), not Judaism (servility and self-pity), but something new under the sun. Now, in America, she hungers to make it real. The stories have never stopped—they buzz and mutter, from dawn to midnight. Alice wants to be a screenwriter. Every day, on her lunch break from the department store where she clerks, she walks past the locked iron gates of the great movie studios. The spikes, thrusting up into the California blue like a skyline, refuse admittance. Then: "Why are you staring?" says a voice from behind her. Alice turns. Seated in a gleaming green roadster is Cecil B. DeMille. Her English is only good for simple sentences. "I want to be in the movies," she says softly. DeMille smiles. His chauffeur guns the motor. "An actress?" he asks. "No," says Alice, "I want to *write* the movies." Cecil B. DeMille tells her he has no job for her as a writer of movies, but offers to take her inside his studio and sign her up as an extra, a face in the crowd. Alice accepts . . .

Three . . . and within six months her English is considerably better and she has begun doing treatments, doctoring scripts, advising her superiors on the merits of potential projects. She leans over her typewriter (it's midnight, she's been working since eight in the morning), and despite the weariness, the frustration of tinkering with the incompetent work of other, lesser writers, she thinks, Yes. And forever yes. She is here, in the land of the free, and free to choose. Heroism is possible. The universe is benevolent. Soviet Russia is an aberration. She has absolutely no doubt of her talent, and absolutely no doubt that she will succeed. She's been meaning to do something about her name, though. Alice Rosenbaum is not a good name for a heroine. Too plain, and too . . . you know. For a month now she has asked her acquaintances to call her Ayn, a Finnish name that appeals to her. Alice looks down at her typewriter, a Remington-Rand. There is always a choice.

Four. Alice is walking across a movie set when she sees him. Amid the hooped skirts, the painted faces, the pasted-on beards, the musty, ridiculous costumes, there is a man. Hair falling over one eye, the eye blue and pure as an eagle's. He is got up as a French sansculotte, but the sham can't disguise what he is. Alice falls in love. How can she meet him? She is not pretty. After a week of agonized mooning and indecision, she impulsively reaches out a foot and trips him. In Hollywood this is called "meeting cute." Conversation follows. His name is Frank. He is eight years older than Alice. They go to the studio cafeteria for coffee. Alice doesn't want to know where he hails from or who his favorite movie stars are. Instead she lights a cigarette and begins to talk, and talk. She talks for an hour without pause, her fierce dark eyes never leaving his face: Man is noble and brave, rationality is his essence and highest calling, his twin subjugations to the tyranny of the State and the tyranny of religion reveal the same moral failing, the refusal to think, for man has a choice, he has free will: he can live morally—that is, for himself—or he can let others do the thinking, he can live *for* others, he can "have faith," faith is the worst curse of mankind. . . . Alice stubs out her fifth cigarette, finally exhausted. Frank is staring at her. Hesitantly he nods his noble head. "Sounds good, I guess." If this were a screenplay, Alice and Frank would need to triumph over considerable misunderstanding and adversity before getting married. But, like so much else in Alice's peculiar life, what happens is stranger than any movie. They simply get married.

Five. Her stories, her truth. The Remington-Rand clatters into the night. Not screenplays—she's given up that onerous apprenticeship—but novels, novellas, plays, all full of grand theorizing. Out they go, back they come. What else is to be expected from malevolent, collectivist publishers and producers, here in the Bolshevik-bedazzled Thirties? Their presumptions to literary criticism ("your English is dreadful"; "clumsy, didactic sentences") obviously spring from the same source, the same depraved metaphysics. Oh, the years fall away, too fast, too easily, like a corny calendar-leaf montage superimposed upon clacking keys. The need for money becomes acute. Frank's acting career remains one of bit-parts, indolently pursued. Alice grimly sets her sights a little lower— and works, truth be told, a little harder on her English. A play, almost a potboiler (though it remains faithful to her philosophy) is produced!. . . is panned, folds. A novel, an allegory of treachery and love in the collectivist state: published! panned, remaindered. Alice almost regrets these premature unveilings. She should have waited for greatness.

It's the middle of the night, and the typewriter is still. Alice is seated stiffly before it. She stares around their small bedroom, made crowded by only a desk and a bureau and the lumpy Sealy. Frank is asleep out on the living room couch. She stabs a cigarette into her black holder, lights it, rubs her eyes. Beyond her desk lamp the room is as dark as a cave. She strains to see. Where is greatness? Her hand falls to the keyboard, her thumb hits the spacebar: *chunka*. She catches a glimpse— a vision—just out of sight beyond the platen, shimmering like light on water, before her, inside her, around her, and it is brighter and stranger, and less like herself, than anything she has yet been able to put into words. Indeed, at this moment some of her words, even her favorite ones, sound wrong: too certain, too arrogant. Is that possible? If only she could see clearly! Again she rubs her eyes, sparks dancing inside her skull; she stares down, q, w, e, r, t, y, and poor Alice begins to think. . . . The words start up again. *See*, of course, is a metaphor, there is nothing to be seen out there but reality, which contains no visions, only physical objects like desk lamps and typewriters. Any vision—again we speak metaphorically—is simply a product of her own thoughts, created by her alone, by her mind, so what else can she do except *think* about it? So she thinks, thinks, thinks . . . and the vision fades. It is replaced by a series of shadows who move left when Alice moves left, right when she moves right. Slowly, determinedly, she inserts a fresh sheet of paper into the typewriter. The words come easily now. Left to right, *bing*. There is nothing wrong with the words.

Six. Alice fires her agent. The agent has told her that the novel-in-progress, the one that at last will tell the story Alice wants to tell—is not commercial. "I fired her," Alice hisses to Frank, "because she could not give *reasons*. She had a *feeling*."

Alice is a stern judge. She doesn't get jokes. Her huge black eyes ("mesmerizing," "extraordinary," "we have never seen such an intelligent and penetrating gaze") widen, and she says in her still heavily accented English, "Explain the humor to me, please." Only the highest aesthetic and moral values have any value at all for her. But Alice loves a certain kind of music. Every single one of her friends—later her disciples, her inner circle—would profess themselves baffled at the spell these tunes cast over the great and austere philosopher. Alice calls it her "tiddlywink music." "Colonel Bogey's March." "C'mon Get Happy." "It's a Long Way to Tipperary," a long way indeed, it's the twenty-fifth day in a row of eighteen-hour days spent at the typewriter, for the climax is approaching, after. . . . No, don't count the years, the fallen leaves. Howard Roark is about ready to dynamite the housing project because they didn't build it according to his design. Alice puts a recording of "I'm an Old Cowhand" on her Victrola. The foolish notes fill the living room. Frank emerges from the bedroom, where he's been dozing, to see Alice twirling and humming amidst the furniture, grinning, entranced, her mesmerizing extraordinary intelligent penetrating eyes shut, carried off and away by her tiddlywink music. "A problem for future biographers."

Seven. Even by Hollywood scriptwriting standards, Alice has probably earned the next development: the saga of Howard Roark is published, is at first ignored, and then slowly becomes a huge bestseller. Despite the reviews. Despite the war, during which Alice's parents die at the Siege of Leningrad. But she doesn't know it, won't learn of it until years later. The papers are full of the heroism of America's Soviet allies. Alice sneers. The very name *Leningrad* is an affront. Not that she'd prefer St. Peter. Paperback rights, film rights. The war ends. There on the screen: Gary Cooper, a perfect Howard Roark in a hideously compromised burlesque of her novel. The adulation of the disciples. "Actually," says Alice to her disciples, "my favorite piece of music is Rachmaninoff's Second Piano Concerto." "Actually," says Alice with a frown, "science has not developed a theory of the meaning and effect of music—yet. I cannot argue for my preferences. But they are right. If you share my philosophy, then you will respond to the same music. Beethoven is malevolent. Mozart's metaphysics are inherently social, that is, non-egoistic, weak, polluted, evil." "I have never," Alice will say to Nathan, lying next to him in the damp-sheeted bed, "had an emotion I could not explain."

Eight. Nathan Blumenthal is twenty-five years younger than Alice. He read her novel about Howard Roark when he was fourteen, and at twenty he still idolizes the heroic architect, and his creator. He writes a fan letter to Alice. Alice, and Frank, decide the letter is unusually well composed. They invite the young fellow to visit them in their fantastic new modern house outside Los Angeles, paid for from the sale of the film rights. If Alice believed in God—which, the idea being irrational, she of course does not—Howard Roark, not namby-pamby Jesus, would be God incarnate. Haughty, driven, merciless. The ideal man. All her life she has wanted to meet a man like that. Frank? She loves him, yes, but she can't ignore the fact that Frank hasn't worked for ten years, that he lounges handsome as a sheik around the living room, brings tea and chocolate for Alice's guests, contributes little to the conversation. But Nathan. Nathan too is good-looking—and intense, and brilliant. He stays until four in the morning. Frank has always agreed with everything Alice says. So does Nathan, but in a different way. He *understands*. And why not, for each and every thought he thinks has been created by Alice, through her novel. Howard Roark, to Alice, is as real as the California sun. Suddenly there appears this young Nathan, just as real, and likewise something of a created character, yet he lives, breathes—and knows who created him.

Nine. For several years, Alice's relationship with young Nathan is Platonic. (A word she would never use, for it was Plato who began the whole disgusting history of philosophical mysticism that she combats—Plato, with his despicable attempts to reduce life on Earth to a dream, a shadow, a poor relation of some trumped-up, unverifiable "Reality"—Plato, whose metaphysics have for two thousand years proved so congenial to the propagandists of organized religion.) ("An intense nonphysical relationship," then.)

Nathan studies for a doctorate in psychology. He intends to construct a vast system of psychological theory and practice based on Alice's philosophy. Oh, the conversations they have about this! two, three, four o'clock in the morning, each fizzing like fuses, Frank going to and fro, bringing goodies from the kitchen, slumping down in his chair with an indulgent, vague smile, often dozing.

As for physical relationships: Nathan marries Barbara, a

fellow student, a fellow disciple. Barbara has chosen to enter the lion's den, the sanctum sanctorum of intellectual evil. She will earn a degree in philosophy, wrest it from the hands of malevolent Platonists and Kantians, all the while maintaining the purity of her allegiance to Alice and her unbending creatures, Howard Roark, Dominique Francon—and now John Galt, who heaves the Earth off his shoulders, the hero of the new novel Alice is working on. Barbara is very bright, yet very unsure of herself. Hands clasped, poised alertly on the middle cushion of the couch, head turning left, then right, she is like a particle energized by the pulsing force-fields that are Alice and Nathan. Alice and Nathan… they argue, reason, build, dream. Nathan changes his name. Now to the world he is Nathaniel, and his new surname is an anagram of "ben Rand," though he will ever deny that this claim to lineage was deliberate. He persuades Alice to accept the offers to lecture, offers she'd always turned down because they came from corrupted left-wing colleges. "You'll be a hit," he assures her . . .

Ten . . . and Nathan, psychologist that he is, is one hundred percent correct. The students love her. She strides to the podium, her black floor-length cape swirling behind her. She wears a huge silver brooch, shaped like a dollar sign, for by now Alice has realized that capitalism is the only logical economic system, its rough justice the fulfillment on Earth of her implacable metaphysics. Her speeches are rousing, rigorous, her accent deceptively charming. Hostile questioners are sliced into tiny strips of stupidity. On the way home from one such speaking engagement, she and Nathan are riding in the back of the car. Barbara is driving, two other disciples are chattering away. She and Nathan begin to touch. Their eyes lock. It is so logical. How could they not, eventually, feel this way about each other? Is not each the embodiment of the other's highest ideals? Sexuality must always be obedient to principles; when it isn't, there's something wrong with you. Alice is fifty. She stuffs a cigarette into her ebony holder. Nathan lights it with his heavy bronze Zippo. Emotion explodes, implodes, zooms back and forth between them with the speed of thought. Up front, Barbara keeps taking little peeks in the rear-view mirror. The other disciples fall uneasily silent. "We didn't blame Barbara for feeling rather nervous, rather—to tell the truth— *put out* about it."

Eleven. And so. Alice and Nathan and Barbara and Frank are seated in Alice's living room. The moon gleams above the city skyline. Alice and Nathan make their presentation: logic, ideals, joy as destiny. Alice does the dialectics, Nathan handles the psychology. "We are only asking one day a week together. An afternoon and an evening. There is no way, rationally, it can harm either of you." "Also," Nathan points out, "this will only last a few years. There is the question of age. . . ." Alice nods firmly in agreement. Yes. Nods firmly in agreement. She has no intention of making herself ridiculous. Nods firmly. Only a few years, and then, of course, it would be ridiculous. Barbara and Frank look at each other. As one, they leap up, protest. "Absolutely not!" says Barbara. "Outrageous!" cries

Frank, trembling. It is eight o'clock. By three in the morning, reason has won out. Alice and Nathan will have their one day a week together. All four have agreed never, under any circumstances, to divulge the arrangement. Think of the damage it would do to Alice's burgeoning philosophical crusade, to Nathan's battle with the Freudians! Even the disciples, Alice admits, would probably not understand. Yet all the arguments are sound. It's just that even the disciples are not quite as sharp as Alice and Nathan. They can't reason things out to their full implications. Only Nathan has a truly first-rate mind. Which is why . . . et cetera. Barbara and Frank don't want to hear it all again.

Twelve. Alice has disciples, indeed: Marty, Alan, Ruth, a dozen others. Bright young people, keen, scathing to the unbelievers, every emotion buttoned down so reason can triumph. They speculate about their futures. Perhaps—no, *for sure*—they will form a new vanguard, a new intellectual movement. Become teachers, leaders, millionaires. Marty pictures himself President of the United States. Alan pictures himself Chairman of the Federal Reserve Board. Ruth pictures herself submissive to one or the other. They speculate about Alice. "We were fascinated by her. Her powers of reasoning were extraordinary. It enraged her that no one took her philosophy or her fiction seriously. She was, we thought, the most important novelist of our time. All her books were savagely reviewed. Not a single critic thought she could write worth a bean. Pretty, no, she wasn't. Her eyes were wonderful. She had great legs. She liked to dress well, and be admired in her flouncy evening clothes. Fury became her. We never saw her in pain. She smoked fifty cigarettes a day, sucking smoke through her black holder and releasing it in swift puffs of conversation. (There was no genuine evidence, she explained to us, that tobacco was bad for the health. It was all unscientific, statistical mumbo jumbo. The Surgeon General was a second-rate mind. We gratefully tapped our ashes into her big pewter ashtray.) Indefatigable—we should say so! It had nothing to do with the Dexamyl. After a lifetime of two-pills-a-day-for-weight-control, her metabolism adjusted, she might as well, if you want our opinion, not have been taking it at all. No, she was *innately* indefatigable. As long as our premises agreed with hers, she would talk all night, teasing apart every argument, examining, checking, building, Roark-like, an edifice of reason. Every now and then some social metaphysician whose premises *didn't* agree with hers would weasel in. She made short work of him. People who disagreed with her premises were not mistaken or pitiable or teachable. They were malevolent. And yet, she could be so tender. If your premises agreed with hers. Do you know what her pet name was for Frank? Cubby-hole." And his for her? "Fluff."

Thirteen. The affair is pretty hard going for Barbara and Frank. (It is not too easy for Alice and Nathan either.) Barbara becomes subject to terrifying anxiety attacks—unable to sleep, popping awake five times a night, her stomach churning, heart galloping, clutching the sheets while Nathan sleeps on. She goes to a psychiatrist, naturally one of the disciples. Since she can't disclose Alice's affair with her husband, the psychiatrist diagnoses her as suffering from one of the new ailments that Nathan's system of psychology has discovered: faulty psycho-epistemology. This means that, since she's having emotions she can't explain, she has failed to choose to be rational. "There is always a choice," he tells her sternly. Barbara guesses that must be so, though a part of her envies those depraved social metaphysicians who presumably would have chosen to kick Nathan's ass out a long time ago.

Dear Cubby-hole is suffering too. When Nathan comes over for his once-a-week assignation, Frank gamely shakes hands and then puts on his overcoat. Alice fusses over him, tells him to be careful crossing the streets. Frank doesn't explain that he's only going as far as the corner bar. The subject of his drinking is not one he cares to dwell on. It's Christmas, the red-and-green traffic lights blend cheerfully with the holiday decor in the shop windows. Alice and Nathan gaze out at the proud, uncaring city. Then at each other. Frank wipes dog manure from his shoe and pushes open the saloon door. Alice and Nathan embrace. On the mantelpiece behind them are two stuffed animals, bear cubs (named—what else?—Cubby-hole and Fluff). To mark the holiday, each cub is wearing a little paper party hat.

Fourteen. Not too easy for Alice and Nathan. . . . Alice believes she can detect a lack of ardor. Has Nathan's love already begun to wane? That would be a monstrous betrayal.

But what other explanation is there? It's not guilt—they've reasoned themselves out of that. Nor is it the twenty-five-year age difference—Nathan has sworn he would love her if she were ninety and confined to a wheelchair. "Love me *passionately*? You must, Nathan!" Nathan soothes her: Yes, my dear, yes, you are the highest embodiment of my sexual ideal. These assurances are starting to come with a wince and a throat-clearing. It was perhaps, he thinks, just a little easier to love Alice when she was a goddess. The physical affair is a strain on his rationality. It remains confined to one meeting a week, but spills over in phone calls, endless discussions of how Nathan isn't living up to his, and Alice's, ideals. I want! I need! Give me more!

"We could see, at the time, that she was frayed, tense, constantly angry. But we put it down to the incredible effort we knew she was expending on the work-in-progress, the fifteen-hundred-page magnum opus she'd been slaving over for almost a dozen years. . . ." and which, when finally finished, almost finishes Alice. It ends the affair with Nathan, at any rate. Publication, stupendous sales, vicious reviews. Dedication: "To Frank and Nathan." Alice is almost beyond caring. The letdown. The reason for living—gone. She feels she will never write again. What is there left to write? Everything she believes, values, can imagine—it's all there in the novel. With a dramatic hand to her brow, she confesses, "I have done what no philosopher has done before: I have *thought everything there is to think*." The disciples look at each other, then bob their heads. She has delivered her final testament, her vision. What is there left of Alice? For twelve years she burned hard and bright. It takes enormous wattage to cast a hundred vivid shadows, all dressed up and given names: John, Dagny, Francisco, character after silhouetted character endowed with desires and destinies, labeled "good" or "evil." Now they are as real as anyone else in Alice's life, as real as Ayn and Nathaniel, and poor Alice has burned out. On a sunless November day, their one-afternoon-and-evening-a-week, she tells Nathan, "I am too depressed to go on with you. I have no strength, no passion. We must go back as we were before." There, there, soothes a vastly relieved Nathan. There, there, agree the equally vastly relieved Barbara and Frank.

Fifteen. But no. Alice the indefatigable: how could anyone imagine that she would remain chained like Prometheus, a prisoner of depression? It takes a rather long time—years, in fact—but slowly Alice pulls out of it. The sudden success of her philosophy helps a lot. You'd go far to find anyone, outside the disciples, who takes Alice seriously as an *artist*, mind you. (The disciples privately wish she'd tone down some of her more extravagant literary pronouncements: "I am the greatest writer of the twentieth century." And the second greatest? "Mickey Spillane.") But as a thinker, a metaphysician, she's catching on in a big way. Lectures, classes, her own monthly magazine, television appearances. She's starting to get bouquets she'd always longed for from those first-rate minds, the establishment intellectuals she'd assumed were beyond redemption: "Her philosophy is the most closely reasoned, consistent, logical system since Thomas Aquinas—if you accept her premises." A compliment to savor, since Alice does have a certain esteem for Aquinas (a disciple not of Plato but of Aristotle, the only real philosopher), though she despises *his* premises, the theological ones. She has Nathan to thank for much of this. He's in charge of the little cottage industry that has sprung up around Alice's books. He runs the magazine, writes the lectures, delivers them. In the eyes of the world, he is her protégé, her vicar. And it's paying off. At sixty, Alice feels she is coming alive again. Even Frank has found a new passion: painting. He is talented—at something! at last!—and furiously whips out oil after oil, there in a world without Alice. Alice takes dancing lessons; she wants to learn the Viennese waltz. What a good sign! The disciples watch her debut, whirling sublimely around the ballroom in Frank's arms. And in Nathan's. She is so happy to be able to say to Nathan, "I am reborn, my love! We can resume." A disastrous problem for Nathan, because there's another woman, a young model named Patrecia. Patrecia does not exactly embody his highest ideals—or rather she *does*—or rather she *doesn't*, not Alice's ideals, which are Nathan's ideals still, aren't they? The waltz has become a madness in three-quarter time. He tries to imagine explaining Patrecia to Alice, and has to trot to the men's room and run cold water over his face to keep his head from exploding.

Sixteen. It is the beginning of the bad years for Alice. Nathan procrastinates and prevaricates—reason after lying reason to postpone the resumption of the affair. Barbara—who knows all about Patrecia, has known and kept silent for months—finally divorces him. He begs her not to tell Alice why. Barbara agrees. It isn't loyalty, exactly. She's certain that Alice will blame her, see her as complicitous. Alice lives in a frozen rage of incomprehension. What is wrong with Nathan? Night after night on the phone she analyzes his faulty psycho-epistemology, while Frank, unable this time to face the impending, familiar nightmare, locks himself in his painting studio. But not to paint; bags and bags of empty bottles will be found hidden there, after his death.

In the end, Nathan can stand it no longer. He writes Alice a letter, telling her the truth. Half the truth: the age difference is insurmountable, he avers. Alice shrieks, hisses, hurls the pewter ashtray, smashes a glass. It's beyond belief, that this man in whom she's reposed her trust, her thought, her love, has proved himself a hypocrite and a Judas. "But do you think," she asks Barbara (still, innocently, seeing her as a confidante), "do you think I am being hasty? Nathan is confused. He has abandoned the vision of his ideals, but perhaps he will choose to regain that vision. There is *always* a choice. What do you think?" Something in Barbara gives up. She strokes Alice's hair, and slowly tells her the rest of the truth: Nathan has chosen a twenty-three-year-old fashion model. Alice sits stunned, and then explodes. "Get him over here! *Get that bastard over here!*" Barbara calls Nathan, and like an automaton he walks through the front door, ready to accept Alice's judgment on him. She calls him everything she can think of, burns, twists, spits. Frank sits on the couch, watching it all expressionlessly. Alice's eyes are ugly, her hands scratch at the air and tremble. Rationality, it would seem, has deserted her. Nathan is dead silent. Alice slaps him as hard as she can, once, twice. Nathan bows his head. "Now get out! I will publicly repudiate you! Never again will you speak for me, for my philosophy! Get out!" Nathan leaves. He has not uttered a single word. They won't meet again. Alice turns to Barbara. "And you— you knew!" Before Alice can crank up the windlass of her fury, Barbara too runs out the door.

Seventeen. The bad years. Alice withdraws from public life. Writes nothing. With Nathan in disgrace, her philosophical movement collapses. The disciples scatter, all but the tiniest inner circle. "We never knew. She sent us a long, bitter communiqué, hinting at every imaginable depravity on Nathan's part, but never said exactly what he'd done. She removed his name from the dedication of all future editions of her great novel. When we visited her, she was impatient, cutting; she searched out every minuscule deviance from her own opinions and promptly excommunicated the deviator. So angry, so cruel. What had become of our joyful rationalist, our indefatigable proclaimer of the Benevolent Universe?" What a noble mind is here o'erthrown. Frank, meanwhile, enters his mid-seventies, and senility. Cubby-hole can no longer concentrate, remember, think. Alice refuses to believe the evidence. It's got to be his psycho-epistemology that's at fault. Night after night, to the horror of her few remaining friends: "Try, Frank. I know you can remember the name if you try. Try harder." As well ask a cripple to walk. Frank snarls feebly, wanders in a daze, drinks. Then, just when Alice has begun to doubt that life can ever again offer her joy, an incredible letter arrives. Her younger sister Nora, whom she has not seen for forty-seven years, has found a photograph of the famous novelist in *Life* magazine, smuggled into Leningrad. "If I can obtain a visa, may I visit you?" Alice is ecstatic: her baby sister, whom she had thought dead with the rest of the Rosenbaums! Like a slow-moving miracle, complete with State Department shenanigans, the visit is arranged. There is Nora, and her timid husband, stepping shakily from the plane. Alice embraces her, tears running down her cheeks. She has decided that Nora must stay, here in the land of the free. Alice has plenty of money, she can offer her refuge from the Soviets. How strange. Nora does not like America. Too many people, too much noise. Too many choices. "Alice, I simply go to the store for a bar of the soap, and the clerk asks me, What *kind*? How am I to know? I say, You decide." The familiar fury begins to engulf Alice. Her own sister is a social metaphysician just like the rest of them. *You decide!*—the abdication of reason. Alice argues, rails, remonstrates, but Nora won't listen. She won't even look at Alice's books. She would rather be back in Russia. The visit is a short one, and afterwards Alice can only spew out vituperation. But surely (a meek suggestion from an old friend) the habits of a lifetime lived under dictatorship—surely they are to blame? Not Nora? And perhaps you came on a bit . . . strong? "How dare you question me! Put down that glass! Get off my sofa! Get out of my sight!" Nora is to blame. The choice was hers, and she chose tyranny.

Eighteen. When Frank dies, Alice feels her own flame flicker in an icy wind. The end was not sudden, but, with Nathan and Barbara and the other disciples long gone, it was Frank to whom she'd increasingly turned, even in his cranky abstraction. "He was the happiest man I have ever known," she tells the *New York Times* obituary writer. The evidence of the empty bottles does not faze her. She claims he used them to mix turpentine in. Survived by? "Myself." No children? "That is correct." Alice clips out the obituary and tucks it away. Each night is endlessly quiet now. She wakes in the darkness, breathless, from a dream in which she *saw* what remains when words have stopped and heartbeats are stilled. Dreams, visions . . . Alice goes back to sleep. Not even a new resurgence of public interest in her philosophy can rouse her. There is one TV talk show host she rather admires, though—he's staunchly anti-Communist—and when he asks her to appear, Alice consents. A pretty lively interview for a seventy-five-year-old widow. Some of the old spark, and the old certitude, is there. Alice praises America, excoriates the collectivist Hippies. Any signs of mellowing? At one juncture, the talk show host asks a provocative thing: "You've made it clear that you're an atheist, but I was wondering: Would you say, Thank God for this country?" Her fans in the audience gasp, waiting for the contemptuous retort. But Alice replies, "Yes: God means 'the highest possible.'" And as she is leaving, he pats her mink-coated arm and says, "God bless you." "Thank you," says Alice shyly; "the same to you."

Nineteen. Alice glares at her doctor. "Stop smoking?" She brandishes her famous cigarette holder. "Give me a reason, a *scientific* reason." The doctor slaps an X-ray down on the desk. Points to a large white patch, and another. Alice stares at the havoc in her lungs, then removes her cigarette from the holder. She firmly stubs it out. "Will it help?" Yes. But the doctor tells her she's also to be operated on. Immediately. Alice finds that she still loves something after all: her life. . . . She swims out from the anesthesia determined not to die. Her doctor is amazed at the strength, the desire. Alice survives. But with most of one lung gone, she's an invalid. Pulmonary problems continue, and one day her heart gives a leap and sends her spinning to the floor, unconscious. Yes, "cardio" and "pulmonary," they go together like tar and feather. Alice, in her final bed, bites her lips to keep from dying. She reminds herself (like that nuisance Socrates): there is nothing to fear, since there is only Nothing. We go from active to static. How meaningless, how. . . . She exerts what little will she has left. Rationality must be regained. Self-pity, of all things, is not the last emotion she wishes to feel on this Earth; surely she's come farther than that. In the name of the highest possible, the best within us . . . Alice closes her eyes, just for a moment . . .

Twenty . . . and wakes from the most extraordinary dream. So many people, and it all seemed so real! Frank, Howard, Nathan, Barbara, John, Nora, Ayn. Ayn. Alice frowns. She *is* Ayn. *That* was not a dream. It was *not* a dream. Oh dear, poor Alice Rosenbaum. Something absolutely horrible begins to happen. Behind her, the dream of Ayn fades, fractures, flickering like a shadow on the wall of a cave, and then vanishes. Before her (and it has always been there, it does not "appear" but rather Alice's eyes are now opened to its radiance) is her vision. At this point, as we well know, there is a choice.

Roaches Crawled Across My Chicken

Right in front of my guests. I was coming out of the kitchen with a bowl of mixed vegetables, and some French bread in a small wicker basket. "What would anyone like to drink?" I asked, and then I saw that my guests were not listening to me. They were staring at the roast chicken.

We all watched in silence. I was trying to think of the correct thing to say, or even a few words that wouldn't be entirely off the track, and I suppose the other three were too. My cousin Lucinda squinted, eyes gone small and distant, as if she'd been given a difficult problem in mathematics to solve. Mrs. Judson (who was my late mother's companion for many years) picked up her napkin and seemed about to flick it toward the chicken. But then she appeared to think better of it. Harry Toole, my pastor, looked pained, but resolute; I had seen the same expression on his face when, one Sunday after Mass, a little boy had pointed out to him a blotch of algae floating in the holy water font.

My cat Nolan rubbed against the legs of my trousers, purring. The chicken and the roaches were beyond the line of his vision. On the stereo I had Kirkpatrick doing Scarlatti, the E major harpsichord sonata. A roach entered my dish of sweet potatoes as the second theme began. It found the mushy terrain difficult to traverse. Clumsily managing to exit the dish, it returned to the chicken (Kirkpatrick took the repeat). Small particles of orange potato clung to its legs.

These roaches . . . their numbers were increasing, and my apartment was alive at night with their whispery expeditions. My hand hesitated when I reached out to pick anything up: a lid, a tissue box, a newspaper. What would dart away from me, and how many? They raced for the drain in droves as I pulled back the shower curtain. I surprised an entire colony of them— seething, writhing—in the back of my silverware drawer. Most of them scaled the drawer's back wall and disappeared before I could gather my wits, and overcome my jaw-clenching distaste. Even the small entranceway of my apartment wasn't free of them; I walked in the front door, flicked the light switch, and saw two or three, the light-brown kind, the color of buttered toast, squeeze themselves down a crack in the floorboards. It was only getting worse. Had the moment come, finally, for *me* to run from *them*? I wanted to, as I stood speechless, clutching my bowl and my basket, and watched them crawl over the pocked brown skin of my chicken.

There was nothing to say. It wasn't funny, nor was there any meaning to be found, clinging to the event like those particles of sweet potato. I couldn't ascribe fancy roles and intentions to any of us, least of all the roaches. These roaches were simply hungry. My guests were embarrassed, angry, and nauseated. So was I, but I could also see where the roaches were coming from (not literally, or I would have taken action to prevent it), and when my guests left, unfed, my stomach was still growling, and I had no money, so I washed the chicken and ate it.

No money, no money. I was so tired of having no money. I'd set myself up as a freelance editor, but the work was sporadic at best, and grotesquely boring: grant proposals and three-hundred-page bibliographies and financial statements of thriving corporations.

Lucinda, by contrast, was paid quite well to research something called algebraic topology at the nearby state university, which she referred to as her "sponsoring institution." She was my second cousin on my mother's side. Her eyebrows were unplucked, furry. She smoked an extraordinary number of long, thin cigarettes and was often lost, or so I imagined, in rarefied thought: her face, at any rate, grew dim, like a bulb going out, and she fingered her temples and stopped breathing for long minutes. When she came out of one of these trances, she seemed convinced of something. She nodded her head, pursed her lips, blinked her eyelashes rapidly. I'd had a crush on her ever since I was eleven and Lucinda was a solemn, thin ten-year-old doodling with a pencil: triangles and parabolas; anagrams and palindromes; brain teasers concerning the activities, addresses, and spouses of Messrs. Green, Brown, and White. Even back then, I wanted to understand what she was thinking about, and when I realized that I never would—I have no head for puzzles—I wanted to bury my face for hours in the fragrant darkness of her hair.

Algebraic topology is a cutting-edge discipline within modern mathematics, I was given to understand. Once, shortly before we became lovers, I remarked to her that there must not be very many other human beings who understood her work. "Twelve," she agreed. Interesting, I said. I suppose you correspond with them? Lucinda frowned and said, "Are you kidding, Vic? I *know* them all *intimately*. They visit me from Munich and Stockholm and Singapore. We're each other's best friends. We call each other all the time—conference calls. We tweet. We remember each other's birthdays. We email Well-Formed Formulae to each other. Our sponsoring institutions pay for the computers."

"That's expensive," I said.

"We text poems to each other." Lucinda never smiled and I had no idea if I was to take this seriously. She may have meant the poetry of formulae (a good Well-Formed one was something of an achievement, apparently), strings of symbols that language-poets would never comprehend but that elevated her and her best friends into the poets' place, the place of ecstasy and communion. Nothing like that ever happened between her and me, though we did hold hands very contentedly in movie theaters. I wanted little more. "Balance," I said to Lucinda once. "I provide balance in your life. I keep you anchored." She stared at me as if I were an Ill-Formed Formula.

The day after my dinner party, Lucinda and I met for

coffee at a Hardee's near her university. The table next to ours had a great many fried-chicken crumbs on it. Almost immediately she told me, "If you don't do something about your roaches I'm never coming there again."

"What do you suggest?" I asked huffily. "I've cleaned and cleaned."

. "Kill them."

"I've tried. You know I've tried."

Lucinda shook her head, frowned at her milky coffee; this was, evidently, the last word in roach algorithms. I remembered that once, several years ago, when we were related only by blood, she had borrowed Nolan to kill a mouse in the crumpling farmhouse her parents had willed to her. She had refused Nolan food and water until he presented her with the twitching lump of brown fur.

"Your roaches." The personal pronoun offended, deeply. In what sense are they mine? I asked myself, driving home from the Hardee's. I don't own them, am not responsible for them, don't regard them as an outgrowth of, or comment on, my character. What can Lucinda mean by giving them to me? Merely a careless formulation? Lucinda, I reflected, did not know many nontechnical words but she used those she knew quite precisely. I was appalled that my lover felt these insects were mine. I don't want them, I said to her, idling at a traffic light. You know that I've already tried to kill them, repeatedly, but they proliferate nonetheless. They have nothing to do with me. If I succeed in killing them I won't feel diminished.

On the contrary, I'll flourish in the absence of hundreds of rustly brown creatures.

I made an appointment with Harry Toole to receive the sacrament of reconciliation. We did it face to face—I couldn't kneel in front of a screen and pretend we didn't know each other—and Harry knuckled his gray old head and nodded twinklingly, making me think of Spencer Tracy, while I went on about Lucinda. It was more a list of *her* sins than mine, I'm afraid. Her unsympathetic command—"Kill them"—had really rankled. Then I told him about the latest cheat I perpetrated on a client. It was easy for me to inflate the hours on my bill, since (this was my justification) I worked so much more quickly and efficiently than the average editor.

This wasn't the first time I'd confessed to cheating. Harry stopped twinkling. Raising a finger and looking off into a corner of the rectory study, he said, "You shouldn't do that, Vic."

"They don't know the difference, Harry," I said. "At least I don't think they do. And I'm broke. I need the money. I have to reach a higher standard of living. I have to move out of that place I'm living in."

"Oh yes," said Harry unhappily.

"By the way, sorry about the other night. Disgusting."

"Are you genuinely sorry?" Harry asked me.

"I certainly am."

"Do you have a firm purpose of amendment?"

Were we talking about roaches or cheating? I hedged: "Haven't I just been saying so?"

Harry nodded and tugged at his ear. "You really ought to stop gouging your clients. That's serious sin." But he smiled. Harry, in general, wanted me to like him, though we both knew this interfered with his efficacy as a confessor. "I suppose you could perform some sort of penance for your roaches while you're at it, but I'm on shaky theological ground here." Now we were both grinning like idiots. But then he said, "And are you willing to marry Lucinda?"

"For God's sake. The question hasn't arisen."

"Then you really ought to stop sleeping with her."

I felt blindsided, and was moved to retaliate. "Look, let's not push it. This is America, not Ireland."

Harry said shyly, "Well, you could pray for some insight into why you cheat and fornicate. Will you do that much?"

"I might. It's hardly recondite, Harry." I was resentful; if there was something amiss in the way I treated Lucinda (and what about the way she treated me?), shaking "fornication" at me was not going to fix it. Furthermore, I realized that he too, just like Lucinda, was assigning the roaches to me.

"Coming on Sunday?" Harry asked. "The folk choir has been rehearsing."

"Perhaps. You've said that before, and they haven't been one bit better." Rather maliciously I added, "I think I'll ask God to remove the roaches. My poor human attempts have failed. Any objection to that?"

Harry refused to take offense. "No, of course not," he said. "Ask Him to do that, by all means. Scriptural precedent, if I'm not mistaken." Here we were, brandishing our grins again. "Um . . . there's a passage in Deuteronomy, I believe. Well, Job and the trials, at any rate."

"Sodom and Gomorrah?" I suggested.

Harry brightened yet further. "There you go. I should imagine those places were *heavy* with roaches. Infested."

I looked at my watch. "You have another appointment, Harry, and I'm meeting a client for dinner. What's my roach penance?"

"Hmmm?" Harry paused and frowned. "It was disgusting, you're absolutely right. Do the Stations of the Cross. Twice."

I agreed—it was just barely possible he meant it—and received absolution.

When I got home that night I thumbed through Deuteronomy (by the moon's glow, afraid to turn the lights on, wondering if the kitchen would scamper to the tune of six thousand chitinous feet on the counters, the floor, the ceiling; the ceiling, that was the most uncomfortable thought—that a battalion of roaches might drop onto my bald spot as I foolhardily entered and reached for the refrigerator door; though roaches in the fridge was not a comfortable thought either—pulling it open, igniting the fridge light and surprising them in the act of annexing my bleu cheese) but I couldn't find the Word of God on the topic that concerned me. I found this curse (Deuteronomy 28:27-30): "The LORD will afflict you with the boils of Egypt and with tumors, festering sores and the itch, from which you cannot be cured. You will be unsuccessful in everything you do; day after day you will be oppressed and robbed, with no one to rescue you. You will be pledged to be married to a woman, but another will take her and ravish her. You will build a house, but you will not live in it." Maybe this was the passage Harry had in mind. It did seem as if it ought to mention roaches, somehow.

I paged back a few verses, trying to get the context of this curse, but found myself floating, rudderless, into the middle of a complicated family disagreement among people whose names I couldn't pronounce, and the recipient of the LORD's ire eluded me. Perhaps the LORD is talking to us all, His very people—this was my thought, as I closed the Bible. Not merely certain malefactors, the odd blasphemer. Would I rather believe that, than believe I'd somehow been singled out? I decided I would. And the last curse, I thought, is the saddest, the weightiest: You will build a house, but you will not live in it. Yes, yes, amen: For the LORD has jammed it to the brim with roaches.

Providentially, Mrs. Judson phoned me later that week with the name of her exterminator. "Good man," she said. "Gets the job done."

"Mrs. Judson, I had no idea. I never noticed a single roach at your house."

"Proves the pudding, then, doesn't it? I had 'em for years, on and off. Mice, as well. He nailed 'em."

"I'm very sorry about the other night."

Mrs. Judson was silent, and then she said, "I'm glad Clara

wasn't there to see it. She liked coming over there. She liked the ceilings."

The ceilings of my apartment were quite high, and the plaster had been worked into swirly designs, like a gesture painting fashioned out of vanilla icing. My mother would often lie down on my sofa (often within minutes of entering my apartment, after the most perfunctory of greetings), fling her shoes across the room with two efficient kicks, cross her wrists behind her hairdo, and smile up into the creamy distance. As I chatted to her about my life, she would fall asleep.

"My mother would have risen above it," I told Mrs. Judson. Her remark had frozen the air between us. For a moment I'd felt we were comrades, partners in infestation, but that illusion was now erased. "A roach or two, between mother and son. . . . Well, I will give this Doctor Favor a call."

"Do that. Damned if he's a doctor, though. Not that it matters. Six of one, a dozen of the other."

"Precisely. Again, many thanks." I waited for Mrs. Judson to invite me to a party, as was her custom, but instead she said, "Well. Bye. Clara didn't think he was a doctor either."

"Doctor Favor is coming," I told Lucinda. We were having dinner at a Chinese restaurant. Lucinda had refused to enter my apartment.

"What?" she asked, chewing an egg roll.

"The roach doctor is coming tomorrow." Our booth and table were very clean. A fresh white carnation had been placed in a small vase next to the soy sauce.

Lucinda finished her egg roll and wiped her fingers with a napkin. She said, "The roach doctor. Weird. But if I follow you, congratulations. You should have done something about it months ago."

"I tried. You know that." I didn't really believe that Lucinda had forgotten all my attempts: the sprays, the bug-bombs, the shiny black deathtraps lining my kitchen counters and bathroom cabinets. None of it had worked. One morning I found the Roach Ranch from Hell covered with a roiling outpost of insects, as if to mock me. They seemed to be dancing. "He said the apartment would be uninhabitable for two nights."

"Come to my place if you want. Although I have a lot of work to do."

"I'll have to bring Nolan," I told Lucinda. Nolan was unhappy about the roaches too. He would begin to settle himself into his favorite chair, intent on meditation, but then would sit up and eye the room, ears cocked, trying to find the source of the endless skittering that we both heard. In the mornings he was up before me, patrolling. I would enter the kitchen to find him hovering over his bowl of dry food. With a fastidious, skillful paw he batted roaches out of the bowl, stunned them, and then ate them alive, glaring at me.

"Fine," said Lucinda. "He's really a doctor?"

"I don't think so. Mrs. Judson recommended him."

"Mrs. Judson is weird."

"You've never warmed to her."

"Clara this and Clara that," said Lucinda meanly. "And

she gets everything wrong. Did you hear her the other night? 'Why, Lucinda, you've barely scratched the tip of the iceberg.'"

I laughed. "To quote her on another occasion: 'Don't judge a book until you've read the cover.'"

"I've read her cover," said Lucinda. "She's weird. This roach doctor is probably a phony. Why don't you google Exterminators and call the one with the best website? That's what I always do when I don't know what I'm doing."

"Too late," I said. "He's coming tomorrow. Let's give him the benefit of the doubt, okay?"

We made plans for my stay at Lucinda's. Ordinarily I avoided spending the night there because I didn't sleep well. Her various communication devices clicked on at odd hours with messages from her far-flung compatriots, and she even refused to turn off the antiquated fax machine. I awakened to hums and buzzes as an endless scroll of topological truths issued forth from Europe or Asia, where it was not the middle of the night. Lucinda snored through these annoyances. Were her dreams similarly lucid, scrolling out in a language only she and twelve other human beings could understand?

The waiter brought our fortune cookies. I cracked mine open and read the fortune out loud: "'Watch for the appearance of an unexpected ally.' Well, I like the sound of that. At least it's not an aphorism. Have you noticed that trend in fortune cookies? Too many aphorisms."

Lucinda was frowning down at hers. "Mine is a regular fortune, too, except it doesn't really apply to me: 'Your money problems will soon come to end.'"

"Oh, that must have been mine," I said. "I can hope so, anyway. We must have picked up each other's fortunes."

We said goodbye outside the restaurant. Lucinda waved a hand as she walked away from me, looking over her shoulder and saying, "Good luck with the roach doctor. I *will* give him the benefit of the doubt. I want to hear all about him tomorrow."

When I arrived home, I heard my landline ringing as I let myself in. I reached for the hall light switch and flicked it on, then looked away—the phone kept ringing—and gave the roaches time to disperse. Then I walked carefully toward my desk. In the doorway to the kitchen I saw what looked like a dark brown puddle, at least a foot in diameter. But it shivered with life—with a thousand lives. Nolan was huddled in a tight ball on the top shelf of my bookcase, legs and tail hidden away beneath him. He gave me a look of unutterable misery. The phone was still ringing. I answered it, standing at my desk, transfixed by the teeming puddle in the kitchen doorway. It was a client, a musicologist for whom I'd just completed a proofreading assignment. He was calling about my bill. "I can't help but feel you've calculated this incorrectly," he told me. I assured him my calculations were correct. The index, I explained, had been extremely time-consuming. I had checked every entry. "Even so. . . ." As I watched, the roaches slowly disbanded, marching off behind the refrigerator. Several ran in the opposite direction, crossing the rug in my dining room and then walking up the wall, where I lost sight of them. I didn't like that: losing sight of them. The musicologist was telling me that he was a man of very little means, that he was financing the publication of his book himself, and that my bill had come as an unexpected and possibly unaffordable shock. "Couldn't we work something out?" Sorry, no, I told him. I had my problems too. I *did* want to help him, but *I needed the money*. In a crushed voice he promised to mail me the check. It was a dreadful conversation.

An hour later, as I fell asleep, I found myself, much to my surprise, obeying Harry's injunction to seek insight. But the only answer I received was the secretive rasp of exoskeletons on plaster. *I don't want to know what they do when I'm in bed*, I whispered to myself. In any event, tomorrow they would die.

Over the phone, Doctor Favor had been terse. A two-day job, yes, he'd informed me after learning the gravity of my problem. His voice was deep, and accented, though I couldn't place the lilt. Vaguely Mediterranean, perhaps, or Middle Eastern. There was no trace of censure in his manner, and I appreciated that. He sounded neither happy nor sad about the roaches, and he never called them mine. He said he would arrive at nine, and that I ought to be prepared to vacate the premises.

With Nolan mourning inside his carrier, I sat in my living room, suitcase packed, and awaited Doctor Favor. I glanced at the ceiling. Two or three spots moved across it, negotiating the swirls and rills like Arctic explorers. Contrary to what I had told Mrs. Judson, my mother would have been greatly upset to see this. One's eyes naturally followed the roaches, and did not dwell on the soothing frozen landscape. She would not have found it restful, nor did I.

Doctor Favor was prompt. He wore clean white overalls, with painter's loops. He was a short man, but no shrimp—big-chested, thick-necked, square-headed—and he wore a carefully trimmed black mustache. He carried an old canvas satchel filled with canisters, bottles, hoses, and, strangely, several books whose titles I couldn't see. I asked him if he needed to know anything more about the situation, and he shook his head curtly.

"I have everything I need," he said, pointing to his satchel. "You may leave the matter in my hands."

"Are those books, uh, reference manuals?" I asked.

Doctor Favor stared at me, eyes stony. "Innocence," he said, or seemed to say.

"Innocence?"

He smiled, showing his gums. "In, a, sense."

"Ah, pardon," I said.

The doctor became businesslike. He walked into my kitchen, stomped briskly on a roach, and began to empty his satchel on the counter. "I will let myself out," he called to me without turning around. "Do you wish to meet me here again tomorrow morning, or may I have a key?"

"I can meet you," I said. But I was reluctant to leave. What would his first foray consist of? Poison gas? Deadly pellets? He placed a thick book, the color of oxblood, next to my dish drainer. Spells?

"I suppose Mrs. Judson's house was quite badly infested?" I said to his back. Doctor Favor grunted, busy with his implements. He turned to the sink and ran water over his capable-looking hands. Then he dried them on a dishtowel, mumbling a few words I couldn't catch. He didn't seem to be talking to me. I watched him unscrew the top of a dull gray cylinder, remove a wafer-like object, and hold it up to the light, mumbling once more. He placed it carefully on the counter, and then turned to face me, arms folded across his muscular chest. He raised his eyebrows.

"Very well then," I said. I picked up Nolan's carrier and my suitcase. "Good luck," I said. Nolan moaned, a long descending note.

Doctor Favor bowed slightly and said, "Have a nice day. Unless you have other plans." He smiled. "Choke."

"Oh, come now," I stuttered. Then I got it, and laughed politely. "A joke. Yes."

The doctor turned his back on me, and opened the oxblood-covered book. I left.

The next morning I arrived wearily at my apartment building. Lucinda and I had stayed up past midnight—she hunching over her computer screen, I pacing the hallway, wishing she would come to bed with me. When she did, she wanted to hear about Doctor Favor: his demeanor, his methods.

"Is this really the right moment?" I asked, entwining my fingers in her soft hair. We were in darkness except for the multiple cue-lights of her many machines, which glowed like tiny eyes, green, red, and ice-blue, from the corners of the room.

"Tell me," Lucinda murmured.

I attempted to conjure up Doctor Favor's burliness, and the lilt of his unplaceable accent. I described how meticulously he'd set out his implements; his abrupt, nearly insulting manner of speech; that fierce, efficient flattening of the stray roach beneath his boot. He had, I said, the smile of a man not to be trifled with. "He'd be a dangerous enemy," I speculated. "I almost feel sorry for the roaches." My account seemed to please Lucinda. She listened in perfect stillness. We then committed the sin of fornication at greater length, and with considerably more verve, than had been our recent custom. I fell asleep happily, but her devices interrupted my sleep several times with their clattering announcements.

When I got off the elevator and rounded the corner of the hallway, Doctor Favor was there waiting for me. His overalls were blue this time. "How did it go?" I asked him, and let us in. I gasped. My apartment smelled like a darkroom. On the floor, the carpets, the tables, were hundreds of shriveled brown corpses. "Oh my God," I said. I could not take another step inside.

Doctor Favor gave me his gum-revealing grin. "As you see," he said, and for the first time I learned something of his attitude toward roaches: he was delighted that they were dead.

"Unbelievable," I said.

Doctor Favor went on smiling. He said, "Don't worry. I will remove them. It is part of the service."

"Thank you," I said helplessly. "What— what more is there to do?"

"Prophylaxis," he said, rolling the R with gusto. "Prevention."

"I see. Will there be any more. . . ?" I gestured at the battlefield.

"Where they fall, you will not see them," Doctor Favor said. "Never again."

"I suppose I should pay you now," I said, patting myself for my wallet. I was still overwhelmed by what I had walked into, and dizzy from lack of sleep.

The doctor shook his head. "I will leave a bill. Mail it in. Or 'PayPal.'" He sounded amused, as if by some quaint foreign term.

"All right. This is— I guess I had no idea."

He swept his eyes around my living room. "Now you know," he said with what I judged to be satisfaction. "Stay away tonight. Tomorrow it will be safe. You and your little kitty-cat can return in triumph." Now I was sure he was mocking me. No doubt he remembered that my Christian name was Victor. Had I appeared weak in his eyes, unmanned by his works?

I decided to challenge him. "And this will really last?" I asked. "They won't come back?"

"Not for as long as you live," he replied solemnly, as if I were a child being told the end of a fairy tale. "And when you die"—he gave a huge, squint-eyed bellow of laughter—"who cares, eh?"

"Well, Harry Toole, my pastor, would take issue with you on that." I am not one of those touchy Catholics, but certain remarks can't go unchallenged. Dragging in Harry to mouth my beliefs for me was of course weak-kneed.

Doctor Favor waved a hand dismissively. "When his rectory becomes a . . . pesthouse, you must recommend my services."

"I'll do that," I mumbled.

I pulled up in front of Lucinda's house to find her sitting in the porch swing, legs tucked beneath her, rocking herself slowly and smoking a cigarette. I rolled down my car window and, even before turning the ignition off, boasted that the roaches were history. Incredibly, Lucinda almost smiled. "I'm so glad, Vic," she called out, and the swing creaked as she got up and walked down the porch steps toward me. "I was in the middle of a thought," she said, "but give me five more minutes. And then." Her eyes were hungry. I killed the motor and walked quietly up the steps behind her. Lucinda sat back down in the swing and resumed her trance. I leaned on the porch rail, watching her respiration slow and then stop.

A few minutes later she came out of it, nodding firmly, and the first thing she said was, "Now. Tell me." Her hand gripped my wrist as I sat beside her in the swing. "Oh, he's earned his doctorate," I began a little giddily. "When it comes to roaches, Doctor Favor is the final solution." I described what I'd seen. "Yes?" said Lucinda. "Yes?" She stared at me, as if she could see each word I uttered. "What else? What more?" I thought back on our encounter, and then repeated Doctor Favor's taunts—if that's what they were. "I must admit," I concluded, "that his manner puts me off. But so what.

Many great men are eccentric. And that odor had better go away. But all in all." Lucinda laughed—a unique occurrence, in my memory. And then she said, "Oh yes, Vic. Now." She pulled me up out of the swing and, with fingernails dug into my forearm, led me down the hallway to her bedroom. I offered a prayer of thanksgiving as we stumbled over her surge-protection box and fell onto the bed: LORD, I thank You for lifting Your malediction. The roaches, I now realized, had been a barrier between Lucinda and me for far too long. Finally I was free of them, and she was free to love me as I wanted and deserved to be loved.

Doctor Favor's word appeared to be good. When I reinhabited the apartment, there was not a roach to be found, quick or dead. Nolan leapt from his carrier, licked at his fur, bad-mouthed me, and stalked over to his eating spot. I poured a bowl of dry food for him. Three days later it remained pristine, uninvaded.

The chemical stench dissipated. The nights were silent. I entered my kitchen with impunity, at any hour, turning on the light to a still-life of saltshaker, spice rack, and dish drainer. Nothing burst into motion, fleeing me. I lost the habit of pausing before entering, and peering anxiously upwards to examine whatever might scurry across the ceiling.

I invited Mrs. Judson, Harry, and Lucinda to dinner, by way of celebration. "Did the job, did he?" Mrs. Judson said when I called to ask her over. "Knew he would. Charged you a kid's ransom, too, I'll bet."

"He's not cheap," I agreed. "What an unusual fellow. I noticed that he doesn't have a website."

"Doesn't need one, obviously. Word of mouth. You'd recommend him, wouldn't you?"

I thought of what he had said about Harry Toole's rectory, which to the best of my knowledge did not need Doctor Favor's services. "I suppose," I said. "Thank you for doing so, at any rate. I'll see you this Saturday."

"Righto," she said.

When I spoke to Harry, he said, "I'd love to. And are you coming on Sunday? I wish you would. The folk choir is really much improved. I mean it this time."

"Oh, all right," I said. "I'll try it."

"I'm looking forward to seeing you. And Lucinda. I don't suppose you've given any thought to, you know, that matter of. . . ."

"Harry, the fact is, Lucinda and I are *doing well*. Our commitment is growing. Things are looking up. I wouldn't speak in terms of permanence, you understand. And of course she's very mathematically minded—it occupies her. But really, I have a lot to be grateful for."

"Oh. Well, I'm both sorry and happy to hear that."

I found this an irritating remark, and said to Harry, "Let's drop it. See you Saturday."

"And your clients?"

I affected not to hear him, and said goodbye.

The past week had been an extraordinarily prosperous one. Clients had flocked to my door bearing quick, simple assignments and had paid my inflated bills with enthusiasm. On an impulse, I even arranged for a redesign of my own meager website. Six months ago Doctor Favor's hefty fee would have virtually bankrupted me, but now I could manage it, wincing. The only roach in the ointment, as it were, was my penurious musicologist, whose check had bounced.

I then called Lucinda. Her phone message told me that she was unable to talk. There followed a list of hypotheticals ("If this is Dieter. . . ."; "If this is TV-or-Car Food. . . ."; "If this is the University of Buenos Aires. . . .") with convoluted responses (" . . . I'm still doing a sweep search for that pi-gamma function, but if you could fax me the tetranomials then I could. . . ."; " . . . your Qwik-Snax were a lifesaver and I was wondering whether you deliver. . . ."; " . . . you haven't sent the room confirmation yet. My sponsoring institution needs to hear from you by. . . .") My name appeared last: "If this is Vic, leave a message." A derisive beep sounded. I asked her phone-mail if Lucinda would come to dinner on Saturday. I still hadn't heard back by nightfall, so I called again. On and on went the various replies, and then the recording said, "If this is Vic: okay." After the beep I said, "Thank you," and broke the connection, regretting my optimistic report to Harry. I decided I would not attempt to see Lucinda before Saturday, and sent her a fax to that effect.

Saturday came. The dinner was not a success, other than negatively, in that there were no roaches to crawl across my roast beef. No one commented on this, although Mrs. Judson smiled at me and said, "Clara was a first-rate cook, too."

Lucinda grimaced. Yes, the evening was strained. Lucinda and I said almost nothing to each other, in a pointed way that I'm sure was all too noticeable. Harry attempted a leprechaun joke that no one laughed at, and shortly before dessert Nolan loudly coughed up a hairball. As a rule he was brusque about hairballs, but that night he turned it into a protracted, somewhat melodramatic affair, over which it was difficult to converse.

As Mrs. Judson was leaving, directly after coffee, she invited me to a small party at her place the following weekend. I accepted gratefully. Harry said, "See you in the morning, Vic," and followed her out. I heard him asking her for a ride back to the rectory as they waited for the elevator.

Lucinda too was reaching for her coat when I came back inside. "Can you stay a few minutes?" I asked her. "I think we should talk."

"What about?"

"You know perfectly well what about. Assuming you received my fax."

"Oh, Vic," said Lucinda. "I'm very involved. You used to understand." She shrugged her coat on.

"I had no choice. But recently everything was starting to seem . . . understandable in a different way. And now I really don't know what's understandable and what isn't."

Lucinda reached out her hand and ran her fingernails gently down my left cheek. "Please don't worry. I want you. Tomorrow. I'll come over tomorrow." Her lips twitched. "But tonight I really need to get some work done on this analysis I'm knocking together for Doctor F- Flores."

"Doctor which?"

"Flores. For next month's convocation in Argentina. All right?"

I made a limp gesture of agreement, and Lucinda buttoned her coat and left.

In the silence of the apartment after they had all gone, I had a hallucination. For an endless, black moment I thought I heard a scampering in the walls—or was it coming from the kitchen counter—or the shower stall? I went rigid in my chair, gripping the arms. But Nolan did not stir from his meditation in the chair opposite me, so I knew I had imagined it.

The next morning, at Mass, one more such hallucination occurred. I approached Harry at the altar, hands folded. The folk choir was indeed improved, almost to the point of being listenable, and Harry's homily had been short. All in all, I was in a good mood, not the least bit edgy or upset, not even about Lucinda. I was overreacting, I'd decided. So: I cupped my hands and received the Host. The Body of Christ, said Harry. Amen, Harry, I said. I placed the Body in my mouth, and queued up for the Blood.

And suddenly the thing in my mouth was alive. It squirmed and wriggled. I knew what it was. I have no idea how I managed to swallow it, but I did, and I felt it struggle and tickle all the way down.

For a moment I considered calling Doctor Favor when I got home and asking him, Do you by any chance have an incantation in your old oxblood-covered book that . . .? But even if he did, I was worried about the price.

A Finger in the Pocket

"Stories," the man said. "Do you like scary stories?" I said I did. "Here's a good one," he said.

I had gone out walking through the small woods that surrounded our apartment complex. I carried a stick, a thin tree limb, and sliced at the bushes along the path as I walked, severing the weakest branches. It was June, school was over, and I felt no need of companions, but I did want to get out of the apartment, because my mother was in one of her overzealous moods, going on at me about doing something with my summer. A "camp" was her favorite idea. The summer seemed perfectly adequate to me without my doing anything with it. I planned to read, teach myself chess, and observe the behaviors of insects, which I'd lately been reading up on. The woods was a fine place to watch butterflies, mantises, inchworms, bumblebees.

Midway along the path, I sat on an overturned tree to rest. Even here, at the woods' heart, the apartment buildings were in plain sight; it wasn't the sort of woods you could get lost in. I watched ants trooping along the dead bark beside me, in a hurry to arrive somewhere. Perhaps they were hungry for honeydew, which they milked from slave-aphids. I saw a shiny black wasp hurl itself onto the back of a caterpillar. The caterpillar, wobbly and pale green, reared up its head and waved it from side to side as the wasp inserted her ovipositor. Then I heard footsteps on the path. A dark-haired man wearing a dull red T–shirt and gray jeans came through the sun and shade. In one hand he was holding a small bag, like those my mother gave me to carry my lunch to school. He said hello.

Sitting next to me on the fallen tree, he put the bag down on the ground and asked my name. When I told him, he nodded as if he approved. Did I live near here? I had certainly been told not to speak to strangers, but he was so friendly that it seemed rude not to reciprocate. I liked his smile, and he was much younger than my father, hardly an adult at all.

He swiveled toward me and raised his sneakers up onto the tree, sitting cross-legged. In answer to his questions, I told him about my parents, my father in the federal government, my mother at home. An only child? Yes, I was, and I added quickly that I liked it very much. "You must get a lot of attention," he said, his thick eyebrows raised as if we shared a joke. Oh yes, I agreed uneasily. "Do you like to read?" he asked me. "I grew up without brothers or sisters too, and I used to spend hours reading." I warmed to him again, and told him yes, I loved to read.

"You're about twelve?" Eleven, I said, and that was when

he asked me if I liked scary stories.

He uncrossed his legs and straddled the log, his eyes bright. "Here's a good one," he said. "Once there was a Christmas party thrown for the students at a medical school. It's being held at a nearby country club. Several jokers decide to play a trick on the other attendees." His voice was interesting: deep, each word carefully pronounced, and there was an odd rhythm to the way he spoke. He paused after each sentence, as if he were reciting them. "They've collected a dozen or so fingers from the corpses used to study anatomy at the medical school. At one point during the party they slip into the cloakroom and place a finger in the overcoat pocket of each classmate they don't like, and then—"

He stopped, and looked at his wristwatch. "Look at the time," he said. "I have to get going." He picked up his bag and stood up. I told him I had to go too. He waved me away as if it didn't much matter to him. "Maybe I'll see you again sometime," he said.

When I came home, I told my mother about the encounter, leaving out the story about the fingers. I don't know why I told her anything at all, for I realized it was a mistake the moment I saw the look on her face. She told me I must never do such a thing again. But I could see that she was more frightened than cross. She wanted to know everything about him. I told her what I could, and tried to emphasize through my tone and descriptions that he'd been a nice man, that I hadn't been frightened myself. It was true; I hadn't found his story about the fingers especially scary (though of course I didn't know how it ended). "This is exactly why you shouldn't be idle," my mother said. "I'm going to speak to your father about it." All the rest of the afternoon she was silent and distracted, her lips grim.

For the next several days I went walking in the woods, wondering if the stranger would be there. I waited on the log, but he didn't come. I left disappointed and relieved. Finally, almost a week later, as I sat there watching two hairstreak butterflies mating, I heard footsteps coming up the path.

He greeted me by name and settled down, straddling the log. He looked exactly the same: dull red T–shirt, gray jeans, sneakers, brown paper bag. He placed the bag on the ground, same as before. I asked him what was in it. "My lunch," he said. That was what I figured, I told him.

"How did that story end? About the fingers?" I asked.

He smiled. "Oh, I don't know. I guess they found the fingers when they were least expecting them. It doesn't matter. Here's a better one. Some medical students are living in a group house, and they aren't getting along with one of the residents. She's not part of their clique, not a student, just a dumb little secretary. They've tried to get her to move out but she won't. So they decide to do something really unpleasant to make her leave. The overhead light in her room operates on a short metal pull-chain. The doctors-to-be go into her room when she's not there and attach a severed hand, stolen from one of those corpses at the medical school, to the pull-chain. Night falls. They gather in the room next door to hers, waiting for her to come home. They hear her footsteps come up the stairs. The door opens. Silence. No scream, no desperate rush out the door. Only silence. It stretches on for minutes. Finally they go out into the hall. Her door is open, the room is lit. They go inside. There on the floor, curled into a ball, driven insane, is the despised housemate. She's eating the hand."

I was glad we were in a sun-dappled clearing, and not in a dark room at night. "Are you a medical student?" I asked him.

He laughed. "Of course not," he said.

"I'd better go now. My mother said I shouldn't. . . ."

"I know," he said. "My mother always said that too." He waved goodbye as I headed back down the path.

This time I said nothing to my mother about meeting the stranger again. His story stayed in my mind. Remembered, it didn't so much frighten me as make me wonder—about him, about adults, about the world I would one day enter. Did such unspeakable things really happen? And did speaking about them help, or was it the very sort of speech that made strangers dangerous to talk to? I was never so glad to have a good book to read that night: a tale of adventure, my favorite kind, with a brave hero I could identify with. It occurred to me that an author was, in a way, a stranger too at first, but then he became a friend, offering stories yet closing his pages willingly, never detaining me longer than I wished to stay. Safe in my bed, able to say with perfect assurance where my parents were and what they were doing, full of satisfaction at the prospect of another day of idleness, and then another, I wondered if my stranger was also in bed, also reading. I wondered if he paused to think about me, as I was thinking about him.

The next time I met him, it was an overcast day, and chilly for June. A breeze blew the scent of loam and honeysuckle up the path. I had on a windbreaker, and so did he; his was a bright plaid. I saw a bulge in one of the side pockets, and a bit of brown paper protruding. "Okay," he said, almost immediately after he'd seated himself. He took the bag out of his pocket and placed it on the ground. "It seems there was a man named Goodman who was terribly jealous and had a terrible temper. When he became angry, he'd shout and curse and hurl things around the room. His wife grew afraid of him. One night she cowered in bed as he stood above her, shouting, cursing. She cringed, her eyes grew wide, she feared she'd lose control of her bladder. Goodman interrupted his rant to ask her what the hell was the matter with her. She told him she was afraid he'd hurt her. Goodman glared. 'I *love* you,' he shouted. 'I'd cut off my right hand'—he held the hand out to her, curled into a fist" (and the stranger held his hand out to me)—"'before I'd ever hurt you.' His wife told him that this was hard to believe. She saw something burst in his eyes, like an explosion. Goodman left the bedroom. Downstairs in the kitchen, he removed a small cleaver from the dish drainer. Placing his right forearm and hand on the counter next to the sink, he raised the cleaver awkwardly with his left hand and brought it down with all his strength. It took him three blows to sever the hand at the wrist. He went back up the stairs at a normal pace. He entered the bedroom and held out the jetting stump. 'See?' he said to his wife."

The storyteller fell silent. Foolishly, I looked at his hands, but of course I would have noticed long before if there'd been one missing. I saw that he wore a gold wedding band, like my father's.

"Wow," I said. "Did that really happen?"

He shrugged.

"So what happened next?"

"Next? Don't you think that's a good ending?"

I shook my head. "I mean, what did she do? Did she scream?"

"Why don't *you* tell it," said the stranger. "Go on, try to guess. Use your imagination."

I was so excited I could scarcely think. But after a minute or two I said, "Okay. What happens next is," and I felt the story come alive inside my mind. I said that Goodman's wife went insane at the sight of her husband swaying before her, his ragged stump gushing red. She ran out of the bedroom. Goodman fainted from loss of blood. She ran through the house, bumping into furniture and walls like a looper moth. She knocked over vases and bruised herself against bookshelves. She made mewing, cooing noises. She wound up in the kitchen. There on the counter was her husband's hand. Two days later, when the police finally broke in, responding to calls about the absent Goodmans, they found Goodman dead in the bedroom, his blood drained, white as a fish. And in the kitchen, hunkered beneath the sink, was Goodman's wife, wide-eyed, slack-jawed. She clutched the hand to her breast (the police saw that a great deal of flesh was missing from it, quite a bit of bone was showing), and as they watched she took another nibble.

The stranger gave me a warm smile, as the rain began to fall, pattering onto the leaves above our heads. "That was wonderful," he said. "You'd better go now. You'll get soaked."

"But was I right? Was that what happened?" His praise of my story and his concern for me were gratifying, but I felt that my imagination had failed me. The stranger's story about the crazy woman in the group house who ate the hand seemed to have taken over my own story as I told it. I felt like a copycat.

Again he smiled. "Maybe. But no one's really sure. Another way I heard it was this: Goodman's wife shrieks once, twice, then leaps from the bed. She removes Goodman's belt from the closet and uses it to tourniquet his maimed arm. Goodman allows it, he stands deadly still, but his eyes never leave her. Every time she looks at him, he's looking back at her. When the tourniquet is tight, she races downstairs to the phone and dials 911. The ambulance arrives, the paramedics listen to her nearly incoherent tale, they charge upstairs and haul Goodman down to the waiting ambulance. Goodman's wife accompanies them, rides in the back with her husband, holds his remaining hand, cleans sweat and blood from his forehead. All his accusations are forgotten . . . or maybe they're not." The storyteller paused and frowned. Then he went on: "She spends the night at the hospital, and the next day, and the next night, doing her best to hold onto herself as Goodman is treated medically and psychiatrically. The prognosis is fair: they won't need to keep him much long-er. Finally she returns home, having neither slept nor eaten. She feels on the brink of madness herself.

She unlocks the front door and enters their house. Blood is everywhere. She goes into the kitchen. In all the commotion of two nights ago, no one had thought to do anything about the severed hand. Goodman's wife has forgotten all about it until the moment she enters the dark kitchen. Then she remembers, and she wants to run away, she wants more than anything in the world not to have to see that hand. She imagines it lying on the counter, covered with roaches. They're scurrying amid the fingers, writhing in the palm, feasting on it. She reaches for the light switch, but then turns and leaves the kitchen. Not tonight, she simply can't face it tonight. She makes up the bed in the guest room (her own bedroom, the one she shared—usually—with her husband, looks like an abattoir) and sleeps for fourteen hours. In the morning, she dresses slowly, and slowly walks downstairs to the kitchen. She sees the gouts of blood on the counter, and the gory cleaver, but the hand is gone. She calls the hospital and insists on speaking to the ambulance crew. No, they did not remove the hand. Her best friend is the only other person, besides Goodman, with a key to the house. She calls her. The best friend knows nothing about the hand, and suggests that she see a doctor. Mrs. Goodman sits alone in the living room. She remembers hearing noises during the night. She should leave the house, leave it all behind, but that isn't possible. She has to stay until she learns what became of the hand." The stranger nodded, and looked up at the sky.

The sun had come back out, and I could smell the moist earth. After a moment I said, "So what happened? Did she find it?" When the stranger did not reply, I tried to prompt him: "I bet it came crawling out from somewhere. Right?"

The stranger said, "I don't know. That's the ending I heard."

"What about Goodman? Did he get out of the hospital? *Oh*," I said, as the idea struck me, "it was him, wasn't it? He came back and—"

"I told you." The stranger's voice was loud. "I told you: I don't know. That's all I know." I suppose he saw the look on my face, because he said softly, "I'm sorry."

I watched him for a moment and then said, "It's okay." We smiled at each other. "It's just that it's not really an ending. I think he should come back and get his hand. And then he could be totally insane, hiding somewhere, and . . . I don't know." I stopped, frustrated again by the limits of my imagination.

But the storyteller sighed and said, "Yes. Yes, I think your ending was what actually happened." He smiled faintly. "They both went mad." He looked at his wristwatch. "Look at the time," he said. He gave me his careless wave and strode down the path. I saw him turn off into a patch of bushes, and then came the sound of urine striking against a tree trunk. As I stood up, I saw that he'd forgotten his bag. I was about to call to him, but the thought of interrupting him while he urinated was fiercely embarrassing. I waited to see if he'd remember and come back for it. I heard the sound of his zipper being pulled up, and again I almost called out, but then he came out from the bushes and I saw him walking away, and soon his bright plaid jacket was lost from sight. I looked down at the bag. I touched it with my foot. The top was rolled up, just like my lunch bags. There was a damp spot on one side. I saw a column of ants begin to take an interest in the bag, circling around it. I reached down and touched the rolled-up part, but then straightened and walked quickly back toward my apartment building. I told myself that the stranger would return for his lunch, and if he found I'd disturbed it, he'd be angry.

That night, I was reading in my room when I heard the phone ring. I put my book down and ran to the wall phone in the kitchen. My father was reading in his armchair in the living room; my mother was watching television in their bedroom.

I picked up the phone, said hello, and gave our name. A man said hello, and asked me how I was.

"Fine."

"I hope I haven't disturbed you."

"No, I was just reading," I told him.

"Are your parents home?"

My mother came into the kitchen. She asked me who it was. I covered the mouthpiece of the phone with my hand and kept the receiver to my ear. I said, "I'm not sure."

"Is it for your father?"

"No, it's for me." There was a click on the line.

"For you? Is it Scott? Or Melinda?" These were school friends of mine.

"No, it's some man," I murmured.

I saw her face tighten. "What do you mean? Let me speak to him."

I heard the dial tone. I handed her the phone. She listened, staring at me, then replaced the receiver in the cradle. "Who was that?" she asked me.

"I don't know," I said.

"Are you sure he wanted to speak to you? Not your father?"

"Yes," I said, though I wasn't sure. My mother didn't believe me, I could tell. So I said what seemed to be true: "It might have been that man. The one who talked to me in the woods."

My mother said, "How did he get our phone number? Did you tell him?"

"No."

She called my father's name, and in a moment he joined us, frowning. Her story sounded unlikely to me—a bad man who'd sweet-talked a boy, then called him up—and my father erased his frown and allowed a calm smile to form as he listened. He did that when my mother needed handling. I was all in favor of her being handled, but wondered why he had never figured out that the calm smile didn't work.

Looking down at me, he asked me if the man on the phone was definitely the man in the woods. "I think it was," I said. "But actually it might not have been—"

"When you talked to him, did you tell him your full name? Our last name?"

I thought about it, and said that I believed I had.

"Well, that explains that," my father said. I knew he meant it was no mystery how the man had gotten our phone number. My mother began to speak but my father put up his hand. "What did he want, just now?" His face was very stern. "Tell me exactly what he said."

"He just asked what I was doing. And then Mom came and took the phone."

My tone was perhaps a bit accusing, for my mother said, "Of course I did! A strange man calls up—"

"Certainly, certainly," my father said to her, again holding up one hand, palm out. I thought of Goodman. We were all still standing in the kitchen, the phone on the wall, the fluorescent light winking. Now my father put his hand down and they both looked at me. My mother's color was high, and her eyes were wet. Her fingers were in motion, up and down the front of her dress. Fingers. My father gave her the smile, then returned his gaze to me: he looked disappointed in me.

"I'm sorry," I said. "I didn't know it would be him. And like I said, it might not have—"

"The point is, you must never talk to strangers," said my father. "Never. If you meet this man again, run home and tell your mother at once."

I said I would.

My mother said hoarsely, "And if he calls again and you answer—"

"—ask him to hold the line and then call one of us to the phone."

I agreed. But I didn't see the point. He would just hang up when he heard my mother's voice, or my father's.

"Those woods aren't safe for you to go wandering," my

mother said, still hoarse. "I don't want you walking there anymore."

"But that's the only good place to watch insects! That's what I'm *doing* this summer!"

"I think perhaps we'd better look into a camp of some kind for you," my father said.

My mother raised her voice to say that that was what she'd been saying all along, and I raised mine to say that I didn't need to go to any summer camp. "We'll talk about it later," my father said, retreating from this double barrage to his armchair. My mother glared at him, then went back to the television. I knew they would argue later, and I knew she would win. I might as well start packing my suitcase.

In my bedroom I pounded both fists into the pillow, giving it a one-two, a left hook, a right cross. My current book lay on the nightstand; I wanted to throw it across the room, bang up against the wall, so my parents would hear. If I destroyed it, so what? My reading days were over. I could imagine what the boys at a summer camp would think of a book-reader. I looked out the window at the moon. It was nearly full, shining above the woods and above the adjacent apartment building, robbing everything of color. My summer had turned colorless too, all my leisure snatched from me. It was now obvious to me that the man on the phone was a true stranger; why in the world had I imagined it was the storyteller? I wished there were some way to tell my mother and father what *my* stranger was really like. Even better, I wished he could pay them a little visit and tell them himself. Then they'd be sorry.

The Liontamer

The technique is the thing, I explain to the curious. The technique is everything. *Emotion* has nothing to do with it, believe me. Nor does *rapport* or *empathy* or *love*. No, madam. Not so, sir. Little boys, little girls: no. Technique is all.

The lion learns the meaning of gestures performed. The hissing sweep of the whip, the stamp of a boot in the dust of the center ring. The lion responds to my signals because he wants rewards. He wants a clean cage, periodic mounting of the lioness, meat. We bring frozen lamb carcasses with us, in the refrigerated car. One is taken out to thaw every thirty-six hours. We hang it, shiny with frost, in the props car. I also make sure that all stray dogs and cats are captured for the lion.

So: rewards. But all must be clear between the lion and me. He must never have to guess at the meaning of one of my gestures. There must be no such thing as a stammer, a lisp, in the sign language of the liontamer. When I raise my gloved right hand, poising it above the peacock-blue plume of my cap . . . when I fold digits into palm, slowly, all command and confidence . . . when I point, banishing the useless ringmaster, the musicians, the multiheaded, muttering distraction of the crowd, calling the lion's golden eyes to me, to me, to *my* head—the clarity of my gestural speech must be flawless. My imperious index finger *enunciates*. It tells the lion: *Hop up upon that stool*. No trembling; my joints and knuckles must not stutter. Technique, you see. The lion must never have to guess.

He hops—a great uncurling of fur—with the daintiness of a house cat landing on a window ledge, and settles himself on the brightly painted trapezoid, front paws supporting his weight as if he were leaning on a lectern. He regards me. I reach for my whip, detaching it from a holster-like clip at my side. Its leather coils dangle before me, from a precise and communicative height: three inches above my heart. The lion takes my meaning. I see his jaws unclamp, revealing black lips and a hint of tongue. I approach him, boots crunching the sawdust, whip still held out before me. Were I to cock my elbow at a slightly altered angle, depending the whip in, as it were, a *foreign accent*, the lion might wonder if some variation in his own behavior were permitted. It is not permitted, no, the performance must take place exactly as rehearsed, for now the gap between muzzle and tangle-bearded chin grows wider, taller, the crowd is hushed, and I allow no blink, no wince of hesitation as I grasp his slick, hot nose and enter that world of darkness and living winds. The lion must never think of improvising, of dining on my brains.

Sometimes our train seems to rattle and groan more annoyingly than usual, and I can't sleep. I leave my berth, pull my fine red silk-and-brass uniform jacket around my shoulders, and go down the shuddering corridor to see the lion. My slippers make no noise, at least none that can be heard above the racket of our journey. Wrapped in crimson, I walk past Honeydew and Indigo, the Siamese Twins of Trapeze Illumination, asleep in a single berth. Bones Jones the Motorcycle Artiste protrudes a skeletal arm from his snore-filled cubicle. I walk past the two doors of the two top turns, who rate privacy in the night: Mr. Walter Covington, the ringmaster, manager, and impresario, and Gabby the Clown (who happens to be deaf and dumb). No light shines beneath either of their doors.

I open the grinding metal door of the lion's cage-car. He hears me, and I feel his yellow eyes. I smell his breath, redolent of strays. The door clangs shut behind me, and my legs vibrate to the pulse of train wheels tumbling through the night. Moonlight enters from a high rectangular aperture, to the right of the cage, splattering the bars with silver. The lion growls, and I see the flick of his ropy tail. Shrugging off the jacket of my uniform, I make a deep bow. My feet kick away their slippers, one after the other. I hear the old leather strike the walls of the car. Then I begin to dance. I caper and pirouette, my faded nightshirt twirling out like a skirt. The chilly air tickles my privates. He growls again, and reaches up to paw at the bars; I hear claw-clicks on steel. Round and about I go, circling the scarlet puddle of my jacket. My hands trace nonsense in the air. The scraping and muttering inside the cage grows more insistent.

This is our secret language. No tented crowd has ever seen such a discourse, nor has Gabby, nor Bones Jones, nor

Mr. Walter Covington. Yet this too is technique, I would say to you, madam, to you, sir, to all you little boys and girls—believe me. It is the technique of the shadow-side. The lion and the liontamer must at times, in the rattling night-journey, speak of what is forbidden.

I conclude my dance, winded, falling to one knee like an impassioned suitor. My arms are spread wide. My head, minus plumed cap, sans toupee, bends before the moon-splashed bars. The lion snaps his jaws so loudly that I feel the snap, at the back of my neck. I shut my eyes.

In a small, untidy zoo, tucked in a corner of a park, also ill kept, that meanders through the center of a city in one of the northern territories—lives the lioness. Every four months we pass through this once-great metropolis, now dirtied and diminished, full of abandoned factories with smokeless smokestacks. Our train squeals into the vaulted station at dawn. A truck awaits us beside the platform. Bars gleam in its back door.

I stand shivering beside the lion's cage-car. Even when we arrive in summer, the dawn here makes my heart feel icy. Gabby, our deaf-and-dumb clown, is always beside me. He pokes my arm and makes a pumping gesture in front of his crotch, grinning. I ignore him. (He is a lewd man, also to be found loitering by the back of the tent whenever Honeydew and Indigo, sweating from their grotesque exertions on the high trapeze, walk crabwise into the showering area.) I watch as the zoo personnel pull aside the bars on the back of the truck, and then affix a complicated tube-like device to the aperture. It is flexible, this device, and serves as a kind of conduit or passageway down which the lion will travel, from car to truck. The zoo people are young, three men in white overalls, university lads perhaps, and always greet me with pleasure, and seem to take a studious interest in our mission. They attach the other end of their jerry-built passage to the end of the lion's car. I squeeze through a cunning flaw in the contraption's metal-mesh sides, and walk along the weird plastic floor of the tunnel until I reach the car door. I open it, and the grating metal echoes along the dim roof of the railway station. Then I unlock the lion's cage, whip in hand.

He knows where we're going, is ready, accepts his reward. With soft padding steps he walks out of the cage-car and descends along the portable passageway, barely glancing through the surrounding mesh at those who watch him: Gabby, still leering; the interested zoo-lads; Mr. Walter Covington, dressed in a sleek tan cashmere overcoat, hands in pockets, gazing from the platform with a frown. Many years ago, he brought me into his private car one evening, offered me a cognac, and interrogated me as to whether this procedure— the transporting of the lion, the mating with the lioness, the integrity and vigilance of all concerned personnel—whether it was all entirely *safe*. He had, I discovered, a vast uneasiness at the thought that his lion (it *is* his lion; the lion and I are his employees) might burst through all these man-made precautions and escape, mauling, slashing, murdering, devouring, and giving a bad name to Mr. Walter Covington's circus. I swallowed his cognac in a gulp, slammed the delicate snifter down onto his traveling escritoire, with its vase of freshly cut orange tulips, the .22-caliber revolver, and the inevitable volume of poetry, and explained that the lion knew, understood, desired the consummation of our efforts. He had no wish to escape. You would do as well to wonder, I sneered, whether Honeydew might someday take up a hatchet and hack her way through the elongated liver that she and Indigo share, thus relieving herself of a no doubt occasionally burdensome twinship. Mr. Walter Covington accepted my assurances with a tense nod, but he was ever present in the dawn, in that railway station, clenching his hands in his cashmered pockets and biting at his mustache as the lion gravely entered the zoo truck.

The lioness, I think, is elderly. Her fur is patchy, her brows grizzled. She eyes the truck as it backs toward her cage, and sniffs at the air with a small and elegant twitch of her muzzle, the nostrils dilating and contracting like the rhythm of a heartbeat. I step down from the truck's cab with painful, early-morning cracks of knees and hips, and the young zoo-men construct their ingenious tube of passage. The lion appears, his mane heavy with intent, sure-footed. We voyeurs are invisible to him, and I briefly long to speak to him with a hand, a finger, a knuckle, to offer even a syllable of— of what? Confirmation that the lioness is his because he and I are, beforehand, also given to each other? Yes, a reminder of some sort. But he's oblivious of everything except the lioness, whose tail now thumps the concrete as she lifts herself half off the gritty floor of her cage, eyes shiny and full of lion.

The new sun pokes an orange rim over the roof of the nearby Reptile House, and a breeze blows some humid scent toward me, an aroma of lion heat, not unlike the puff of air that escapes from our human blankets, our human couplings. The lion and the lioness perform a curt and courteous sniffing-dance, and then he leaps, bright penis protruding, to grasp her flanks with his great paws. As she is mounted, the lioness growls, and lids her eyes. Their coupling is swift. They stagger about the cage, tails lashing. And the lion roars, at the moment of his deepest thrust. My eyes water.

Mr. Walter Covington, that evening many years ago, made to refill my snifter (I placed a hand over it) and asked me whether the lion had ever injured me. His tone was intimate, as if we were discussing an adultery. He was concerned still for the reputation of his circus, for the possibilities of lion-riot, so I only shook my head disgustedly. The truth is that, yes, once I received a wound from the lion. We were rehearsing his leap through a hoop of fire. I held my torch to the kerosene-soaked rags that sheathed the metal circle. With a soft, implosive whump, flames raced round and joined themselves. Kneeling to set my torch on the ground (a gesture the lion had seen many times, had watched me perform as precisely as a word is spelled), I then extended my hand to him, making a pass toward the crackling hoop: *Jump.* Instead, the lion reached out a paw and touched my hand. I proffered the other hand, made the same gesture, more emphatically: *Jump!* He jumped, calmly, and returned unscorched to his trapezoidal stool. I unfurled my whip, spoke two familiar cr-aa-cks! and the lion walked out of the ring. Then I looked at my hand. (The cut was to require seventeen stitches, which I took without anesthetic.) I grabbed up a towel and wiped away the blood. I saw the shape and size of the orifice, its depth, the way the flesh was peeled back like lips. Ladies, little boys and girls, turn away. But you men: I tell you that the lion had given me the wound of Eve—had torn it from my flesh with one touch of his claw.

Gabby, his mute salaciousness piqued by the lion's zoo visits, looks at me longingly when we return. He wants a report, full of broad and vulgar miming, which I have never given him. Rebuffed, he assassinates me with a look, scratches his belly and slouches off. He has no further interest in the lion, and returns to his gargoyle world of greasepaint and pratfalls.

Bones Jones, however, wants to watch the lion eat, and often I oblige him. Jones's joints poke out like the knobs of gristle at the end of a turkey drumstick. He is a ghastly mantis, fully six feet four and weighing, perhaps, a bit over one hundred pounds. How can his frame withstand the punishing vibrations of his motorcycle? He swoops along the high wires, gunning the engine, folding himself over the handlebars like an origami.

I hurl a lamb carcass into the cage. The lion pads over to it, cuffs it, then settles himself down, encircles the marbled maroon flesh with his forefeet, and begins to gnaw. Jones gazes at the feeding lion. His rock of an Adam's apple falls and rises. Jones wishes that I would not execute the stray cats and dogs before presenting them to the lion. Just once, he has told me, just once he would like to see the lion murder his lunch before devouring it. What is there to say? If the matter is not self-evident (to encourage the lion's taste for live prey would be to endanger my own neck!) then it isn't worth the breath to explain it. Yet I tolerate Jones's visits at feeding time. This gaunt stick-insect, whose empty swallowing is such an eloquent counterpoint to the blood-filled gulps of the lion, earns my pity.

The lion has munched down a dachshund. The odd chunk of skull, a dollop or two of guts, remain before him. His beard is gory. Bones Jones wipes his own chin, staring, and I am moved. I touch his sharp shoulder blade before I go for the hose. The lion seizes a cranium fragment and cracks it between his teeth like a walnut shell.

The train is gliding, rolling, roaring. It is the dead of winter, deep in the night. I am fast asleep and dreaming, after a restless insomnia which was finally lulled by a walk down the drafty passageways, a visit to the lion. We spoke of what was forbidden—I think I have never danced so feverishly—he polished his claws on the bars—and I returned to my berth.

I am dreaming that a new artiste has been hired by the circus. Mr. Walter Covington refuses to be precise in his description of the newcomer—he and his mustache smile craftily and turn away—but I know this artiste will destroy us all. It is necessary to stop the train! I say to the sleek tan back. Suddenly I am wrenched awake by a shuddering and a tilt. I find I have tumbled against the window. Tumbled against the window!—yes, the car is nearly on its side, the train is not moving, we have upended, derailed. I see snow packed tight against the glass. Alarms are blaring. I struggle to disentangle myself from the blankets. A fist thrusts aside the curtain of my berth. It's Mr. Walter Covington, looking down the incline of the train's slant at me, and I am too disoriented to hear more than a few words (or perhaps he is too distraught to do more than gabble): snowdrifts, ice, an accident, injuries. I scramble up, out, down, and pull on my scarlet jacket. I locate my slippers where they have rolled beneath the berth and slide them onto my feet. Someone is wailing nearby.

In the corridor, all the lights are out, and it is drafty and chill. (With the perfect irrelevance that disaster inspires, I wish for my toupee; my pate is cold.) Snowdrifts are piled against the windows, but a little moonlight spills into the train. The wailing grows louder, joined by sobs and gruff instructions. Madam, sir, I know my circus compatriots, I'm used to their freakishness. This is fortunate, for I'm able to accept and assimilate the scene in the shadowed corridor; you, it would drive mad. Little children, it is your most hysterical nightmare come true. Mr. Walter Covington and I attempt to navigate the passageway, fighting for balance against the floor's unnatural tilt. A squirming dwarf dangles upside-down out of an upper berth, its feet snagged by the sheets. We move on, are halted by a scrambling, moaning thing, naked, with too many limbs, plucking at our legs with four hands. Honeydew and Indigo have met with some injury. *Cold* . . . I hear one of their identical voices whisper, and watch a dozen fingers crawl like centipede legs over the glistening band of flesh that stretches between the two torsos. Mr. Covington sidesteps their agony, pulls me along with him, but in passing I too reach out a hand and touch that connective band. We take a few steps and stumble over Bones Jones, seated against one corridor wall, knees pulled up like spikes against his chest. One arm hangs down at an impossible backwards angle between his legs, the other is intertwined with his shins. Mr. Covington bumps this sharp-limbed tangle as he passes, and Jones screams, cowering. The bony man has broken a bone. Train personnel are cursing, pushing, trying to restore order. Instead, they appear to be doing more damage. They jostle, knock heads, tread on hands, throw us circus people into a panic. Mr. Covington refuses to stop to receive the instructions of the authorities. He has a harsh grip on my forearm, yanking me after him. We are almost through the sleeping cars. At the exit from the final car, there is a shape, holding itself upright with a palm on either side of the passage. Gabby stares at us, his face as garish as a whore's. He has donned his full panoply of makeup, and on his head is a floppy pink cap topped with a puff-ball of bright chartreuse. Mr. Covington gestures to him to go back down the cars, to help the others. Gabby does not move. He bites his painted lower lip, and blood trickles out of the false redness and cuts a line down the powder of his chin. Mr. Covington brushes past him with an oath, and Gabby gazes at me like a lover and whispers, *"I heard what you said,"* but I am beyond astonishment. I walk on, turning once to look over my shoulder and seeing the right hand of the erstwhile mute slowly disappear beneath the waistband of his clown-drawers.

In the gap between cars, Mr. Covington pauses and turns to me. "The lion!" he breathes. "We must—" "Yes," I say, "of course." From the moment I saw his fist yank the curtains of my berth aside, I knew where we were going. His mustache is sharply etched in the moonlight, and I am seized with the desire to rip it out by the roots.

We pass through the props car—a Pandora's box of up-ended cargo and frosty lambs—and reach the door of the cage-car. Mr. Covington hurls it open, and I hear him groan. He staggers, and I move him aside impatiently and enter the car. The bars of the lion's cage have torn free of the floor and the ceiling, and lie topsy-turvy like pickup sticks. The car is silent and empty—no, it is loud and full with the absence of the lion.

"Is he somewhere on the train?" Mr. Covington pants. "Look," I say, pointing. The aperture, high and to the right of the cage, has been torn open and widened. Splinters of wood hang at violent angles. I walk over and peer outside. There is a confusion of snow and wreckage; aimless markings and depressions in the drifts; and then a clear set of paw tracks.

I feel Mr. Covington at my side. "Can you find him? Can you coax him back? For God's sake, don't tell me we have to call the law! My gun— I'll get my gun, yes? We have nets, ropes— Do you want me to—?"

I cut off his questions with a shove to the sternum, turn, and walk out of the car, onto the tiny exposed platform which joins the props car. I pause for breath—my heart is leaping and roaring in my ears—and jump off the train into the snow.

Quickly, before I can feel the frigid shock, I begin walking. My naked ankles and shins plow through the drifts. I follow the lion's tracks, buttoning my uniform jacket. Behind me I hear Mr. Covington trudging to catch up.

Our accident has taken place in the wilderness. A dozen or so yards beyond the railway tracks, a forest begins, the trees heavy and gleaming with snow. The lion has made straight for this protection. At the point where his trail enters the woods, I can see that the underbrush has been trampled down, small saplings broken, low-hanging tree limbs knocked clean of snow. The lion has made a tunnel into the dark forest.

I enter the tunnel, pushing aside those branches that are higher than a pacing lion. The moonlight is weak and dappled through the snow-heavy canopy of trees, but I can find my way. In a few minutes, the woods grow less dense, and once again I am following paw-tracks rather than a crushed lion-tunnel. I place each slippered foot into the hollow of a lion-print. Behind me Mr. Covington curses a tree root. We enter a clearing.

The lion crouches beside a small pond, its iced surface shining in the moonlight. His forelegs are stretched out before him. He raises his head at my approach, and I see the jets of steam rise from his nostrils.

Clumsy footsteps grow louder behind me. I turn and snap, "Stay back!" The footsteps cease. Slowly I walk toward the lion. My hands are ungloved, I lack my plumed cap, I have no whip. Were I to stamp my numb, slippered foot, only a weak crunch of snow would echo in this clearing. It occurs to me that I am a fool.

Three yards, two yards separate us—and then the lion growls. I imagine that we are after all in a circus ring. The silent trees are our audience. Is the ringmaster not with us, useless as ever, panting at the edge of the clearing? I raise my right hand in a practiced gesture, thumb and forefinger speaking two words: *Stand up.* The lion heaves himself out of the snow. He shakes white crystals from his mane.

At the conclusion of our usual act, I have a certain sweeping, ushering motion that I perform, involving both arms, to tell the lion: *Return to your cage.* That is what I say to him now, but the cold sends a shiver through my body, at just the wrong moment, and my gesture is awkward, tongue-tied. The lion glances at the route he traveled to come here, then lifts his muzzle and emits a short, soft roar. He takes a step toward me.

Mr. Walter Covington's voice: "You're crazy. I'm going back, I'll get the others, the ropes, the nets. I'll bring my gun." I hear him moving quickly away from us, back down the lion's path.

Now we are alone, and an unease seems to overcome the lion. He paws the snow, watches me, snorts and mutters. I am finally afraid. The lion raises a paw and makes a patting motion at the air. He is worrying the bars of his cage, sharpening his claws on imaginary steel. His next growl sounds a clear note of warning.

I bow. He growls again, less urgently. I can't feel my feet, but I force the muscles of my legs to kick, and one after the other my slippers fly off. They land on the frozen pond and go sliding off in eerie single file. Snow sprays from my naked toes as I begin my dance. The lion settles down, back into a relaxed crouch, and watches me. My nightshirt flares out around me. Faster and faster I twirl and curtsy, afraid that at any moment I will trip myself and collapse into a snowdrift. The lion—I see him in snapshots, over a shoulder, under an arm—breathes white clouds of steam, and often raises his paw to scratch at what has always separated us when we spoke in this way. Each claw is distinct in its nest of fur.

When I can dance no more, I fall gracelessly to one knee, arms thrown out. My throat aches with the frigid gulps of air I must take. I look into the lion's eyes (strange how moonlight and snow turn the world gray—where is the gold in his gaze?) and ask him with my heart, with the only language left to us: *Return with me.*

The lion gently parts his lips. Wider and wider, the yawning orifice grows. I see his tongue palpitating behind gusts of breath-clouds. Somewhere far off I imagine I hear voices, ugly commotion, the chaos of rescue.

I struggle forward on my knees, trembling with love. I place a hand softly on each side of his ice-bright mane and enter the darkness.

Acknowledgments

Grateful thanks to:

Robbie Murphy, who helped these stories at every step of the way.

Catrina Neiman for meticulous editing.

Matt Brinkley for good eyes and good suggestions.

Most of all . . . Katie Fisher, *come di fiamma ardore*.